He asked the obvious questions.

I gave the only answers.

Blood. Human. As much as possible.

Then I gave him some. And he liked it. Hell, we all like it. Just some can't stand the *thought* that we like it. And what we have to do to get it.

Tap as many veins as you like. Draw off just enough and leave behind a confused mugging victim or a zonked-out junkie. Hustle the blood banks, buy some green scrubs and lurk around the hospitals. Find a sweet Lucy who'll open a vein for you as often as she can just because she loves to be used that way. Try lapping at your own slit wrists or sucking on a decapitated rat and get sick as a man guzzling seawater. Try it all to put off the one thing you don't want to do, but sooner or later you'll do it.

And once you do, once you pop a blade through warm, healthy skin and feel the hot gush of living blood hit the back of your tongue, you'll wonder why you waited so long.

And then you'll curse at how long you're gonna have to wait till the next time. As few of us as there are running around, it's still too many. We all start picking off civilians whenever we feel hard up, this island's gonna be an abattoir. That happens, the lid blows off.

BY CHARLIE HUSTON

*Already Dead*

*No Dominion*

*Half the Blood of Brooklyn*

# HALF THE BLOOD OF BROOKLYN

CHARLIE HUSTON

www.orbitbooks.net

ORBIT

First published in the United States in 2007 by Del Rey Books,
an imprint of The Random House Publishing Group, a division of
Random House, Inc., New York
First published in Great Britain in 2008 by Orbit



A CIP catalogue record for this book
is available from the British Library.

ISBN 978-1-84149-680-1

Papers used by Orbit are natural, recyclable products made from
wood grown in sustainable forests and certified in accordance with
the rules of the Forest Stewardship Council.

Printed and bound in Great Britain by
Mackays of Chatham plc, Chatham, Kent
Paper supplied by Hellefoss AS, Norway

Orbit
An imprint of
Little, Brown Book Group
100 Victoria Embankment
London EC4Y 0DY

An Hachette Livre UK Company

www.orbitbooks.net

*To Mr. Stoker and Mr. Chandler.*

*With my greatest thanks.*

*And apologies for the liberties taken.*

NEW JERSEY
MANHATTAN
Williamsburg Bridge
WILLIAMSBURG NORTHSIDE
WILLIAMSBURG SOUTHSIDE
Brooklyn Bridge
Manhattan Bridge
Broadway
Ellis Island
Statue of Liberty/ Liberty Island
Brooklyn-Battery Tunnel
BROOKLYN HEIGHTS
DOWN-TOWN
FORT GREENE
CLINTON HILL
NAVY YARD
DUMBO
Flatbush Ave.
Flushing Ave.
Bedford Ave.
Myrtle Ave.
Humboldt Ave.
Lafayette Ave.
COBBLE HILL
BOERUM HILL
CARROLL GARDENS
Atlantic Ave.
BEDFORD-STUYVESANT
Fulton St.
RED HOOK
THE DOCKS
GOWANUS
PARK SLOPE
PROSPECT HEIGHTS
WEEKSVILLE
Eastern Pkwy.
4th Ave.
9th St.
CROWN HEIGHTS
Empire Blvd.
Prospect Park
Prospect Expwy.
Upper New York Bay
Gowanus Expwy.
Greenwood Cemetery
WINDSOR TERRACE
Linden Blvd.
Church Ave.
39th St.
SUNSET
Greenwood Cemetery
FLATBUSH
Clarendon Rd.
Coney Island Ave.
McDonald Ave.
Ocean Ave.
Foster Ave.
Utica Ave.
5th Ave.
7th Ave.
14th Ave.
BOROUGH PARK
Ditmas Ave.
BAY RIDGE
Shore Pkwy. (Leif Ericson Dr.)
4th Ave.
85th St.
New Utrecht Ave.
Ridge Pkwy.
BROOKL
Ocean Pkwy.
Nostrand Ave.
MIDWOOD
FORT HAMILTON
BENSONHURST
THE CHOSEN
MARINE PARK
Verrazano-Narrows Bridge
Dyker Beach Park
18th Ave.
Bay Pkwy.
Ave. P
Kings Hwy.
Stillwell Ave.
KINGS HIGHWAY
Shore Pkwy. (Belt Pkwy.)
STATEN ISLAND
Ave. U
GRAVES-END
SHEEPSHEAD BAY
GERRITSEN BEACH
Lower New York Bay
Neptune Ave.
BRIGHTON BEACH
MANHATTAN BEACH
CONEY ISLAND
THE FREAKS

Coalition Sighting? In Queens??
The Rebbe
Gravesite
Gravesend Park
Washington Cemetery
Friends field
Ambush
THE CHOSEN
Chester R.I.P.
THE FREAKS

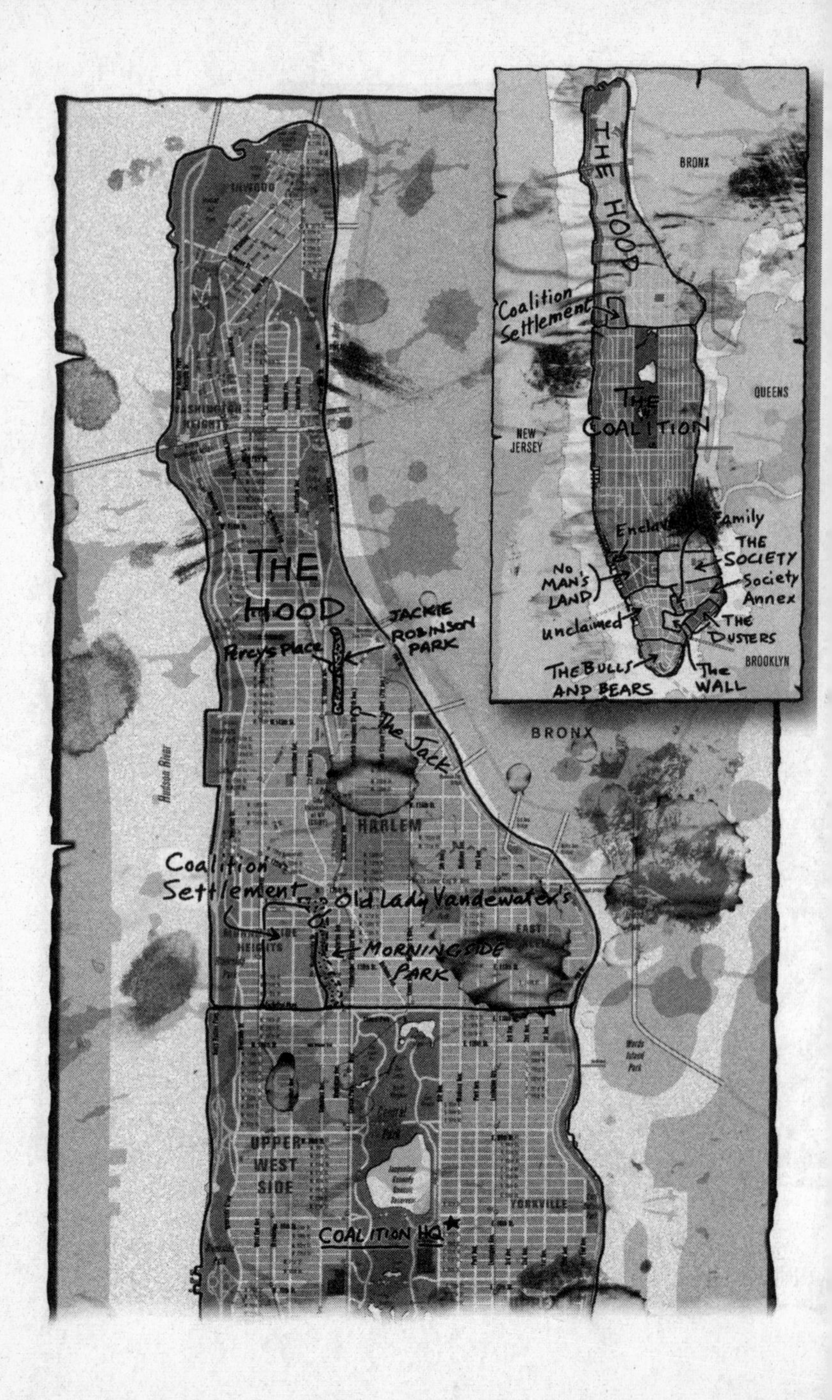

THE HOOD
BRONX
Coalition Settlement
THE COALITION
QUEENS
NEW JERSEY
Enclave
Family
THE SOCIETY
Society Annex
No MAN'S LAND
unclaimed
THE DUSTERS
THE BULLS AND BEARS
The WALL
BROOKLYN
THE HOOD
JACKIE ROBINSON PARK
Percy's Place
The Jack
BRONX
Hudson River
HARLEM
Coalition Settlement
Old Lady Vandewater's
MORNINGSIDE PARK
UPPER WEST SIDE
YORKVILLE
COALITION HQ

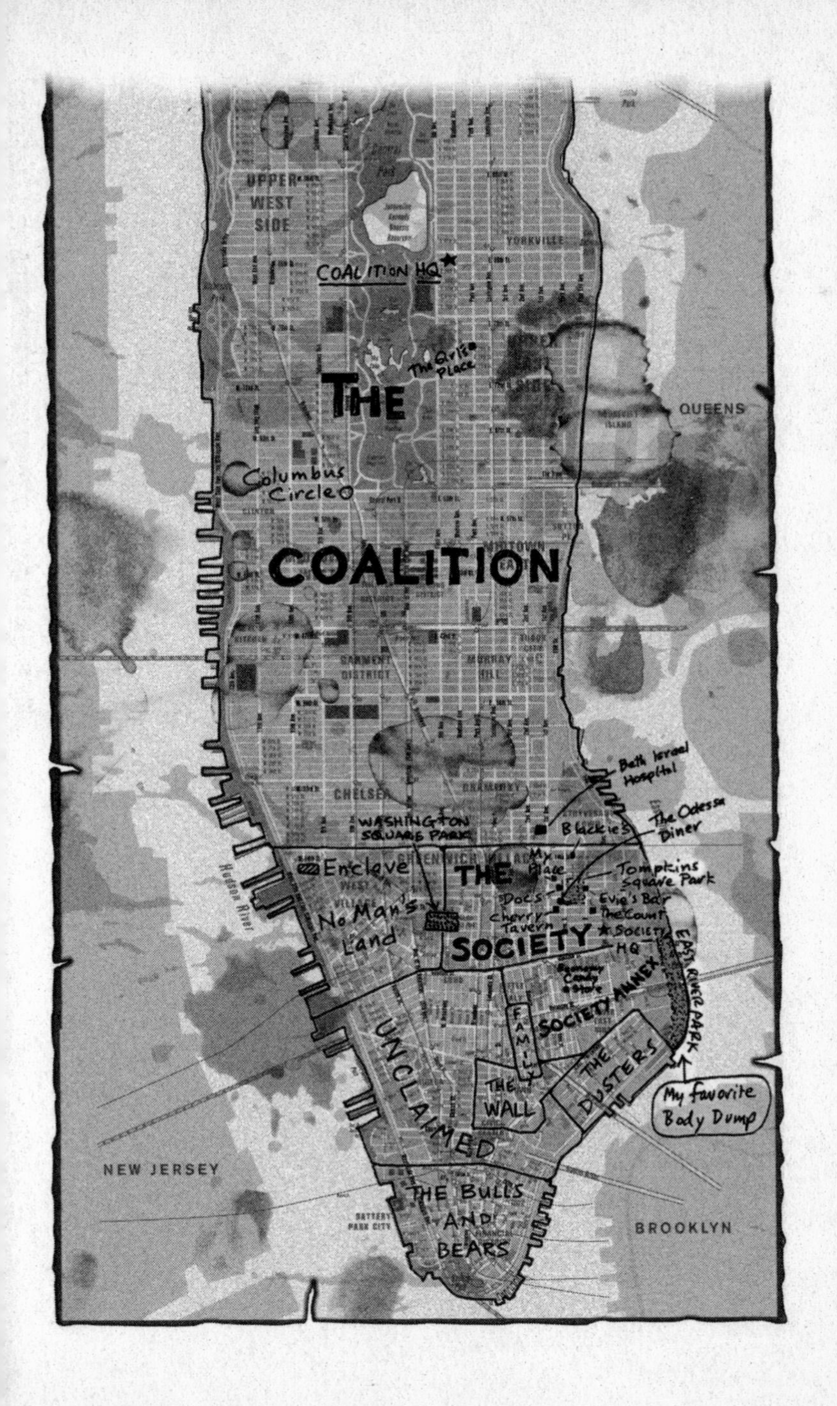

UPPER WEST SIDE
YORKVILLE
COALITION HQ
The Grill Place
THE COALITION
QUEENS
Columbus Circle
MIDTOWN
GARMENT DISTRICT
MURRAY HILL
CHELSEA
GRAMERCY
Beth Israel Hospital
WASHINGTON SQUARE PARK
Blackie's
The Odessa Diner
My Place
Tompkins Square Park
Enclave
Hudson River
No Man's Land
Docs
Cherry Tavern
Evie's Bar
The Count
SOCIETY HQ
THE SOCIETY
EAST RIVER PARK
SOCIETY ANNEX
FAMILY
UNCLAIMED
THE WALL
THE DUSTERS
My favorite Body Dump
NEW JERSEY
THE BULLS AND BEARS
BATTERY PARK CITY
BROOKLYN

I DON'T LIKE HIM.

I don't like the way he smells. I don't like the way he looks. I don't like his shoes. If I stuck a blade in him and drank the blood that shot out of the open wound, I wouldn't like the way he tastes.

But Terry told me to be cool.

So I don't kill the guy.

—You can't get somethin' for nothin', is all I'm sayin'.

Terry nods, waves some of the thick cigar smoke away from his face.

—No doubt, no doubt.

The guy I don't like blows another cloud off his stogie.

—If I bring the Docks into your thing, I got to know what's in it for my members. Not like I'm here for my own self. I'm an elected representative, it's the members decide these things, and they decide nothin' they don't know what they got comin' on their end of the deal.

Terry coughs into his hand.

—Well, like I say, the way we work here, the way we, you know, like to go about this kind of thing, is with the understanding that we're all working toward a greater good. The Society, it's not just, you know, a Clan in the traditional sense. We're not just trying to get along and go along. We've got goals. We're all about, and I'm not telling you anything you don't already know, but we're all about empowerment for anyone and everyone infected with the Vyrus. And does that mean folks that aren't even in the Society? You bet it does. But does that also mean achieving our goal will be easier with as united a front as possible? Absolutely. What I'm, you know, getting at is, whether you bring the Docks into the Society or not, you'll still reap the rewards when we break through one day, but, man, we could sure use as much help as possible right now.

The Docks Boss nods, ponders, chews the frayed end of his hand-rolled Dominican, and glances at the goon he brought with him.

—I think he's tellin' me there ain't shit in it for us.

The goon shifts the baseball bat perched on his shoulder.

—Sounds like it.

—Sounds like he's tellin' me he wants somethin' for nothin'.

The goon nods.

—Sounds like it.

The Docks Boss takes the cigar from his mouth, points it at Terry.

—That what you're tellin' me, Bird?

Terry presses the palms of his hands together and puts the tips of his fingers at his chin, a prayerful moment.

—What I'm trying to get across is that there's something in it for all of us. Me, you, your man there, Joe here, your members, the Society, all the Clans and Rogues and even the folks out there that never heard of the Vyrus. I'm talking about how we're gonna make the world a bigger and more wondrous place when the day comes we go public and let them know we're here. I'm saying that there's something in it for everyone. Every person on Mother Earth, man.

The goon raises a finger, a point's been proved.

—Yeah, he's saying there ain't nothin' in it for us.

The Docks Boss pushes his chair back, stands, drops the smoldering stub on the floor and stomps on it.

—C'mon, Gooch, let's get the boys and get the fuck out of here.

Terry shrugs, rises.

—Well, I can't say I'm not disappointed, but it's not the first time we've been turned down.

He puts out his hand.

—And I just want you to know, we're still fighting for you, man. Anytime you want to join the struggle, we'll be happy to have you by our side.

The Docks Boss looks Terry up and down, from his

Birkenstocks, past his hemp jeans and his FUR IS MURDER t-shirt, up to his graying ponytail.

—You're a freak, Bird. We ain't never gonna have nothin' to do with you and your hippies and your college kids and your queers and the rest.

He pulls out one of the cigars that stick up from the breast pocket of his cheap suit, bites the end off and spits it at Terry's feet.

—And I'm gonna tell Predo as much when I go see him.

He scrapes a match alight on the surface of the kitchen table and puffs the cigar to life.

—The Docks are a serious Clan. We make the move over the bridge here and swing our weight behind someone, they're gonna know their backs are covered. You don't want to give somethin' back for that security, to hell with you. Predo knows value. And he'll pay for it.

He drops the match.

—Hell, I only came to see you out of curiosity. Had to see for myself it was true what they say. How one of the top Clans over here is run by a pansy.

Terry tugs at the soul patch below his lower lip.

—Well, if that's how you see things, that's how you see things. Probably all for the best that you set up housekeeping with the Coalition. And still, still, I wish you nothing but health and happiness, man.

The Docks Boss rolls his eyes and heads for the door.

—Fuck you, Bird.

Terry looks at me.

—You mind showing them out, Joe?

I open the door.

—Sure, no problem.

I close the door behind us and lead the Boss and Gooch down the hall toward the front room where his other two boys are cooling their heels.

The Boss steps alongside me.

—A guy like you, a regular-lookin' fella, what the fuck are you doin' with that clown?

I crack a knuckle.

—It's a job.

Gooch laughs.

—A job? Hope you get paid through the nose, havin' to live in the middle of this freak show.

I stop at the front-room door, rest my hand on the knob.

—What you gonna do, it's all I know.

—Too bad for you.

—If you say so.

I open the door and stand aside to let the Docks Boss step into the room ahead of me.

Stupid fuck that he is, he goes right in and only stops when he sees the headless bodies of his boys on the floor, and Hurley swinging a fire axe at his face. I got to give it to him, he does manage to get his arm in front of his head before the blade comes down.

As his arm is hitting the floor and Hurley is going into his backswing, the Boss has got his remaining hand in his jacket, going for the iron bulging at his side. Hurley takes his hack Lou Gehrig style and the other arm comes off and slaps into the wall, the gun dropping.

The Boss stomps, splinters the floorboards beneath the sheets of plastic Hurley spread before he went to work. He kicks the body of one of his headless bodyguards.

—Fucker! Useless faggot!

He stands in the middle of the room, the spray from his stumps slowing to a steady trickle as the Vyrus clots the blood, scabs visibly forming over the wounds.

He looks at Hurley, spits blood at him.

—That all you good for, pussy, a fuckin' ambush? Come on! I can take it.

He sets his feet, turns his face upward, eyes wide open.

—Come on, pussy!

Hurley hefts the axe over his head.

—Just as ya say, den.

The Docks Boss screams as the blade drops. He stops when it splits his head down the middle.

Stupid fucker.

All those cigars, they kept him from smelling anything else. Otherwise he'd have whiffed the reek of blood the second I opened the kitchen door; he would have known there was a problem. In that tight hallway, he could have taken me apart. Another reason to like smoking.

Gooch leans into the room and looks at his boss flopping on the floor. He ducks back as a last jet of arterial blood sprays the ceiling and the dead thing goes still.

—Jesus, that's gonna be hell to clean up.

Hurley gives the axe a jerk and pulls it from the Docks Boss' face.

—Ayuh.

Gooch points at the mess.

—I ain't helpin' ta clean this. That wasn't part of the deal.

Hurley wipes the blade of the axe on the Boss' shirtfront, sees the cigars and pulls one from the dead man's pocket.

—No one said ya gotta clean nuttin'.

—Just so it's clear.

Hurley finds a match, thumbs a flame from it and puts it to the cigar.

—It's plenty clear, boyo.

Gooch points his baseball bat at the corpses.

—So you guys clean up your mess and I'll round up the rest of the Docks and let them know we're joinin' with ya.

Hurley looks at the cigar, wrinkles his nose, and drops it to hiss in the Boss' blood.

—Boyo, the way ya fellas sell one 'nother out, we would nae have ya ta clean our privies.

Gooch is about as quick as Boss was. He gets the bat up in a hurry to block Hurley's axe. But the axe never leaves Hurley's shoulder.

I tickle Gooch's earlobe with the barrel of his dead boss' revolver.

—Hey, Gooch.

He doesn't move.

—Yeah?

—I like this freak show.

I put a bullet in his ear. And when he's on the floor, I put a couple more in.

Hurley shakes his head.

—What's da point a dat, Joe?

—No point. Just that he was an asshole.

Terry comes down the hall and looks at the mess.

He takes off his glasses and bows his head.

—What a waste.

I put a Lucky in my mouth.

—If you say so.

—Labor should be our natural ally. They could have been a big help.

—A big help fucking things up. If this is the best Brooklyn has to offer, we don't have much to worry about.

Terry slips the glasses up his nose and gives me a look.

—The best isn't the problem, Joe.

He heads back down the hall toward the kitchen.

—The worst is what we have to worry about. The worst is still over the bridge.

He turns in the doorway.

—But they'll be coming.

I don't got enough problems.

I don't got enough problems dealing with the day-to-day shit that rains from the sky in Manhattan, now I got to start worrying about it being shipped in from Brooklyn. That's what happens when you get a regular job, other people's shit becomes your problem. 'Course, by the time you got that figured, it's up around your ears and you're just trying to keep your fucking mouth shut.

—Cat got your tongue?

I look up from the square of linoleum between my shoes and try a smile. It doesn't work.

—No, babe, just tired.

—You didn't have to come by.

—Sure I did. What else am I gonna do?

—You know how to flatter a girl, Joe.

—Not what I meant.

—I know. Just kidding.

Evie reaches out and takes my hand. The IV hose hooks around her pinkie and I pull it free so it won't get tangled.

—The one on your cheek looks better.

She pokes the tip of her tongue into the pocket of her cheek, pushing out the spot where the first of her Kaposi lesions appeared.

—Yeah. Pretty cool. Now if I can just get rid of the other thirty-six I'll be in business.

A nurse comes in, looks at the IV, checks the cunna in Evie's arm, fakes something that might have looked like a smile when she started this job and walks back out.

Evie shows me her teeth.

—I love that one, she's so sweet. Not a bitch like the others.

—A real Florence Nightingale.

—Yep, she's the one told me how to use the diuretic suppositories, used visual aids and everything.

She makes a fist with one hand and forces the index finger of her other hand into its grip.

—Very helpful.

She runs a hand through what's left of her red hair, dozens of strands coming loose, clinging to her fingers.

—Fuck. Fucking hell.

I look at the old lady on the other side of the tiny room, reading her *Women's Wear Daily,* sucking down her own chemo, head rolled up in a turban, trying to ignore Evie's curses, wondering how much longer she's going to have to stay in this room before they find her another. Just like the two others before her.

—Fucking, fuck, fuck. Hair. My goddamn hair.

—Babe.

—My hair, Joe.

—I know.

—Do I got to lose my hair?

—They said it'll grow back.

She shakes her hand over the edge of the bed, the strands of bright red floating free.

—Fuck them. They said the vinblastine would help. They said the mouth ulcers would stop after the first couple treatments. They said fewer than one in ten had constipation. They said my white count was plenty high to start the chemo. They said not to worry about the anemia, we'd just do more transfusions. They said I was a healthy girl and properly treated HIV didn't have to become AIDS at all. Fuck them and what they say. They know shit.

She waves at the old lady.

—Hey, I look like I got no AIDS to you, lady? What'd they tell you? What line of shit they feed you before they started in?

The old lady has the magazine out of her lap and in front of her face, blocking Evie out; blocking out the bright purple tumors, the patchy hair, the graying teeth.

—Babe.

—What? Am I making a scene? Am I embarrassing you, Joe? Don't want to be seen with me? All you gotta do is go.

I stand, bend and put my mouth against hers.

She kisses back for a moment, then moves away.

—Don't.

I lay a fingertip on one of the sores that rim her mouth.

—Hurts?

—No. It's just. It's so gross. I'm so gross. I'm a fucking monster.

—Baby, you're not even close.

And I kiss her again.

She coughs and I taste the bile from her empty stomach and the blood from the ulcers inside her lungs.

She pulls back again.

—Bowl. Bowl.

I get the plastic bowl and hold it in front of her and she heaves a couple times and nothing comes out.

—Fuck. Goddamn fuck.

I put the bowl aside.

—It's cool, baby.

She turns from me.

—Bullshit. It's not. It's not cool. I'm sick. I'm so sick of this.

—You can take it, baby.

—Are you? I can take it? You have no fucking.

She rolls on her back, talks to the ceiling.

—Go away, Joe.

I don't go away.

She looks at me.

—Goddamn it, if you can't do something to help me, go away! You think this helps? Standing there, looking at me like that? You think I feel better about what's happening, having your sorry ass here moping over me? Do something! Fucking do something!

I reach out to touch her.

She slaps my hand.

—Don't touch me. You said you wanted to take care of me. Then fucking take care of me. Fucker! Fucker! What use are you? I'm sick. I'm fucking dying and you're standing there. You, you. Always doing things. Your fucking job. Your job, and you can't help me. All you can do is put more blood in me for this fucking disease to live in. You don't help. You.

She's sitting up now, her pajama top slipping off her boney shoulder, showing the pale skin and freckles.

I stand there.

She yanks on the hose in her arm.

—Fuck this. This can't make me better. Nothing can make me better. You can't. You can't.

She throws the dripping needle at me.

—Go do something! Save me, goddamn it! Fucking save me!

The nurse comes in, sees the mess, shakes her head, gets to work.

Evie flops back into the pillows.

—See, this bitch, at least she can do something. She cleans up after me. She brings me crap food I can't eat. If I could take a shit, she'd wipe my ass for me.

The nurse glances my way, shoots her eyes toward the door.

I look at Evie's feet, sticking from beneath the sheet.

—I'll come by tomorrow.

She has her hands over her face.

—God, I want to be alone. Please let me be alone. Leave me alone. Don't ask me for anything. I don't want to do it anymore. I don't want to think about anyone else anymore. I'm no good at it. Leave me alone, Joe. Let me die alone. Go away. Go away.

The nurse faces me, places a hand on my arm, points at the door.

I think about taking her head between my hands and twisting her neck and spitting in her face as I kill her.

The old lady peeks from behind her magazine as I leave, shaking her head.

On the street I fire up a Lucky and look at the people walking around: on their way home after a late workday, on their way back out because it's Friday night, whatever. Normal stuff. Stuff Evie can't do these days.

I think about killing them all.

It wouldn't change things, not for my girl up there on the HIV ward of Beth Israel. But it would make me feel better. A dead body for every blood-corrupting cell invader in her would just about even things out with the world as far as I'm concerned.

A sense of proportion not being something I have much of a grip on.

A Harley grumbles up to the curb and the leather-coated rider touches the brim of his top hat.

—Joe.

I watch a guy walk past with his girl on his arm, both of them giggling at some stupid shit they think is cute. I skip asking what's so fucking funny and go talk to Christian instead.

—What's up?

He pulls the aviator goggles from his eyes and lets them hang from his neck.

—Something needs looking at below Houston.

—Off my beat.

Christian takes one of the smokes I offer him. I pop open my Zippo and hold out the flame.

—Not for long, I hear.

—What's that mean?

—Means everyone knows Terry is talking to faces from over the bridge. Those bridge-and-tunnel types start coming into the Society, Bird's gonna have to find turf for them somewhere.

—Where you hear that?

He grins.

—Seriously, man, you think Bird could move his action that close to Pike Street, and me and the boys wouldn't know what's what?

—Even if it's so, I only look after Society business.

He takes a drag.

—Joe, we go back?

It's a stupid question.

We go back to the night I peeled him off the sidewalk after the Chinatown Wall had shredded his gang and left him broken. Some asshole cut his vein and bled him and then bled into him. Thought it'd be cute to leave him breathing. See if the Vyrus would take root and keep him alive. Alive or the next best thing, anyway. Lameass probably figured if Christian died it'd be no harm, no foul. If he lived he'd freak out, be torn up over what happened to his boys and do himself. Go out colorful. Didn't figure I'd make the scene, do the right thing and clean up the mess before any cops or civilians got involved and found Christian still kicking.

I could have bled him out. Could have tumbled him into the East River, just another floater for the patrol boats to fish out. But there was a time someone could have made the same call on me, so I figured I was due to pay that one off. Figured I'd get him on his feet, give him the score on the Vyrus and let him make his own call.

Well I gave him the score. Filled him in on how the Vyrus was cultivating him. How it'd keep him sharp and strong and fast and pretty goddamn youthful for that matter, as long as he kept it fed.

He asked the obvious questions.

I gave the only answers.

Blood. Human. As much as possible.

Then I gave him some. And he liked it. Hell, we all like it. Just some can't stand the *thought* that we like it. And what we have to do to get it.

Tap as many veins as you like. Draw off just enough and leave behind a confused mugging victim or a zonked-out junkie. Hustle the blood banks, buy some green scrubs and lurk around the hospitals. Find a sweet Lucy who'll open a vein for you as often as she can just because she loves to be used that way. Try lapping at your own slit wrists or sucking on a decapitated rat and get sick as a man guzzling seawater. Try it all to put off the one thing you don't want to do, but sooner or later you'll do it.

And once you do, once you pop a blade through warm, healthy skin and feel the hot gush of living blood hit the back of your tongue, you'll wonder why you waited so long.

And then you'll curse at how long you're gonna have to wait till the next time. As few of us as there are running around, it's still too many. We all start picking off civilians whenever we feel hard up, this island's gonna be an abattoir. That happens, the lid blows off.

We let them know we're here, we let the real people know what's lurking just underneath their lives, and we won't last another night.

We'll all be in the sun.

And what the Vyrus does to its host when it gets hit by the sun, it makes what my girl's going through look easy.

And it ain't. That shit ain't easy at all.

I smoke and look at Christian and remember how he handled it when he was back on his feet. Way he handled it is, he found what was left of his gang, the Dusters. He managed to infect a couple. And they infected a couple more. After some months, when they had their shit together, they got on their hogs and hit the Wall. Massacre ain't the word. I don't know the word for what they did down in Chinatown. But the Dusters own Pike Street now.

They haven't been acknowledged as a Clan, but they could give fuckall as long as no one messes in their shit. And no one does.

I flick a butt into traffic.

—Yeah, sure, we go back.

He fits his goggles over his eyes.

—Then believe me when I say, What I got to show you, this kind of thing is everybody's business.

I get on the back of the bike.

—Where we going?

—Rivington off Essex.

I put my feet on the bitch pegs.

—Not the fucking Candy Man?

He taps his toe on the shifter.

—Yeah, the fucking Candy Man.

And he takes me for a ride below Houston.

The basement reeks of blood and ammonia and candy.

—What do you think, Joe?

—What do I think?

I take another look at the poor slob spread all over the floor: arms and legs and hands and feet and head and bisected torso and ripped-out heart all laid pretty much where they should be, but with about a foot or so between various parts that should be connected.

—I think we got a fucking Van Helsing on our hands.

Christian claps his hands to his cheeks and bugs his eyes.

—A Van Helsing? Ya think?

I look at the big white Maytag refrigerator in the corner of the basement. Blood is smeared around the handle and drips from the seal at the bottom of the door, pooling on the floor.

—Don't be a smartass, Christian. Nobody likes a smartass.

—You would know.

I go to the fridge and tug on the silver handle. The blood around the seal makes a noise: two pieces of overused flypaper being peeled from each other.

Two dozen slashed blood bags drip the last of their contents over the stainless steel shelves. A small flood of it washes out onto the floor.

Christian walks over.

—Any of it still good?

I pick up one of the bags and hand it to him.

He smells the ammonia it was laced with, the same ammonia that's been splashed around the basement.

He drops the bag.

—That's fucked up. What's he think, the ammonia's gonna hurt us?

I dab my index finger in some of the blood.

—Make for one hell of a stomachache. If he hadn't poisoned it, I'd be licking the fridge clean right now.

He pushes his top hat to the back of his head.

—Well, sure, me too, man.

He considers.

—And still, might be worth the sick to have a drink.

I smell the blood on my fingertip.

—Won't do you any good, ammonia killed it. Vyrus won't want it.

He kicks the fridge door closed.

—Fuck.

I wipe my finger on a piece of old newspaper I peel from a stack under the stairs.

—Can you get a scent?

He flares his nostrils, inhales, grimaces.

—Ammonia's overpowering most of it. You?

I shake my head. I've been sniffing around like a hound and can't get one good trace of whoever did it. The mess spilling from what used to be Solomon's belly, the ammonia and the basement over-stock are killing the subtler human traces of sweat and skin. If I'd had some blood today the Vyrus might be running strong enough to peak my senses, but I didn't. And Sol's is making me damn hungry.

I toe the head on the floor and watch it rock back and forth.

—When'd you find him?

Christian is skirting a spill of intestine.

—Swineheart and Tenderhooks rolled over here right after sun-down looking to score. They didn't know the shop closed for Sabbath and rattled the gates for a while before they went round to the alley side and banged on the trap. Smelled the blood. Twisted the lock off the trap and came down here. Saw this shit and freaked out. Came and got me.

I poke around some boxes, shifting them, looking for God knows what. Moving the boxes releases sugary pink smells.

—Swineheart and Tenderhooks got freaked?

Christian points at the corpse.

—This shit? You bet they did. Who wants to fuck with a Van Helsing?

The answer is *no one*.

Fuck with some kid who stumbled onto the wrong scene at the wrong time and managed to get out alive and declares a war on the undead and comes after you armed with holy water, garlic, and a crucifix? Sure, no problem. Holy water's just gonna get you wet, garlic's just gonna make your breath rank, and a crucifix is just a stick with a guy nailed to it. Nothing special. A Van Helsing like that comes after you, all you got to do is get him someplace dark and give his head a twist. After that, it's all a matter of how much of his blood do you drink right away and how much do you drain off and mix with an anticlotting agent so you can drink it later.

But a real Van Helsing? That's a different matter. A real Van Helsing knows that you bring a Vampyre down the same way you bring anyone down; only more so. A well-fed Vampyre won't like taking a bullet in the leg, but it won't stop him, not unless it hits the femoral artery and he bleeds out before he can stick a finger in there to plug the hole while it heals. And it'll heal. Fast. A Van Helsing that knows that? Knows to put some large-caliber rounds into a Vampyre's face, neck, chest? Or maybe to cut his or her head off? Or strangle him long enough to starve the brain of oxygen? Or has a handy tub of cement around to plant their feet in before dumping them off a bridge? Or has a big truck to run into them and roll back and forth over the broken body before the bleeding wounds can close and the bones knit? A Van Helsing who knows how weak we can become when unfed? Or how vulnerable to the sun? One who knows to look for the signs of feeding, the high mugging rates, the mysterious disappearances, the rumors among the squatters and the winos? A Van Helsing who really deserves the name? No one wants to fuck with that.

I put a couple boxes of Sugar Daddies back in place.

—Yeah, no one wants to mess with that. Funny, though.

Christian is looking in the hole in the guy's chest.

—How's that?

I start up the stairs to the shop above.

—Funny a Van Helsing gets all old school with the evisceration and the beheading, and the guy he's carving up ain't even infected.

He follows me.

—Yeah. Thought about that myself.

He jerks a thumb back at the corpse.

—Old Solomon never was a lucky one.

I reach the top of the stairs and push the door open and the smells of roasted nuts and dried fruits and caramel and chocolate and high-fructose corn syrup and red dye number 5 and pure cacao and refined sugar and gelatin and all the other stuff that goes into the stock of the Economy Candy Store hits me in the nose.

—Yeah, but he ran a great fucking candy shop.

Christian walks past a counter, reaches into a glass jar, grabs a jawbreaker and tosses it into his mouth.

—No lie there.

Bottle Caps, Big League Chew, Pop Rocks, Almond Joy, Gold Mine bubble gum, candy cigarettes, Pixy Stix, 100 Grand bars, Chunkys and a couple hundred other varieties of packaged candies. And in barrels: roasted and raw cashews, peanuts, almonds, brazils, hazelnuts, pistachios and filberts. And in plastic buckets: dried cherries, apricots, apple rings, peaches and pineapple. And laid out on wax paper inside the glass cases at the front of the crowded shop: bricks of dark Belgian chocolate, turtles, white truffles, chocolate-covered pretzels and strawberries and orange slices.

He bites down on the jawbreaker; his perfect teeth, polished and hardened by the Vyrus, crush it like an eggshell.

—Before I got infected, 'bout half the teeth in my head were ready to fall out because of this place. Growing up off Water Street, my mom used to bring me and my sister up here after church on Sundays. Give us a buck to split between us.

He rips open a Fun Dip packet, licks the white candy wand, dips it into the sugar powder inside and pops it in his mouth and sucks on it.

—Still got that sweet tooth, man. When I first found out the business old man Solomon ran in the basement, the real moneymaker, I was a little disillusioned. Got to say. Kiddies upstairs getting fixed on sugar, Vampyres in the basement scoring. That's kind of jacked up. Even in my book.

I pick up a necklace, beads of pastel candies strung on a choker of elastic.

—You got over it.

He takes the candy wand out of his mouth.

—Hey, get hard up enough, who isn't gonna come see the Candy Man? Telling me you never darkened his doorway?

I drop the necklace in the side pocket of my leather coat.

—I was a Rogue. I didn't have a Clan or a gang backing me up if I went off my home turf. Coming down here before I hooked back up with Terry, that wasn't an option.

He waves the wand.

—Shit, Joe, we would have had your back.

I go behind the counter and poke around in the drawers and the register.

—Yeah, and that would have cost me something.

He dips up more of the purple powder.

—Never said nothing in life wasn't free.

I find the hogleg back of the counter and put it next to the register.

—Never said you did.

He points at the sawed-off double barrel.

—Loaded?

I pick up the gun and crack the breech and show him the two 12-gauge shells inside.

He shakes his head.

—Imagine keeping something like that around in a shop fulla kids.

I snap it closed and tuck it into my belt at the small of my back, letting the coat fall over it.

He takes a look.

—Pretty good conceal. Long as you don't start doing jumping jacks it won't show too bad.

I find a half-full box of shells and put it in the pocket with the necklace.

Christian drops the remains of the Fun Dip in a wastebasket and wipes the back of his hand over his purple-stained lips.

—Makes you wonder, though.

—Huh?

—Why he kept the gauge up here with the kiddies instead of downstairs where the real dangerous types were coming in.

I walk to the stairs.

—Solomon wasn't stupid. Some junkie walked in here looking to clear out the register, he could handle that just by showing him the gun. Downstairs? Any infected stupid enough to try and knock out the only dependable dealer south of Houston would have to be stone strung out. Shotgun wouldn't have been worth a shit. Hit a burner with both barrels, take his head off, his fucking body will walk across the room and rip you in half.

—Know that for a fact, Joe?

I'm half down the stairs. I stop and look back up at his silhouette at the top.

—I know it.

He starts down.

—Still and all.

—Yeah?

—Shame he didn't have it down here today.

We hit the bottom and look at the corpse of the Candy Man.

—Shit, Christian, he wasn't one of us. Fuck did he think he had to worry about from real people?

—Got a point.

There's a box of garbage bags in the corner with the cleaning supplies.

I pick up a mop.

—Ready to get started?

—Sure.

He tears a bag out of the box.

—Why you think they done it?

I stick the mop bucket under the tap in a big slop sink.

—Could be the Van Helsing is only half smart. Killed him before he realized he wasn't infected. More like, he knew Solomon was the Candy Man. Knew it would cause a shitload of trouble cutting off the supply down here. Did it Stoker style to make a point. Something like that. Fits with poisoning the blood in the fridge.

He squats and starts picking up the smaller pieces.

—Sounds about right.

He drops a hand in the bag.

—Sorry, Sol, you were a hell of a confectioner.

Evie won't talk to me.

When I call, the night nurse says she's fine, watching TV, but doesn't want to talk to anyone.

That could mean anything from she really is watching TV to she's bent over her plastic bowl with chemo-heaves. I know which is more likely, but I try to pretend it's the other.

Not that she wants my sympathy. Not that she wants me lying in bed staring at the ceiling, chaining Luckys and thinking about the virus that's eating her alive. Far as she's concerned, I can fuck off whenever I want and just stop hovering around asking how she's feeling.

Or I can do something to save her.

Not that I take it seriously, all that shit. That's just the chemo talking. The misery and the pain and the acid they're pouring into her. She doesn't really think I can do anything. She's just fucking desperate.

She's just sick.

Girl was sick the night I met her. I knew the score then and I got in the game anyway. Nothing's changed between us. She's still sick. We still don't sleep together. I still eat my heart out every time I look at her.

The pity party's in the other room if you feel like joining it.

I won't be in.

Only thing that's changed is she's dying faster. Faster than she was before. And faster than me. She's dying really fucking fast.

'Course, she doesn't know I'm dying. She doesn't know shit about me. The nighttime schedule she chalks up to a sun allergy, solar urticaria. The guns and the rough and tumble and the padlocked fridge in my apartment and the donor blood I get deposited on her behalf so she always has enough for the transfusions she needs because of the anemia caused by the chemo? That's all because of my job.

Organ courier.

Transporter of healthy tissues between those with perfect kidneys, healthy corneas, melanoma-free skin, pink lungs, unperforated intestines; and the miserable disease-wracked bastards with nothing but money. Nice work if you can get it.

Except that it's a lie.

Yeah, I told my girl a lie. Just one on a long list. Once you skip over telling someone the part about needing to consume blood in order to feed the Vyrus that's keeping you alive, there isn't much room for truth in a relationship.

So it's built on lies. So if she knew what I am, what I do, she'd slap her hands to her face, scream *NOOOOOOOOO* and run from the room crying for help. Or not. Being Evie, she might just kick me in the balls for lying to her. Then she might ask a lot of questions. Then she might ask me if having the Vyrus in her would kill the virus in her.

And I'd have to tell her the truth for a change.

It would. The Vyrus will kill what's in her. It will kill anything that invades and attacks its host.

It will save her.

No more puking. No more hair loss. No more oral ulcers. No more loose teeth. No more chemo. No more Kaposi. No more AIDS.

No more cold showers. No more hand jobs. No more dry humping like the high school kid I never was.

Just me and her and all the time you could want, as healthy as a human being can be. Healthier. As healthy as something not quite human and not quite alive can be. For just as long as we can keep it together. For just as long as we can score and lay low and live with the constant scrabble to find the next hit. For as long as we can stay out of the sun.

It's a life.

And who am I to bitch. I may not have asked to be infected, but I haven't hurried to get out of the deal. Been over thirty years now, and I can bow out anytime. A bullet is still a bullet, whether it goes through your brainpan or mine. And dead is still dead. Or so I'm told. I'll know for sure soon enough. Just like everyone else.

We're all going the same place.

I'm just taking a different road.

If the scenery sucks, I can drive into a ditch whenever I want.

And I can take Evie with me. All I got to do is one simple thing. I just got to do what she's begging me for. I just got to save her.

I get off the bed, stub my smoke out in the tray on the night-stand and throw down the last swallow of Old Grand-Dad in the water glass there. I take Solomon's hogleg from my dresser and put it and the shells in my gun safe with a couple other pieces I've acquired in the last year. Used to be I had a pair of handguns that suited me more or less to a tee. The work I've been doing lately, I've found I go through them in a hurry. It pays to collect an extra or two when you get the chance.

The phone rings and I answer it and talk to someone and hang up.

I head for the door, in a hurry to be somewhere else, to be doing something else. To be thinking about anything else. I go fast and I leave the guns behind.

I won't need one where I'm headed.

Unless I plan on shooting my boss.

God knows I've had worse ideas.

Organ courier.

I wish.

Freelance. My own boss. The way I used to have it.

That was cherry.

It was a scrabble being a Rogue, not having a Clan to look out for you and keep you in the drink, but no one looks over your shoulder and tells you what to do. You fuck up, someone's gonna put you down. Nothing but blood, sweat and tears. And damn little blood.

Hell, I pine for it.

—The Candy Man? That's a real bummer.

I get out of my own head and look at Terry, the man whose dime I've been on for the last year. Not that he'd put it that way. He'd say I'm simply a pledged member of the Society, serving the greater good. But I know better. After all, it may be a dog's life, and I may be the dog, but I know whose hand is holding the leash.

—Yeah, whole bunch of SoHo ragtags are gonna have to find a new hookup.

He holds his index finger and thumb an inch apart.

—You're still taking the short view.

He spreads his arms wide.

—What I'm trying to get you to see is the big picture. Expand your vision, get into your peripherals, man. See the vistas. The trees, they're beautiful. But the forest, when you see the whole thing? That's a mindblower.

He shades his eyes with a flat hand, gazing into the distances beyond the walls of this tenement kitchen.

—When you really open your perceptions and take it all in, the view is breathtaking.

I look at Lydia. She's got her eyes squeezed shut, fingers rubbing her temples.

I tilt my chin at her.

—Got a headache?

She peels her eyes open and flips her hand in Terry's direction.

—You don't?

I check out Terry, his eyes still shaded, smiling at us.

—I've been listening to it for a long time. Guess I'm building an immunity.

Terry drops his hand.

—An immunity to truth, Joe? I hope not, man. I hope not.

I fiddle with the unlit smoke in my hand. Terry and Lydia don't like me to smoke in Society headquarters. Like secondhand smoke is gonna kill them. The *principle* of the thing, they'd say. Like there's any principle involved in breathing smoke other than it tastes good.

—The big picture, Ter, I'm missing it, so fill me in.

He lowers himself to the floor, slowly bending his legs till he's folded into a full lotus.

—The Candy Man is dead.

—Got that.

—Sure, sure you do, that's basic. The Candy Man is dead. Which, you know, he was a guy in a high-risk market. The blood, I mean, not the candy. So getting murdered isn't like a statistical improbability or anything. But, and this is the *down the rabbit hole* part, he's killed in a fashion that suggests a pretty well-versed Van Helsing was involved. A Van Helsing with enough, I don't know, foresight, savvy, whatever, to poison the Candy Man's stock so no one could scavenge it. And then the final tree in this, well, not really forest, but grove, maybe, or *copse* is a better word. The final tree in this copse is the really relevant fact that Solomon wasn't what a Van Helsing would call a, you know, a *vampire*. So that's our copse, our thicket of trees within the forest. The question is, What's out of place here? What tree, or shrub even, doesn't belong in the thicket?

I light my cigarette.

—You lost me at copse.

Lydia points at the NO SMOKING sign above the door.

—You mind?

I take another drag.

—Sister, if you can get through this without a smoke or a drink, more power to you. Me, I'm made of weaker stuff.

She crosses to a black-painted window over the sink, pinches the heads of the thirty penny nails driven through the frame into the sill, draws them out with a squeak, the upside-down pink triangle tattooed on her shoulder jumping as her muscles flex, and shoves the window open.

—I'm not your sister. My sisters share my values and concerns. They don't put money into the pockets of death merchants.

She drops the nails on the sill.

—And, Terry, a little support on the no-smoking policy would be appreciated.

He rests his hands palms up on the points of his knees.

—Trees, guys. Forest. Copse.

Lydia folds her arms.

—The Candy Man wasn't infected. The Van Helsing killed him like he was infected. He or *she* knew all this other stuff, but didn't know Solomon was a civilian. That's your odd tree.

He snaps his fingers.

—That's it, that's what I'm talking about. That particular piece of foliage seen on its own is just another fragment of the ecosystem, just another link in the chain of life. But in context of *our* forest? It stands out like a sequoia in the Amazon. An uninfected dealer in the forest of the Vyrus. Solomon has always been an exotic, yeah? So now, now something happens, someone yanks that tree, uproots it and salts the earth. But the way they go about it, it looks like they got a handle on the terrain, like they should maybe know better. So why kill that tree like it's a, and I don't like this analogy any better than you will, Lydia, but I'm talking here from this *gardener's* point of view, why kill this tree like it's a weed? Seeing as you know the difference. The Van Helsing I'm talking here.

I flick my butt and it arcs out the open window and between the bars of the security gate.

—Because he's an idiot, Terry. Because he's the kind of asshole goes around hacking people's heads off when he could just shoot them. Because he's a fucked-up nut job who knows just enough about us to be dangerous, but not enough to know Solomon was clean.

Lydia is pointing at the window.

—You planning to go out there and pick that up? Litter doesn't throw itself in the garbage, you know.

I pull out a fresh smoke.

—It bothers you, go toss it in a can.

—I swear, Joe, sometimes I think Tom was right about you, sometimes I think you're working for the Coalition, trying to subvert everything we do down here.

—And we all know where thinking like that got Tom.

She comes away from the window.

—That a threat?

That a threat? Am I threatening the head of the Lesbian Gay and Other Gendered Alliance? Am I throwing down on a woman I might not be able to take one on one, let alone if she comes at me with a couple of her bulls behind her?

Fucking no, I am not.

But I have shit manners.

—Fuck you, Lydia.

—Fuck you twice, Joe. Fuck you all over if you ever come close to threatening me. Tom was a spy. A scumbag subverter and a counterrevolutionary and a real asshole. He got what he asked for. But you ever come close to threatening me with the sun again, I'll bring fury down on you.

—You'll bring *fury* down on me? What the hell is that supposed to—

Terry looks at the ceiling.

—Forest! Forest! Forest!

I crush the cigarette in my hand.

—Brooklyn. OK? I get it. Lydia gets it. Brooklyn is what's going on. Brooklyn is the big picture. So what the fuck? What's that got to do with the Candy Man?

Terry smiles.

—See, you do have wider vision, man. That's great.

Knowing it's the kingdom of the blind around here, what's that say about me and my vision?

I open my hand and spill tobacco and shredded bits of white paper on the tabletop.

—Great, now we got that sorted out, can I blow?

Terry untangles his legs, straightening them, rising erect.

—Joe. Lydia. Just as we are negotiating possible alliances with these, I guess they have to be called pseudo Clans at this point, just as we're initiating *talks*, a Van Helsing appears. On our back porch. An apparently seasoned and knowledgeable Van Helsing who kills in a, you know, *potent* style. But he does this—

Lydia coughs.

—We don't know it's a man. Can we please not *assume* the male pronoun for a change?

—Right. So the Van Helsing, he or she, kills an uninfected guy like the guy was infected. If he or she does it out of ignorance, it's kind of, well, *incongruous*, to use a five-dollar word. So maybe it's an *accident*. Or maybe it's a *message* that even an uninfected isn't safe if he's trucking with the likes of us. Or maybe, maybe, it's done just to stir up some shit.

The phone rings.

—I mean, these are delicate times. New faces coming over the bridge. Elements no one has had contact with in, like, decades, man. Talking complex ramifications here. Talking old growth forests getting new seedlings. Talking shifts in the balance of power.

The phone rings.

—And the Candy Man, for all his, no pun here, all his sweetness, he was a hard-core businessman. He was a stone reliable dealer below Houston. The only one down there all those Rogues and odd bits of Clans could rely on in a pinch.

The phone rings.

—Think that's not gonna stir concern down there? I mean, Christian finds out about this, what's he do? He doesn't burn the store like would have maybe been the easy thing, he comes and gets Joe. He looks north. He sees a potentially troubling situation near his club's turf and reaches out for some Clan involvement.

The phone rings.

—He looks for some people who can stabilize a situation and bring a little balance *before* things can get knocked off kilter. He knows.

His riders relied on the Candy Man. So he knows what this could mean.

The phone rings.

—And, yeah, maybe it's all as simple and screwed up as a Van Helsing. Maybe we can get him, or her, before a little panic takes place. And then, well, market forces will take over and someone will fill Solomon's void and it'll all be cool.

The phone rings.

—But maybe, and I'm not talking from any secret well of knowledge here, I'm just saying, maybe.

The phone rings.

—Maybe it's someone fucking with us.

The phone rings again and Terry grabs it from its cradle on the wall.

—Hello? Hey. Hello. Yeah. How 'bout that? Been a while. OK, OK, the usual. Yeah? Wow. That was fast. Sure. Hey, we all got our ways. Who? No. Not them. Sure the Freaks did. No surprise, but not them. Uh-huh. I know. Old times, kind of. Well, sure, you know, that was different. Yeah. Uh-huh. Hang on.

He holds the phone out to me.

—It's for you.

I take the phone and put it to my ear.

—Yeah.

—Pitt, it's Predo. I understand there is a Van Helsing in your midst. We will need to address this. Come see me.

Fucker.

Little fucking fucker Predo is, he keeps me waiting in the lobby with nothing but back issues of *The New Yorker* and *Town & Country* to read.

I fiddle a Lucky out of the pack and stick it in my mouth.

—Uh-uh.

I look at the giant behind the reception desk.

—*Uh-uh* what?

He waves his pen back and forth.

—Not in here.

I take out my Zippo.

—What's with everybody? It's smoke. It doesn't hurt us. It's like the best part about the Vyrus. Look, Ma, no cancer.

I snap the lighter open.

He places the pen on his desk, aligning it perfectly with the vertical edge of his blotter.

—Don't even think about it.

I tap the tip of the unlit cigarette.

—Buddy, it's too fucking late for that, I'm thinking about it.

He smiles, no doubt dying for me to light up so he can stop dicking around with the boss' PowerPoint presentation and go to work on me instead.

—Then you best find something new to think about.

I size him up. It doesn't take long. A guy built like that, you'd have to be blind not to be able to size him up from about half a mile out. I'm a big guy, but one of his suits, the jacket would make a nice overcoat for me. Still, I long to try it, see if I could put a couple in his face before he tears the desk in two, jumps across the room, digs his finger into my sternum and pulls my rib cage out.

Not that I got anything to prove, but the fucker pisses me off. Way he backed up Predo that time they broke into my place and tossed me around, that made me not like him. Not that I ever did in the first place. Piece of Coalition enforcer shit that he is.

But I didn't bring a gun. And I don't have the stones to try it even if I was packing.

I drop the Zippo back in my pocket, take a big drag off the unlit cigarette, pull it from my mouth, blow a huge cloud of no smoke in his direction.

—Gotta rule against this?

He slits his eyes.

—Sooner or later.

—What? Sooner or later you're gonna sprout something from the brain stem that keeps your lungs pumping?

He rises. If we were outside, if it was daytime, he'd blot out the sun.

—Sooner or later you are going to fuck up and be back on the street again. Sooner or later you won't have Clan protection anymore. Sooner or later you're going to be a Rogue again. And nobody will care what happens to you. Nobody will care when I pick you up by the ankles and wishbone you.

What's a guy gonna say to that? Especially seeing as it's likely true.

Wish I had that gun.

The phone on his desk buzzes. He presses a button on it and picks up the handset.

—Yes. I'll send him up. Yes, Mr. Predo.

He closes his eyes, frowns.

—Yes, I will, sir. Unforgivable. It won't happen again.

He puts the phone down, opens his eyes, keeps the frown.

—Mr. Predo will see you now.

I get up.

—And we were just getting to know each other so well.

He looks me in the eye.

—And I am to offer my apologies for my threats. I went far beyond the limits of my duties. A simple request not to smoke would have been more than enough.

He sits, picks up his pen and starts pretending to do something in an appointment book.

I walk to his desk and stand there.

He looks up.

—Yes?

—I never heard the actual words *I'm sorry.*

His fingers tense, the stainless steel barrel of his pen flattens between them.

—I'm *sorry.*

I tap invisible ash onto his desktop and make for the doorway that leads to the stairs.

—Keep your fucking apology. First time I get the chance, I'm gonna see how many bullets I can fit in that empty head of yours.

He presses the buzzer that lets me pull the door open, masking whatever it is he's muttering about my mother.

Like I ever gave a shit about her.

—I'm wondering, Pitt.

I'm remembering what it was like when I was a kid, the handful of times I attended school, the way those days inevitably ended in the principal's office or a police station. The lectures. The rhetorical questions. The, *What were you thinking?* The, *How do you expect to get anywhere doing things like that?* The, *Is this how you act at home?* The, *Do you think you're scoring any points with that attitude?*

—I'm wondering, is there anything you care about at all?

Nights like this, it's easy to remember those days.

I stop picking at the knot tangling my bootlace.

—I care about getting out of here as soon as possible.

Predo places the pen on his desk, aligning it perfectly with the vertical edge of his blotter.

—If that is your goal, you might try paying attention for a few moments.

I point at the pen.

—You know your receptionist did that the exact same way. What do you think that's about?

—I wouldn't know.

—Hunh.

He watches me, the bright blue eyes in his smooth boyish face looking at me, slouched in the uncomfortable small wood chair across from him.

—Any other random thoughts, Pitt?

I give up on the knot and uncross my legs.

—Nothing just now. Why don't we get to your thing.

—*Thing*. My *thing*. That is what I am talking about. A Van Helsing, well versed from what I hear, at large, and you evaluate it as a *thing*. An object or idea of no value relative to any other *thing*. No better. No worse. Of no greater concern than a rock or a tree, perhaps.

—What is it with people and trees tonight?

—Excuse me?

—Nothing.

He brushes the flop of dark bangs from his forehead.

—Someone was talking about trees?

I shrug.

The corner of his mouth twitches upward.

—Was Bird speaking on the subjects of forests and trees?

—What's it to you?

The corner of his mouth straightens.

—Nothing. I have heard similar lectures in the past.

I look back at the knot, give it a tug, pulling the wrong end and drawing it tighter.

—Pitt?

I keep my eyes down. Thinking about Terry and Predo. Hippie Terry. Head of the Society. Revolutionary who organized all the downtown riffraff and Rogues almost forty years back, got them on the same page and broke off a piece of Coalition turf to make their own. And old man Predo. God knows how old, but so well fed, so blooded up he still looks twenty-five. Coalition whip and public face of their Secretariat. The one who straightens the rank and file. Head of the enforcers. The man who counters the Society's drive to unite all the infecteds and take us public with the Coalition's doctrine to unite in utter secrecy. A couple of true believers in separate corners. Guys taking potshots at each other every chance they get.

They go back.

Back to a time when Terry was up here. A time when they

worked the same side. A time maybe only they and a couple other people know about. Like me.

A time I figure they'd kill to keep hidden.

I put the thoughts away. Blink. And look up into the spymaster's eyes.

—I'm Society, Predo. I was out, now I'm back in. You want to fish for what goes on behind closed doors, find another place to drop your line. I don't run your errands anymore and I don't give up skinny on my people. You want to know do I care about anything, now you know.

His eyes widen.

—Heaven's, Mr. Pitt, have you seen the light? Are you a believer again? Forgive my surprise. I was under the impression that you had taken over Society security because it was the only way Terry would tolerate you on their turf anymore. My apologies if I've been mistaken. I never meant to impugn your devotion to your cause.

—Impugn my ass and tell me what the hell you want.

—There, that is the Pitt I am most familiar with, the one I have come to know and manipulate with such ease in the past.

I think about throwing my chair through the covered window behind him and pushing him after it. But it's probably safety glass and I doubt the chair would break it. And we're only on the second floor of the Coalition's Upper East Side brownstone anyway. So what the hell good would it do? Not like the sun's shining out there or anything.

—Thinking about hurting me, Pitt?

I nod.

—Most of the time.

—Naturally. It is your nature to think ill of your betters. As to what I want, well, simple professionalism. You handle security for your Clan, I oversee somewhat larger and more complex operations of a similar nature for mine. In an era of détente such as we now enjoy, I merely wish to keep open the lines of communication between our offices when threats emerge that might endanger the well-being of all. Something like a Van Helsing, I would have hoped to receive a direct call rather than having to find out about it through sources of my own.

—While we're on the subject.

—Yes?

—What sources of your own are spilling news about what happens below Fourteenth?

—Below Houston is open territory. We have alliances just as you do.

—Still dancing with the Bulls and Bears?

He blanks his eyes.

—Anything you want to know, Pitt, ask it directly. Attempt to winnow information from me and you will only become frustrated and waste your limited resources.

—Seemed that was a direct question.

He ignores it anyway.

—What can you tell me about the Van Helsing?

I hold up my hand, tick a finger off.

—He killed the Candy Man.

I tick another finger.

—He did it old school.

Another finger.

—He tainted a load of blood.

And my last point I tick off on my thumb.

—And he dumped ammonia around to get rid of his scent.

Leaving me showing him one finger.

—And that's it.

He nods, looks at a couple papers on his pin-neat desk, ignores the finger, and makes a couple notes.

—Well, then. Dismembered corpse. Two dozen tainted pints. And you are on the job. Very well.

He places a paper in his out-box.

—Good luck finding him.

I lower my finger.

—That it?

He glances up.

—Of course. As I said, a consultation was all I wanted. I have no interest in prying into a matter that lies so close to Society turf.

I get up.

—Yeah, sure, because that would be out of character for you.

He looks back at his papers.

—Have it as you wish. *My* wish is simply to facilitate the secrecy the Coalition believes is in all of our best interests. I have no desire to advance the goals of the Society, but interfering in a matter like this can only lead to unwanted publicity. That said, should you require any assistance in your investigation, you have only to call.

The fingers of one hand waft in the direction of the office door.

—Until next time.

I look at him, illuminated by the green shade lamp on his desk, surrounded by hardwood filing cabinets, the walls decorated by black-and-white photos of former holders of this office. All of it as it has been for more years than I learned to count in school. And I make for the door.

—Yeah, sure, next time.

—Pitt.

I stop with the door half open.

—Yeah?

—How did things go with the Docks?

I hesitate. It's a heartbeat. Less than a heartbeat. But I hesitate.

—Docks?

—The Brooklyn Clan that's looking for a Manhattan ally.

—Sure, I know who they are, just haven't seen them myself.

—Odd.

—How's that?

He taps a finger against his chin.

—We had scheduled a meeting with them. Understanding that they were to meet with the Society first.

—News to me. How'd that go?

—They never arrived.

—Hunh.

He watches me.

I shrug.

—Bridge-and-tunnelers, guess they got bad manners.

He lifts an eyebrow.

—I suppose so.

I start to go out the door, turn back again.

—Hey, that thing.

He looks up again.

—*Thing?*

I point at his desk.

—The thing with the pen, the way you put it there, all perfect. The way your boy downstairs does it the same exact way. I got a theory about that.

—Yes?

I purse my lips.

—He's studying you. Marking your moves, the way you go about it.

—About?

—Your business.

I pistol my fingers at him.

—He's trying it on, Predo, seeing how the job would fit him. Yours, that is.

And I'm out the door and down the stairs and through the lobby past the giant who's gonna have Predo's eyes in the back of his head from here on out, and on the street where I can breathe.

I light a smoke.

Did it tell him anything? That hesitation, did it spill what went down with the Docks? I don't know. But he's better at this than I am. He's better at everything than I am. It probably told him every fucking thing he wanted to know. Every goddamn thing he got me up here to find out from me.

I'm getting screwed.

Figure I know that much. God knows I should recognize the feeling when Predo slips it in. Scumbag's had his action in my ass often enough.

*Manipulate,* he said.

Guess that's the way the polite folks are saying *fucked over* these days.

Like to say he's got it all wrong. Like to say he's never had my number. Never pulled it over on me. Never made me dance on his strings. But I'd be lying. And lying to yourself pays out nothing. Not that it's ever stopped me before.

Terry and his damn forest. Well, he was right about that. Way Predo snagged me at the end there, asking about the Docks, figure he's seeing the same landscape as Terry. Both of them looking across the Brooklyn Bridge at all that territory, the couple thousand infecteds that have been living in the bush out there, and how they've suddenly started crossing the bridge looking to come back into civilization.

A Van Helsing?

Like Predo could give a fuck.

Pull my ass up here, drag me across 14th Street for a *consultation* he knows Terry won't let me bow out of. Do that for a lone whackjob? Bullshit.

Do that to fish for what Terry's up to with Brooklyn? Yeah, figure that's how Predo plays his games. And figure Terry's got that figured just as well.

Now I'm supposed to go home, turn in my report, tell him how it went down so he can take a read on Predo's hand.

Both of them trying to get an idea of the other guy's cards by looking at my face.

Fucking job!

Oh. Fuck me.

Two dozen pints. He said, *Two dozen pints.* Fucker knew what Solomon had in stock. Predo. Van Helsing. Would he do that? Send one of his enforcers down to do a job that looks like a Van Helsing? Do that to get me in his office where he can look me over? Hell yes, he would.

Or.

Shit.

Or it could have been Terry. Could have been he had Solomon done, knowing Predo would try to play me. Terry could have done it to get me in Predo's office so he could . . .

What?

Fuckers!

Try to think like them, try to make your thoughts slither and creep like theirs, all you get is tangled and lost. Screw it. Keep it simple.

The Van Helsing is just a Van Helsing, till further notice.

Predo is just an asshole, till further notice.

Terry is just my boss and my oldest friend and a man who I don't trust for shit, till further notice.

I can't afford to figure it any other way. I can't afford to try and play it any other way. Start playing someone else's game, you've already lost. Besides, I got more important things to worry about.

I got a sick girl.

—Joe.

I stop kicking the can I've been chasing down the dark Central Park footpath. I look at the woman blocking my way.

She's black and she's beautiful and she's built like a brick shit house.

—Sela.

She toes the can with the point of her glossy black knee-high boots, the slit in her skirt falling open over a bare, muscle-rippled thigh.

—Got a minute you can spare?

I look at my watch.

—Not really.

A long red nail scratches the back of her neck just below the line of cropped, tight black curls.

—Too bad.

I make to go around her.

—Yeah, too bad. See ya around.

She nudges the can in front of me and steps into my path.

—Not what I meant.

I look down at the can, back up at her.

—How did you mean?

Her big shoulders roll under the designer leather of her tailored jacket.

—I meant *too bad* in the sense that it doesn't matter if you've got a minute to spare or not. I need it anyway.

I take her in: the new uptown threads, the salon cut, the makeup so flawlessly applied that you only know it's there because you can't see it. I think about the last time I laid eyes on her: in an Alphabet City tenement, the ripped jeans she'd had on, the Patti Smith T, the mohawk she'd sported then. I don't have to inhale to smell the money all over her, or the hand it came from. I got no interest in seeing that hand again.

Christ, why didn't I bring a gun?

—Sela, long time no see, you were a champ that time I needed a hand, but I could give a fuck what you want my minutes for. They're mine. Top of that, I'm up here on business. Got a transit from Predo. You want to fuck with me, that's who you'll have to deal with.

Her tongue wets her lips.

—Look at you. Look at you. Joe Pitt, hiding behind Dexter Predo's skirt. How's a thing like that happen? How's a man like you get that low? Lose himself that deep? Got to be a story there.

I flip my Zippo open and closed a few times.

—Last time I checked, I'm not the one disavowed the Society. I'm not the one came up here and pledged Coalition.

—I didn't come up here for politics.

I kick the can from between our feet and go around her.

—Like I give a shit.

She doesn't move.

—I came up for the girl.

I keep walking, kicking the can.

She stays where she is.

—She wants to see you, Joe.

I kick the can, follow it down the path.

—I don't want to see her.

—She knows, Joe. She knows it all.

I freeze, my leg cocked.

—How's she know?

Sela pulls the ends of the belt on her coat, drawing it tighter over her waist.

—I told her.

I kick the can and watch it sail into the darkness away from the path.

—Why the fuck did you do a thing like that?

She walks past me toward a limo that has pulled to the curb where the path is cut by the 65th Street Transverse.

—Because she asked.

I watch her back.

—You could have lied.

She stops at the limo, turns to me.

—You don't lie to people you love, Joe. It doesn't work.

She opens the door.

—Now get in the fucking car so I don't have to drag you in.

I get in the car.

—You shouldn't be mad at Sela.

—Who says I'm mad at Sela?

—No one.

—Right. Know why? Because I'm not mad at Sela, that's why.

The girl flicks her fingertips at the jagged line of bangs on her forehead, keeping them mussed just so.

—You are *soooo* mad at Sela. Know how I know you're mad at Sela?

—No. I don't.

—I *know* you're mad at Sela because you didn't check out her ass when she went out of the room. And *everyone* checks out Sela's ass.

—Except me, I guess.

—No, *you too*. Because your eyes kind of *flicked over* to check out her ass, and then you remembered how *mad* you are at her so you didn't look. Like that was showing *her* or something. Which is *really* funny because all you did was cheat yourself out of a good look at an *amazing* ass. I should know. I look at it all the time.

She cranes her neck around and looks down her back at her own bottom.

—I do *all* the same exercises as her. I mean, not the same weights, she's *way* stronger than me. *Obviously.* But I do all the calf raises and presses and leg curls and *everything* that's supposed to make your ass pop, and mine just stays where it is. Flatflatflat. I want an ass like Sela's. *Everyone* wants an ass like Sela's. One way or another.

She looks at me, the bangs back in her eyes.

—But yeah, you *maybe* don't want her ass. I hear you have a *girlfriend* or something. I mean, I don't really *believe* you wouldn't want Sela's ass, but *maybe* you don't.

—She's got a dick.

She frowns.

—Huh?

—Last I heard, Sela was pre-op. She's got a dick.

She shakes her head.

—*So?* What's that got to do with her *ass*?

I put a cigarette in my mouth.

—Christ if I know.

She watches while I light up and take a drag and blow smoke. She watches while I do that, while I stand there and itch all over from the need to get the hell out and do something for Evie and try not to look like I've got a care. She watches until there's a long ash hanging from the end of the cigarette and I'm looking for a tray.

She smiles and points at a low table next to an Eames chair and ottoman.

—Over there.

I walk over, my hand cupped below the ash, and knock it into the silver tray on the table and stand there and smoke some more.

She points.

—Can I have one of those?

I dig the pack from my pocket and shake a smoke out and toss it to her. She catches it and places it in her mouth and walks down the room until she's right in front of me.

—Light?

I snap the Zippo in front of her.

She places the tips of her fingers on the back of my hand, guiding the flame closer to her, the unbuttoned cuff of her long-sleeve blouse sliding up her forearm and revealing the lone silver bracelet torn from a pair of handcuffs locked around her right wrist.

Her eyes flick from the bracelet and the few links of dangling chain to my eyes and she catches me looking at the cuff, remembering how it got there.

She gives a little smile, like she's just scored a point, and she draws on the filterless Lucky, and immediately starts hacking.

She doubles, choking and heaving, holding the smoke out at arm's length.

I pluck it from her fingers and put it in my face as I cross to the bar and pour a glass of ice water from a crystal pitcher and bring it back to her.

I hold it out and she shakes her head, tears steaming down her cheeks, huge phlegmy hacks shuddering her little body. I push the glass against her lips and tilt it up and she's forced to open her mouth and swallow, half of it running down her chin. The coughs subside into little hiccups and she knocks my hand aside. I take the glass to the bar and set it there and watch while she wipes her running mascara with the tails of her top.

I drop the cigarette in my hand into the water at the bottom of the glass and pluck the one she started on from between my lips and tally her score.

—You almost had it down, you know.

She looks up at me, the makeup smeared from her face, the teenager beneath it revealed.

—Had what down?

—Your mom's act.

She stops wiping her face, walks around me behind the bar, drops a couple ice cubes in a glass, pours some kind of triple-distilled boutique vodka from Romania or someplace over it, and tosses the drink down her throat and pours another.

I smoke the cigarette I took from her mouth.

—See, that's not bad. You got the drinking down pretty good. Except your mom probably wouldn't have bothered with the ice. But you're what, seventeen? So you got time to develop. Another twenty years and you'll be a perfect Upper East Side white trash burnout with a real grown-up booze jones, a trophy husband, a stable of gigolos, and a perfect ass.

She sips her second drink, her breath raising mist from the ice.

—And when I'm just like my mom, will you kill me just like you killed her?

I take a drag. Taste her lipstick. Remember her mother's kiss.

I drop the butt in the bar sink.

—One other difference, she would have offered me a drink.

She finishes her own and puts the glass on the bar.

—Well, like you said.

She starts for the door at the far end of the room, unbuttoning her blouse as she goes.

—I'm not her. Get your own drink. I'm gonna go change.

—I won't be here when you get back.

She stops at the door and drops her blouse on the floor.

—Now who's pretending, Joseph? I mean, of course you'll be here. You just can't wait to hear why I had Sela bring you up here. And to see how I've grown up.

And so Amanda Horde goes out of the room smiling, wearing thousand-dollar jeans, a scrap of black lace, and the handcuff I once took from my own wrist and put on hers.

Damn me. Damn me if she isn't right.

* * *

Yeah, I killed her mom.

Sort of.

Mostly she was dead before I broke her neck. Mostly she was infected with a bacteria that was turning her into something. Something you can call a zombie. For lack of a better word that describes something that goes around eating people's brains. Mostly she wanted to die. Afraid as she was that if she was around much longer she'd eat her own kid.

Far as I'm concerned, parents eating their kids sounds like more of the same. Doesn't mean I want to watch it happen or anything. Killing the woman just seemed like the right thing to do at the time. The right thing, or the best option.

But she did ask me to do it.

And she did kiss me.

It was a complicated night.

Think about a night like that often enough, you'll ask a lot of questions. Most of them about yourself. The kind of person you are. What you'll do and why and when you'll do it. What you believe in. What you really believe in.

In the movies, a vampire can't see himself in a mirror. Just because I can, that don't mean I got to like looking. What's inside is inside for a reason. Because you're not supposed to see it.

The girl, she's a girl. A kid. She doesn't know any better. And I know fuckall about what she really wants because she's a teenage girl and who the hell knows what goes through her mind. Figure she wants everything. She wants to see everything the world has to offer. And being a rich kid, she wants to *own* it all.

Ah, youth.

I make myself a drink. She comes back after I've made a couple more.

—Sela can't get drunk.

I watch her come to the bar; she's kept the jeans, pulled on a tight pink tuxedo shirt with ruffles down the front, reapplied the makeup, and resprayed her retro-80s-rocker-grrl-shag cut.

I top off my bourbon and cross to the windows and look down at Park Avenue.

—Then she's not trying.

Amanda laughs.

—*Seriously,* she can't.

—We can all get drunk. We just have to work real hard at it. Get enough booze in the system before the Vyrus can clean it out.

—Yeah, *sure,* she told me that, but I mean in a *normal* way she can't get drunk. Because she's an *alcoholic.* So she doesn't drink. That's what I *really* meant, she can't *drink.* Alcohol, I mean. Not the *other* stuff. She drinks *that.*

I drink whiskey, pretend to watch the street while I look at her reflection in the glass, next to mine.

She crosses to the Eames and drops into it.

—But she *has* to drink *that.*

I keep my back to her.

She opens a box on the table next to the chair and takes out a clove cigarette.

—Which, it doesn't *gross* me out or anything, but I do think it kinda *sucks.* No pun or anything. I mean, *really,* when you think about it, people eat cows and chickens and pigs and whatever they *want,* so what's the *dif*? Especially with someone like Sela who's *totally* got her shit together. I mean, with what I pay her as my trainer and my bodyguard, she can just *buy* what she needs. She never has to think about *hurting* anyone. It would just be *so* much easier if she could go to a *store* or something.

She lights her clove with a silver table lighter shaped like a thorn-circled sacred heart.

—Can you imagine, like, blood *boutiques*? People would get all *sniffy* about where they bought their blood and stuff. And *someone* would be making money. And, like, *anyone* could sell their blood and make some *money* and it wouldn't matter if they were *sick* or anything because you guys can't *get* sick.

She blows a cloud of smoke without coughing.

—But it will probably *never* happen that way.

She sticks her tongue out, an onyx stud dots its tip.

—Because most people are *such* fucking prudes. They don't *get* anything. They think that if something's *different,* that means it's like it's abnormal. Like there's any such thing as *normal.*

She leans back in the chair.

—Like when people see me and *Sela* out. If they see us having *dinner* together, a teenage *white chick* and a big *black* woman, they can't *help* but think it's all fucked up. And if they notice her *Adam's apple*? If they're *clued in* enough to know she was born with a *penis,* you can *see* the freak-out all over their faces. And the way they *love* it. The way they just *love* staring and whispering and thinking how much *better* than her they are. People just *suck* that way.

I don't argue with her about it.

She pulls her bare feet up on the chair.

—So it will probably *never* be like that. Like with all of you getting to live like everybody else.

She hugs her legs to her chest.

—Not unless someone finds a cure.

I turn around.

She rests her cheek against the tops of her knees.

—Did you know I just won a *lawsuit*? It was kind of a big deal. In the *Journal* and *everything.*

—Must have missed it on my way to the funny pages.

—Uh-huh. Well, I *won* and I got the terms of my trust *altered.*

She winks at me.

—You're right, you know. I mean, I'm kind of *surprised* you remembered, but you're right, I *am* seventeen. But in a couple months, I'm gonna be *eighteen.* Know what that means?

She bites her lower lip.

—It means that since I won my *suit,* I start to come into my *inher-*

*itance*. It means all the lawyers and all the board members and all the presidents and the CEOs and *everybody* has to get out of my *ass*. It means that all the *business* and *finance* classes I've been taking at prep, all the *biochem* courses I've audited online, all the *tutors* I've run circles around because they can't keep up with how *smart* I am, it means that's *all* gonna pay off.

She smiles ear to ear.

—Because when I'm *eighteen*, I'm gonna exercise my voting shares and *take over* Horde Bio Tech Incorporated. And I'm gonna put it to work finding a *cure* for the Vyrus. Because, you know what?

She takes a drag.

—I'm not just my mom's daughter. I'm also my daddy's little girl.

She blows smoke out her nostrils.

—And he was a genius.

I polish off my drink.

—He was a fucking loon.

She flutters her fingertips.

—Well, *yeah*.

I head for the bar.

—And you're following right in his footsteps with that crap.

She puts her feet on the floor.

—Where are you off to?

I put my glass on the bar and look at her.

—Figure I know now what you wanted to talk about. Figure I know you've grown up spoiled as your mother and whacked as your father. Figure my curiosity is sated and I'm leaving now.

—No, that's not it.

I snag the bottle I've been drinking from off the bar and turn my back to her. I'm on my way out.

—Mind if I take this for the road?

—Oh, *Joseph*, you're just afraid.

I hear her stand behind me.

—Is it the *girlfriend* thing?

I stop.

I turn.

She drags off her clove.

—Cuz I get that. *Sela* says that *Lydia* says that you have a *girlfriend* and *Lydia* thinks that she has *AIDS* and that you *take care* of her. Which *Sela* says *Lydia* can hardly *believe* and she thinks you *must* be using her as a Lucy or *something,* but I *totally* believe it because I *know* what you can be like. I know you like to have *something* to take care of. But what I *don't* get is, Do you really not *fuck* her? Because that's what *Sela* says *Lydia* thinks because of the way you talk about the Vyrus like it's something you can catch from a *toilet seat* or something.

I think about the night I saved her life. I think about that, and it keeps me from doing something to shut her up, something to shut her up forever.

She stubs her clove in the silver ashtray.

—Because *you can't,* you know. You can't get the Vyrus from a toilet seat. Or from *fucking.* If you could, Sela would have given it to me by now. Not that that's *scientific* or anything. But it's true. You can only get it from the *blood.* I've learned *that much* so far. But you're probably just *scared* of fucking her because you're scared of, you know, *intimacy* and all that. Because you *know* you're gonna die horribly and you don't want to take her with you or *whatever* stupid *cliché.* But here's the cool part.

She walks toward me.

—If you *did* give it to her, if you bled into her and made her like you, that would *cure* the AIDS. And *then.*

She stops and reaches for the bottle in my hand.

—If I really can cure the *Vyrus* like I think I *can.*

She takes the bottle from me.

—You could give her the *cure.* And she wouldn't be sick at *all* anymore. And neither would you. And you could do *anything.* You could be as *normal* as anyone, whatever that means.

She taps the stud in her tongue against the mouth of the bottle and drinks.

—If normal's what you *want.*

This child, standing in front of me, talking about things I might want, talking like she knows something about anything, talking about my little life like she understands what any of her words mean or could mean to me.

This child, I do my utter best not to kill.

But that doesn't stay my hand.

I slap the bottle from her and it shatters against the wall and I bring my palm across her face and send her to the floor.

She looks up at me, blood trickling from her nostril and the corner of her mouth.

—Who's my mama now?

I'm on my way out when Sela comes through the door. Her jacket's off, she's wearing a leather vest over her implants, the muscles in her shoulders and arms cut by iron.

I plant myself and get ready to put my boot in her balls and she blows past me straight for the girl.

—Baby.

—I'm OK.

—Stay there, I'll get some ice.

—I'm OK.

She props herself up on her elbows.

—He didn't do anything I haven't had done to me before.

Sela comes from the bar with a towel full of ice and cradles the girl's head.

I start for the door.

Amanda bares her teeth, blood smeared across them.

—Don't leave so soon. We haven't even talked about what happened that night.

I'm on my way.

She's still talking.

—I always thought they were nightmares. Till Sela told me what she knew.

Halfway to the door.

—But she doesn't know much. Only you know all of it. Do you know what I dream about? I bet you do.

At the door.

—Do you dream about it? Is the cold shadow in your dreams too?

I stop.

I turn.

I wish again for a gun, to shut her up.

—Don't talk about it. It knows you. Never talk about it.

She touches the bracelet on her wrist.

—I dream about you too, Joe. Should I be afraid of you?

But I'm not listening anymore. I'm gone.

What's inside is inside for a reason.

What's hidden is hidden for a reason.

What's buried is buried for a reason.

The cab gets me back down to 10th Street. The keys get me back in my apartment. The code turns on my alarms. The trap door takes me down to the basement room where I live in secret. The combination opens the safe and puts a gun in my hand.

But none of it will protect me.

It's been in here before.

Doors and locks don't matter. Hiding places are where it lives. A gun won't stop it. But I stand there in the middle of the room with a gun in my hand anyway, scenting for it. Searching for dead spots in the air, places where odor has been drawn from the atmosphere by its passing. Dreading that talking about it might have brought it back. Keeping myself from diving beneath the covers to hide from it.

The Wraith.

And to hide from the other things little Amanda Horde had to say.

To be normal.

Like I was ever normal. Like I was ever any different from how I am now. A cure won't make me better. It'll just make me more like a regular son of a bitch. Like the Vyrus makes you into something else. It doesn't. If you get it, if you survive, it's because you were already the kind of person who will drink blood.

And how do you know if you're that kind of person? You don't, not till your mouth covers a fresh wound and you find yourself jamming your tongue in it and sucking.

Is that the kind of person Evie is? If there was a cure, I maybe wouldn't have to find out.

If a cure is possible.

Now that I got a gun in my hand, I'm gonna go talk to someone about it.

—Jeez, Joe, am I glad ya came by. Been calling you since I got here.

—How long's he been this way?

—I don't know. I came around, he was like this.

—Uh-huh. You just dropping by?

Phil rubs his nose.

—Sure, I guess. Just paying a visit.

—'Cause you guys are tight that way. You pop in every now and then.

—Well. Well. Didn't say we were *tight*. Sure we're friendly, but *tight* might be a little of a, you know, an overstatement.

—You carrying, Phil?

He runs hands over all his pockets.

—I look like I'm carrying? Don't I wish.

—Not for you, for him.

He reams out his ear with a fingertip.

—Aw, well, not, not just this moment. But, sure, from time to time Mr. Bird passes me something to bring up here. Not that I know how he comes by the stuff.

—*Mr. Bird*.

I size him up. A pasty jumble of limbs in latex-tight sharkskin slacks with three inches of white socks showing at the ankles above two-tone patent leather, a jacket matching the slacks stretched over narrow shoulders and an embroidered cowboy shirt with silver caps on the points of the collar, a bolo tie featuring a cockroach frozen in amber snug around his throat.

He fidgets with the bleach-blond pompadour that crests his head and adds eight inches to his height.

—So, long as you're here to, you know, make sure he's OK and all, I should get going.

He jitters toward the door.

I clear my throat.

—Phil, you got any idea how many times tonight I've wished I had a gun and didn't?

He flashes eyes at the door and back to me.

—Uh, no, no, got me.

—A lot. Know what else?

—Um, no.

—If you piss me off and make me start wishing I had a gun in my hand so I can shoot you in the knee just because it will make me feel better, my wish will come true.

He chews a fingernail.

—So, um, you're saying you're packing, right?

I nod.

—That's what I'm saying.

—And I'm supposed to stay here, right?

—Yeah, that's it.

He swallows a piece of cuticle.

—Well, just threaten a man, why can't you? You make it all complicated like that and I sometimes don't know what I gotta do to keep from getting slapped around.

I walk toward the Count where he's pressed naked into the corner of the loft, his lips moving, a jumble of syllables pouring out between them.

—My bad, I figured it'd just be an instinct for you by now.

Phil follows behind.

—Hey, I appreciate the benefit of the doubt and all, Joe, but really, man, unless I'm high you really shouldn't count on me thinking too straight.

I stop outside the circle of symbols the Count has scrawled in his own blood and feces.

I point with the toe of my boot.

—Any idea what this shit is?

Phil gives a little sniff.

—Just regular old shit, yeah?

—The pictures, Phil, not what they're drawn in.

—Right, uh, no, no clue. Just crazy stuff, right?

Crazy stuff. Sounds about right.

I squat and put myself on eye level with the Count. His eyes keep spinning, dancing around the patterns on the floor and walls and ceiling, resting for a beat of every orbit on the blade of the knife pressed to his wrist.

—Count.

His eyes flick over me, pass back, continue on their way.

—Count.

No reaction at all this time.

I look at the maul of flesh where his right foot used to be. The knob of half-healed meat, nubbins of bone poking out of it where the Vyrus tried to sprout new toes. But it was too much damage, shattered bone and muscle and skin ripped away, the kind of wound even the Vyrus can't make entirely right.

I wonder if putting a bullet in his other foot will get him to pay attention to me like it did when I shot that one off.

Instead, I poke in a pile of trash on the floor and find a rat-gnawed chopstick.

I hold it in the air before my face.

—Count.

Nothing.

I whip it down and drag it through the circle of nonsense on the floor.

—No! Nonononononono!

He draws the blade of the knife across his wrist, blood runs free as he scuttles forward on all fours and starts painting fresh the lines I've broken.

—No, no, no, no, Joe! Joe, Joe, Joe, Joe, no!

He freezes, studies the repairs, holds his wrist over the floor to drip the last drops as the Vyrus draws the wound closed.

I tap the chopstick on the floor.

—You're not looking too good, Count.

He points his gaze at me. His mouth falls open and he tilts his head back and laughs.

—No, not looking too good. Hunh, hunh, hunh! Not too good, Joe.

His teeth snap closed and his head drops down and he points the knife at me.

—Hey, hey, Joe, Joe, Joe Pitt. Know what?

—What?

He cups a hand at his mouth, sharing a secret.

—You gotta rep.

—No kidding?

—Know, know, know what it is, is?

—Nope.

He glances at Phil, leans closer, keeping his body within the lines of his circle.

—You gotta rep, says you kill people.

—Huh, go figure.

He slaps the flat of the blade to his cheek, presses the steel against his filthy skin.

—Wanna do me a favor, Joe Pitt?

I shrug.

—Won't know till you ask me.

He puts the point of the blade in his left nostril, the handle angled toward me.

—Kill me, would ya? Please, Joe. Pretty please?

I do think about it. About slapping my open palm against the knife and driving it through his sinus and up into his brain. But it wouldn't kill him, not right away. The angle is wrong. It'd hurt like a fucker and turn him into a retard, but it wouldn't cut the medulla.

Of course, looking at him, it's hard to say he'd be worse off.

—Count, I need some information.

His eyebrows jump.

—Sure, great, a swap! Kill me and I'll tell ya anything you want to know, huh?

I rub my chin.

—How 'bout a compromise?

His eyes narrow, looking for a trick.

—Like what?

—How 'bout you tell me what I need to know and then I kill you, sound good?

His eyes close. They open. He takes the knife out of his nose.

—OK, OK, OK, but no funny stuff. None of your trickery, Mr. Joseph Pitt. If that is your real name.

It's not my real name. But the Count isn't his. So who cares anyway.

—Sure, no trickery.

I keep my eyes on his and point the chopstick over my shoulder.

—Get lost, Phil.

—Lost? Like, for real or?

—Go sit in the can and cover your ears and hum real loud so you can't hear what we're talking about.

—Uh.

—It's not code, it's literal. Go do it.

I wait until I hear the bathroom door close and the sound of "Sweet Caroline" hummed nasal and out of tune.

The Count's eyes keep trying to peel away from mine. I clap my hands in front of his face and they pull back to me.

—Yeah, kill me, kill me, kill me.

—Soon enough, Count. Questions first.

I point at a pile of textbooks and back issues of quarterly medical journals heaped within the circle.

—Been keeping up on your studies?

—Yeah, yeah, good question. Yeah, I have. More, more, give me more like that.

I watch the pulse jumping in his neck at death-metal tempo; feel the heat coming off his body; smell the sweaty tang under the shit and blood that speaks of a metabolism careening brakeless.

—When's the last time you ate?

He purses his lips.

—Ooooh, toughie, toughie. Good one, stumper. But I can get it, I got this one, I got it. Uuummmm. Two weeks? A little more? Yeah, yeah, two weeks, a little more than two weeks. Maybe three?

Two weeks, maybe three. Fuck. Two weeks with no fresh blood. And he's been painting the place with his own. He's beyond starving.

I look at the closed bathroom door where the tune has changed to "Summer Wind."

—Why didn't you drink Phil?

He scratches his balls with dirty cracked nails.

—Phil? Phil? Jesus, drink Phil? Who'd drink Phil? Guy's a Renfield. Total Renfield. I don't want any of that. Nononono.

—Bull. You're far enough to try drinking me.

He gives his fingers a sniff.

—Don't wanna drink you, Joe. Don't wanna drink Phil. Don't wanna drink anyone.

—When's the last time you fixed?

A shudder runs up his body, his bowels open and try to void, but nothing is left in them.

He coughs.

—Sorry about that. Pretty gross. Pretty impolite. Not myself today.

—When'd you have your last anathema, Count?

He bites the air, clacking his teeth.

—It's bad in there. The anathema is cold, man. It shows you things. I'm on the inside now, man. I don't wanna be. I don't wanna know. Want out. Gotta get out. No more on the inside. No more blood, no more blood. Out! Out! Get it out!

He jabs the tip of the knife into his thigh, poking a few holes and watching a sluggish welling of blood before the Vyrus seals them, coveting what little it has left.

I grab his wrist.

—Cool it, man.

He stops jabbing, looks at my hand, looks at the point where I've reached across his circle, tries to twist free.

—You've broken it! It's broken! Things get in! No more! Out! I want out! Get it all out! Get out! Get out!

—I'll get it out, Count, I'll get all the blood out of you. Listen, cool it and listen.

He jerks and twitches and the muscles in his belly writhe.

—Listen? Listen? I hear it all, man, all of it.

His skin is burning my hand. Air whistles over his teeth and down his throat. Starving the Vyrus, he's driving it to the edge, pushing it into a corner, forcing it to defend itself. Anytime now, it'll frenzy and attack.

I put my free hand on the butt of my gun.

—Hear this, man. I need to know, Is it possible? If someone had the resources, is it possible, could there be a cure?

He stops twisting, just his stomach crawling beneath the skin.

—A cure? A cure? Yeah, yeah, yeah, easy one, the old one. Just gotta get it all out, just gotta get the blood out.

I pull the gun, show it to him.

—Sure, gonna cure you, man, but tell me first. A cure? A real cure, could that happen?

His eyes lock, his breath falters, his body goes rigid.

I hear his heart stop beating.

Fuck.

—Phil!

The bathroom door doesn't open, but the humming stops.

I stand, gun pointed at the Count.

—Philip! Get out here!

The door stays closed.

—Um, kinda busy in here right now.

I back away from the Count.

—Philip, get your fucking ass out here!

The door swings open and he comes out, tugging his slacks up over his skinny ass, a scrap of toilet paper stuck to the sole of his shoe.

—What, what? Jesus, man, you send a guy to the john to meditate, you can't blame him when nature calls.

—Come here, Phil.

He's crosses the room, looking at me pointing my gun at the Count.

—Jeez, you shoot him or something? Not that I heard it or know anything, seeing as where I was and all.

He comes alongside me.

—Why you still drawing down on him if he's stiff?

I hear something move in the Count's chest.

He jerks erect as if strings had pulled him.

Phil takes a step back.

—Oh, oh, shit, I gotta go.

I reach out and grab the leather strands of his bolo tie and yank them up, hauling him to his tiptoes.

He chokes and gurgles.

The Count vibrates, his nostrils flare, his eyes find Phil's stretched neck and stay there. He takes a step, a flicker, his foot landing outside the circle, and he howls. Another step, speed blurred. Another howl. He shakes all over, every spasm strobed by the impossible flood of adrenaline the Vyrus has released.

I give the bolo a jerk and it scrapes Phil's skin and the scent of blood hits the air.

The Count comes for him.

He's too fast to follow, so I don't try. I keep the gun aimed at a point he'll have to cross to get to Phil's blood, and I start pulling the trigger.

Two bullets hit him before he hits Phil and drags him from my grasp, the thin cord of the bolo cutting twin stripes across my palm.

Phil is silent, beyond screaming, eyes wide, mouth stretched, tongue stuck out.

The Count ignores the holes in his stomach and opens his own mouth and lunges to bite out Phil's jutting tongue.

I shoot him twice in the back and he twists off Phil and flings himself at me, raking his nails at my eyes, wrapping his legs around my waist and squeezing, everything too fast for me to stop it.

But some things the Vyrus can't change. It's made him strong and fast and desperate, but it hasn't made him any more a fighter than he ever was.

His elbow clips my shoulder and I feel it dislocate. Blood runs down my face. He licks it, finds it poison to him, and wails and spits. I wrap my left hand around his throat and squeeze and fall forward and land on top of him and jam my knee into his gut-shot belly and choke the air from him and he bucks and roils and tears half my left ear off. And I choke him and choke him and choke him.

When he's still, I get up and find my gun and hold it.

Phil sits up, rubbing his throat.

—Fuck! What the fuck was that? What the hell was that about, man? That wasn't cool. That wasn't cool at all.

I look at the floor, find the Count's knife and pick it up.

—Yeah, well, I needed some bait to distract him.

Phil is on his feet.

—No shit! I got that. See, don't know if you missed this part, man, but I was the bait you used. That was so far from cool. That was like, whatever the opposite of cool is, that's what that was.

I tuck the gun in my belt.

—Uncool.

Phil points.

—Totally uncool!

The Count makes a wet sound, blood sputters from between his lips.

Phil takes a step toward him and stares.

—Fucker's not dead, man.

He looks at me as I come over.

—Better put a couple in his brain, man, fucker's not dead.

I look at the holes in the Count's stomach. They're not healing.

—Yeah, not yet, but he's close.

I tap the blade of the knife against my thigh.

—Hey, Phil?

He's trying to untwist his collar and his bolo.

—Yeah?

I bring the knife up.

—Speaking of uncool, I really need him to live.

He's looking down, focused on the ends of the tie.

—Hey, go ahead and First Aid away. Think you're crazy, but do what you gotta do.

I place the tip of the knife on his chest and he looks up.

—What I gotta do, Phil, is I gotta feed him.

His jaw drops, his head tilts.

—No way, man. Seriously uncool! Seriously uncool!

I grab his wrist and twirl the knife.

—Stop being a pussy, man. I'm not gonna take it all.

If it was just a matter of blood, I'd slash Phil's wrist and stick it in the Count's mouth and let him suck the fucker dry.

Phil's lucky it's more complicated than that.

He's also lucky I had some blood yesterday and got a healthy stash at home. There've been times, after a scrum like that, I'd have tapped him dry. Not that I want to drink Phil's blood any more than the Count, but the niceties go by the wayside when you're hard up. As it is, I spill a couple pints in an empty takeout coffee cup and pour it down the Count's mouth.

No surprise, it rouses him.

No surprise, he wants more.

But I've kicked Phil out by then, a fifty in his pocket for his troubles. With nothing to eat in the room, the Count goes haywire and tries to jump out the window so he can get at all the blood he can smell down on the streets where the night owls are taking the air. I've got my boot planted on his neck and I throttle him and pistol-whip him until he settles down.

Phil's blood is keeping him in the game, the holes in his belly and back aren't leaking anymore, but he's a long way from out of the woods. And it's not like more blood is gonna take care of everything that ails him. I want to get him talking straight, I'll need him healed, fed and fixed. But the fix he needs, I don't got. The fix he needs, I don't got time to find. And I never will.

And that leaves one option. Get him clean. And only one place to do that.

—He was going cold turkey.

Daniel casts his eyes on the Count's body cradled in my arms, half-wrapped in the sleeping bag I stuffed him in before dropping it in the trunk of the cab that brought me to the West Side.

—Really?

He bends and looks at the Count's crap-smeared face.

He looks at me.

—A friend of yours?

—Hardly.

He scuffs the floor with his foot.

—Well. Bring him in.

He brushes his fingers at the Enclave manning the door and it slides open, revealing the dark cavern of the warehouse.

I stay on the loading dock.

Daniel takes a step toward me.

—Something giving you pause, Simon?

I shift my feet, hating it when he uses my real name, but not wanting to get into it again.

—Yeah, see, I need him alive.

He raises the skin where his eyebrows used to be.

—Alive. In truth, he's rather close to actual life in this state.

—Daniel, I need him alive in the usual sense. I need him alive and awake and able to talk to me in all the usual senses of the words. I need to know if I bring him in there you're not going to decide he's a pariah or some shit and drain him and burn his body and make the ashes into tea or whatever you do.

A smile jumps across his face.

—*A pariah?*

—Whatever, I don't know the lingo.

A frown follows the smile.

—You may as well bring him in, Simon. We won't sacrifice him to our dark gods or anything. And it's too late for you to do much else.

I bring him in and pass him to the waiting arms of another Enclave and watch him carried away into the candlelit darkness. White shapes move deep inside the concrete-and-steel chamber. Bodies drawn thin by fasting, paled to ivory, shedding hair.

I think of Evie.

Daniel walks out and drops his mantis body on the edge of the loading dock, legs dangling, hands tucked beneath his thighs, a thin white poncho made from an old sheet draped over his shoulders hanging to his knees.

—Nice night.

I tug my jacket close.

—It's fucking freezing.

He looks up at me.

—Still a nice night.

He pats the concrete.

—Have a seat.

I stay on my feet, light a smoke.

Daniel looks away from me and to the gray glow above the rooftops.

—What's his name?

—Calls himself the Count. Don't know what his real name is. I told you about him before.

—Did you? Hm, I've forgotten.

I blow smoke and steam into the cold air.

—You don't forget shit, Daniel.

He closes his eyes.

—Don't I?

He opens them.

—It seems to me that's all I do these days. And what a relief it is. All the nonsense washing out on the tide. I'm a bit confused by the common perception that it leaves one cloudy, old age. I've found a great deal of clarity. The years refining my mind, focusing it on a single thought.

I sidelong him.

—A bit past old age, aren't you?

He swings his legs, bounces his heels off the painted front of the loading dock.

—Well, it's all relative. I'd be inclined to say that I'm pretty damn young as this all goes.

He waves a hand at the universe.

—But that's a sorry cliché. Overused. And maybe not even accurate.

I tap some ash from the tip of my cigarette.

—How old are you, Daniel?

He ducks his head.

—Old enough to know better. At least that old. And old enough to forget. So remind me. The Count?

I spit a flake of tobacco from my tongue.

—Spy. Coalition spy. Got sent down to the Society to cause trouble. Terry flipped him. He's got a load of money in some trusts. Terry flipped him to get at the money.

—And the state he's in?

—I didn't like some things he did. So I hit him with a heavy shot of anathema. Hooked him to the bad dose.

The corners of his mouth drop down, drawing the skin tighter over his skull. If you can draw skin tighter over a skull when it looks painted there in the first place.

—And the procurement?

—Not my problem.

Not my problem. The going out and finding some slob to infect, someone who the Vyrus doesn't kill outright, and harvesting his infected blood and getting it to the Count while it's still fresh enough to shoot, the entire manufacture of anathema, not my problem. But it's been happening anyway. After I declined, Terry had to have someone doing it. Hurley, I'd imagine. Keeping the Count alive and on the bad dose, keeping access to his fat accounts open.

Daniel keeps his frown.

I drop my butt.

—It bothers you?

He looks at his feet.

—Not the deaths. The useless cattle the Vyrus rejects aren't to be mourned. I pity them perhaps, for the half-lives they've been given. But the ones harvested for the anathema, the ones the Vyrus takes and doesn't cast off, they have been wasted. It all smacks of waste. And manipulation of the Vyrus. I know that's my own perception, and a limited one, but I feel it nonetheless. Even though I know the Vyrus cannot be manipulated. It uses us, not the other way around.

I grunt. At a loss for anything else to say.

He taps my thigh with a finger.

—But no lectures tonight, yes?

—Fine by me.

He stretches his neck.

—I'm tired. Finish the story. Why do you need him?

I look at him, see Evie again, wasting in her bed.

—He was premed in school. Terry loaded him up with medical books. Had him studying. Trying to maybe figure out some stuff about the Vyrus.

He sighs.

—*Medical books*. Poor Terry. He's so . . . material.

He brings his feet up on the dock and rises.

—And if that's what you need from him, his medical knowledge of the Vyrus, you should have let him die. In the usual sense.

I look at the litter in the gutter.

—I have to ask him some stuff.

—Well, whether you had *stuff* to ask him or not, we'd help him.

—Didn't know ministering to the weak was your new line.

He gestures at the darkness in the warehouse.

—It's not, but he's Enclave.

—The fuck?

He scratches his head.

—Not that I knew him before, but, yes, he's one of ours.

—So, what, you look at him and you just know he's in the club?

He shrugs.

—That's all it took when I first met you. You're either Enclave or you're not, it can't be hidden or mistaken. Believe in Enclave or not, it believes in you. And the Vyrus tells me.

—The things you believe, Daniel, I don't know how you remember how to stay out of the sun.

—And what do I believe, Simon?

—Got me, man. Got me.

He shakes his head.

—It wasn't a rhetorical question. I'm asking for you to articulate it, my beliefs. You want my help, this is what I'm asking for. Tell me what I believe.

I look around, at everything but him.

—It's, man, it's complicated.

—No, it's simple.

—You, you guys, Enclave, you believe the Vyrus is, what, spiritual? Supernatural. You believe it, man, it consumes us and when we die we pass into its world. You believe that if you starve it, take in just enough blood to keep it alive as it consumes you, that you can be made, Jesus fuck, I don't know, into something like it, but stay in this world. For what reason you'd want that, I do not fucking know.

He stares at the ground.

—One by one, Simon, all Enclave test their limits. Wean themselves from this world, give up more of their physical selves to the Vyrus by forcing it to consume more of its host than it would do were it fed well. One by one, reaching their limit, they fail, wracked by their own insufficiencies, dying in the dark. But it will not always be that way. This is what will happen, Simon.

He puts his mouth close to my ear, the heat off his body far more intense than what I felt from the Count, his burning unlimited.

—One day, as many have before, one of us will open the doors of this place and in the bright light of morning, will walk out naked. And not be burned. The Vyrus having consumed entire its vessel and made of it something not earthly. When it happens, when one of us crosses into the Vyrus' plane, but retains corporeality, that one will guide the others through the same path. And we will be true vessels for the Vyrus. Uncorruptible to the sun, intangible to the weapons of this world, able to project the Vyrus through our physical selves at will. We will bring it to all, the great and the meek. And make the world Enclave, make it Vyrus. As it is meant to be. As it already truly is.

He's at my side, burning me and crazier than fuck.

I don't move.

—There's only a hundred of you.

He steps away, raises his hands.

—Well, we'll just have to see what we can do.

He turns to go.

—Daniel?

—Mmm?

—The way you know the Count is Enclave?

—Yes?

I watch his back.

—The way you say the Vyrus told you that? Does it tell you other stuff?

His shoulders rise and drop.

—How so?

—If you met someone, could you tell, by looking, could you tell if the Vyrus would kill them? Or, the other thing, infect them? Make them like us.

His head tilts back. I can see the seam of bone where the quarters of his skull meet under the skin.

—Yes. Actually, yes, I can do that.

—If I brought someone here?

He lifts a hand.

—Come back in the morning, Simon. Your friend will be sensible by then. Come in the morning and talk to him. Ask him questions. And anything you'd like me to look at, bring it with you.

He walks into the darkness.

I take a step toward the doorway.

—The morning?

His white shade is fading.

—Just before sunrise. I'll be going out after that.

I take another step.

—Going out?

A candle flame reflects a last flicker of him.

—I'm done here, Simon. I kept telling you I was failing. Did you think I could hold out forever? Time for me to find out what the Vyrus wants from me. And the sun will show the way.

I step close to the darkness, but I don't go in there.

Instead I walk east, headed out of the no-man's-land that surrounds Enclave turf. Turf I've always crossed alone, because no one else wants anything to do with it. I think about coming back across it before sunrise.

But not coming alone.

—Joe.

I look up. My foot has just hit the east side of University Place, the edge of Society turf, and Hurley's waiting for me.

—Hurl.

He moves his toothpick to the corner of his mouth, juts it eastward.

—Terry's bin callin' ya.

—I wasn't home.

—Dat's what he said.

—Man's fucking psychic or something.

—Must be, told me ta look fer ya comin' offa Enclave turf. Me, niver woulda figured anyone ta be over der.

—Yeah. Well. Tell Terry I'll catch him later, got some things to do.

I move around him and he drops his hand on my shoulder and almost knocks it back out of its socket.

—Said, Terry wants ta see ya.

I look at the hand weighing my shoulder down.

—With all due respect, Hurley, you want to get your hand the fuck off me?

He takes the toothpick from his mouth with his free hand.

—Let's nae fook aboat, Joe. Yer head o' security, sure, but Terry's dah boss, an' when he calls, ya come to 'im. So, an wit all due respect fer ya an' yer job an' all, come da fook wit me er I'm gonna have ta beat ya till ya do.

I lick my lips.

—Sounds important.

He puts the toothpick back in his mouth.

—Fook do I know, I'm just da fookin' help.

The pie at the Odessa Diner is shit. But I ordered it anyway.

Terry ordered the veggie pirogies.

—Really, Joe, it's just the kind of thing we have to start getting used to. Whether we like it or not, our world is getting bigger. Trying to stay on our turf won't change that. And, think about this, if we try to just stay in our space, just kind of cling to what we have from Houston to Fourteenth between the river and Fifth Ave. while the world outside that patch is getting bigger, well, we'll just be getting smaller the whole time. Think about that, and see if it doesn't blow your mind.

I pick up my fork, poke the pie, but it doesn't look any better than it did when the waiter put it in front of me.

I put the fork down.

—However big the world's gonna get between now and tomorrow night, it's gonna have to do it without me being involved. I got other things I'm working on, and I am sure as fuck not going to Brooklyn tonight.

Terry cuts a pirogi in half and dips it in applesauce.

—I hear you, man, I hear you. Brooklyn. Wow. I mean, how many years have we been talking about that place like it's a different world. The undiscovered country. Like only Lewis and Clark would know how to handle a land like that, right? Going to Brooklyn? I must be crazy asking you to do that at a moment's notice. Something like that, man, we should be planning an expedition with, like, Sherpas and stuff.

He pops the piece of pirogi in his mouth and chews and swallows.

—Problem is, problem is, our debate with the Docks Boss and his people last night, that seems to have caused some ripples.

He pushes the other half of the pirogi through the applesauce and watches me.

I point at his plate.

—Those things are better with sour cream.

He nods.

—I'm trying to stay away from dairy.

I poke my pie again. It's clearly store bought. The crust flat and shiny, the overhead fluorescents reflecting off it. The filling gelatinous, dotted with three or four clots of apple puree.

He eats the last piece of pirogi and wipes his mouth with a paper napkin.

—So, ripples. Like, the Docks weren't the first of the Brooklyn Clans to get in touch with us.

—I gathered.

—Right. And now, this other group, well, they seem to have, and I'm not saying I know how this happened, but they seem to have gotten ideas of how we handled our differences with the Docks. And this has made them, I don't know, leery, I guess. And they want, well, some assurance. Some direct contact with the Society. And they want it soon. Like, and this is where the urgency comes from, they want it tonight. They're willing to send a representative, but they want us to handle transportation.

I dig my fork into the pie and put it in my mouth. It's as bad as I thought it would be. I wash it down with thin black coffee.

—So go give them some direct contact. Last time I checked, diplomatic missions weren't something I specialized in.

He pushes his plate to the side and wraps his fingers around his cup of chamomile tea.

—There's nothing diplomatic involved. You go, you get their representative, you bring their representative back here, and after the meeting you provide return transit. And hey, you know, I wish I *could* go. First contact, man. I mean, direct face-to-face contact, I'm not saying it's Nixon in China or anything, but it's a pretty major deal.

I look past Terry, out the big front windows of the diner, and watch the Friday-night barhoppers parading up and down Avenue A.

I glance at the clock above the front door. Well past midnight. Way past visiting hours at the hospital. If I call the night nurse she'll shine me on again, tell me Evie is fine no matter how she is.

The taste of the crap pie and the lousy coffee is still in my mouth.

I look at Terry, blow some air, give with a big helpless shrug.

—Sure, Terry, I get it, and I don't mean to make light or anything, but I have security issues here on our turf. That's why you gave me the job, right, to take care of things right here at home? Way I remember it, the deal was I do things the way I think they should be done. Right now, I got to tell you, this Van Helsing is the real deal. What I've been poking into tonight, the tension out there in the community is high. Word is spreading and people are freaked out. Those are our folks out there, living in fear, I can't do something to make them feel safe, well, I should just hand the job to someone else. That's not even taking into account how riled Predo was when

I went up to see him, guy's got a serious bug up his ass over this. I don't take care of it quickly, it could screw up all the quiet we've been enjoying lately. Just, hey man, just priorities.

The waiter places the check between us, fair warning that he wants his fucking table back. Terry flips the check, looks at the total, goes in his pocket.

—Yeah, the Van Helsing. That's, sure, that's a concern. Thing is, thing is, and you know how I feel about pointing fingers, and I could be wrong, but the thing is, Joe, this problem in Brooklyn, it didn't really exist until you went up to see Predo.

I remember that pause, that half second when Predo mentioned the Docks to me. That one moment when I cracked open and he read me cover to cover.

Sharp bastard.

He places some bills and change on the check, a precise ten percent tip included.

—And, you know, these things happen. He can ferret information with the best, so I'm not saying you could help it. Predo, he's just doing what comes naturally and putting whatever he got from you to use. If I were to guess, I'd imagine he maybe placed a call to these folks he knows we're in contact with and suggested that we might be, I don't know, untrustworthy in negotiations. Which, I'll grant in this case may have been true, but generally we're a much safer bet than the Coalition. But try telling that to new faces when the story going around is that we, I don't know, used a *containment strategy* on the Docks. Which was really best for everyone. Their attitude and values may get by in Brooklyn, but things are far more sophisticated here. A lead pipe mentality like theirs would have caused trouble for all the Clans.

—Yeah, well, we'll never know one way or another, what with how they were *contained* and all.

He recounts the money on the check.

—You can be flippant about it if you like, Joe.

—*Flippant?*

—But I can't. I have to take these situations seriously. That forest we were talking about before? That metaphor can be extended pretty far. The forest, the ecosystem, it needs to be kept in balance. Too many new species enter the ecosystem at once, they throw it out of balance. Species that have been there for eons, they can find themselves at risk.

He takes fifty cents off the check and puts it back in his pocket.

I look at the clock again. There's an orderly at the hospital, if I pass him a pint of gin he'll get me on Evie's ward. I try to remember when his shift ends.

—Yeah, ecosystem, unbalanced, got it. All the more reason I need to stay here and deal with the Van Helsing.

I start to get up.

Terry puts a hand on my wrist.

—Joe, sorry, I'm being unclear. Let me focus this a little for you.

He pushes his glasses up his nose.

—Fuck the Van Helsing.

He looks at my chair. I sit in it.

He nods.

—Predo doesn't give a damn about the Van Helsing. People out there don't know about the Van Helsing. You haven't been looking for the Van Helsing. What you have been doing, what you did do, was you went up to Predo and let him, you know, work you. However it played, you tipped him and he knows how we handled the Docks, and he's pissed. He knows they would have thrown in with the Coalition and he's pissed we, well, intervened or whatever. Now he's getting kind of childish and trying to do the same thing with us, and the situation needs to be dealt with.

I watch the waiter come and take a look at the check and the money. I watch the sour look on his face get more sour as he eyes the money. I watch him clear every last plate and glass and piece of silver from our table, leaving the check.

He makes to take the teacup from Terry's hand and Terry looks up at him.

—I'm not finished. When I'm finished you can have the cup and the table. Until then, stay the fuck away from us. And if you want a better tip, refill the water glasses every now and then.

The waiter takes a step back, touches the ring in his right eyebrow, turns and walks away.

Terry turns his eyes to me.

—Sorry about that, I'm a little, man, a little stressed, I guess.

I wait while he works out the stress.

—See, and that stress, a lot of it has to do with all this Brooklyn stuff. And I'd really like to bring some stability to the situation so I can, you know, decompress. I don't want to spend my time taking out my issues on innocent bystanders like that kid. So for the sake of everyone around me, before I, I don't know, start taking people's heads off or whatever, I need to have this thing dealt with right away.

I remember what it was like, back in the day, when Terry would take someone's head off. I look at him, old man hippie, and know it's still in there. The head-taker. One of the best.

I lean in.

—Bullshit.

His forehead creases.

—Um. Excuse me?

—Bullshit, Terry. You didn't want me to tip our hand to Predo, you wouldn't have let me go up there. I've been played by you two before, I know what it feels like. Whatever you really want, it has fuckall to do with me running to Brooklyn. The Van Helsing? I know that doesn't mean shit. I already got that figured. I don't know who's play it was, yours or Predo's, but I know we've seen the last of him. You want me to do a little dance? Fine. Tell me the tune. Show me the steps. Draw them out on the floor so I know exactly where to put my feet. Because I am goddamned if I'm gonna let you two jerk me all over town again getting my head bounced off hard stuff.

I lean back in my chair and light a smoke.

Terry scratches his cheek.

—Wow. Wow. That was, that was very honestly put. That was a real, I don't want to say breakthrough, because I've always felt like we get each other, but that was such an honest and feeling piece of communication. I'm, I don't know, touched. Thanks, Joe. Thanks for that.

I go to tip some ash in the tray, find the waiter took it with everything else.

—Whatever, man. As long as we're clear.

Terry waves a hand.

—Oh yeah, we're clear, man.

He strokes his chin.

—Thing is, thing is, you have no idea what you're talking about.

He raises a finger.

—Playing you? Would it were so, my friend, but no, that's not the case. I let you go up to talk to Predo because I figured you'd been around enough by now to be ready for his game playing. But you're not ready to deal with Predo on those terms. Enough said. No shame in that. Lesson learned by us both. No, I just really, really need to take care of business.

He leans in.

—It occur to you, Joe, all these Brooklyn Clans coming to us and to the Coalition, it occur to you to ask why? I mean, what's up, right? And I'll skip waiting for an answer you don't have, because rhetoriality is the last thing we need right now. What's up is that they're scared, man. Scared bad. Someone over there, someone's pushing, grabbing turf, squeezing out the little Clans. Years now, guys like the Docks, they wanted nothing to do with, you know, us Manhattanites. Wasn't just a matter of no one from the Island wanting to cross the river, they had no interest in coming this way. Now they got no choice. They need allies and they got no choice. And if they're getting squeezed over the river, if sociopolitical forces are sending these refugees our way, we need to make arrangements now. Or we'll be sitting in the middle of a humanitarian disaster. By which I mean at least a few hundred new infecteds on the Island, all of them looking for blood. That is the kind of impact our little ecosystem cannot absorb. They have to work with the Clans here. There has to be some organization. Everyone knows it, but there's still gonna be some jockeying. We're all gonna get a little bigger. And it's important no one gets too big. In terms of the ecosphere, that'd totally screw shit up. This Clan we're in touch with, the Freaks?

—*Freaks*. That's promising.

—Let's not start making judgments based on something as flimsy as semantics. Regardless of how they've chosen to represent themselves to the world in language, they apparently carry a membership of several dozen. That's more than enough to cause waves or swing a slight advantage in numbers. They cannot be, you know, disregarded.

He points the finger at me.

—So now, I need the head of Society security to do his job and go out to Brooklyn and clean up a little mess that is, when you get right down to it, pretty much his own damn fault, and make sure the Freaks understand that we offer them their best opportunity for seamless integration into Manhattan.

He drops the finger.

—As for what you're up to, well, your private life, Joe, this girl you, I don't know, *take care of*, that's all well and good. From what I hear she brings out a real nurturing side in you. And I guess I've heard things aren't going well with her. I'm sorry about that. God knows the Society is more than sympathetic to anyone with any kind of illness, but, you know, some hit closer to home than others. That, however, is neither, you know, here nor there. There's a security problem that needs to be tended to. The Society needs you to tend to it. If you can't tend to it, you need to let me know and we'll, for lack of a better solution, dissolve this relationship and you can go back to your old status. And all that.

He leans back.

I think about *all that.*

On my own dime again. No more Terry breathing down my neck. No more sit-downs with Predo. No more taking care of everyone else's business before my own.

Yeah.

And no more easy blood. No more stipend from the Society coffers. Scuffling. Scraping for my own blood, let alone the stuff for Evie's transfusions. And, sure, no more sit-downs with Predo, but probably seeing him sooner than later. Once I'm out from Society sanction, he'll be sending his giant to collect me. For accounts past due.

Rogue.

Alone.

God I want it.

*God I want to be alone. Please let me be alone. Leave me alone. Don't ask me for anything. I don't want to do it anymore. I don't want to think about anyone else anymore. I'm no good at it.*

I reach out and drop the butt of my Lucky in Terry's teacup.

—Where am I going?

He slides the cup away.

—Coney Island.

Coney Island. The far edge of the world. Where the land runs out. Put it on a map, you'd be scrawling *Here there be fucking monsters* across it.

I don't say anything, I don't have to.

Terry holds up a hand.

—Yeah, it's a bit of a haul. But you'll have wheels. And company.

—*Company.* So why the fuck do *I* have to go?

He picks up his cup, remembers I dropped my smoke in it, frowns.

—The company is exactly why you're going, Joe.

He holds a finger up to signal the waiter who turns his back and continues flirting with the cashier.

He sets the cup on the table.

—My own fault for being a dick. There's karma for you, Joe.

I look at the clock one last time. If I hurry, I'm pretty sure I can catch the drunk orderly.

—Why I'm going, man? Company?

He pushes the cup away.

—Yeah, company. Well, like I say, their person, the Freaks', is coming here, but, they're you know, leery, so, one of ours has to stay with them.

I rise, lean over the table.

—Fuck. No.

—Easy, man.

—I am not going out there to be tied up and sit in a basement with a bag over my face waiting to find out if it all goes cool so I don't get my head sawed off. You want a pawn, send one. Hurley's around here someplace.

He puts his hand over his heart.

—Hurley? No, not for this. And you? Sit hostage? No way. Man, that's like the whole point. They're sending someone from their hierarchy, Joe. We have to do the same. That's why you got to go, to make sure she gets back. I can't rely on Hurley if any, you know, subtlety is called for.

I stay on my feet.

—She?

He glances at his watch.

—Yeah. And she's, you know, a valuable asset, so handle with care, right?

—I don't appreciate being discussed like I'm property.

We both look at Lydia.

Terry rises.

—Man, I wish I could be in on this. It's like a brave new world.

Lydia points at the check and money on the table.

—Is that what you're leaving for a tip? You know what someone makes in the service industry, Terry? There's no minimum wage, no health benefits, no pension plan. You ever waited tables?

Terry digs in his pocket.

—My bad. My bad.

I rub my forehead, look at Terry.

—It has to be tonight?

—Yeah. See, these aggressors I'm talking about, imperialists really, they're kind of everywhere out there from what we hear.

—Great.

Lydia puts her hands in the pockets of her Carhartt jacket.

—Except on Friday night. So if we don't want to mess with them we go now.

Why couldn't it have been Hurley?

—It's political. Not that I'm saying any decision isn't political, but in this case it's more so. Every time you put one of those things in your mouth and light it and inhale and then blow the smoke for other people to breathe, that's a political decision.

With Hurley I could have smoked without getting this shit.

—And don't look at me like that. Just because it can't affect me or you, that doesn't make it OK. We may be afflicted, we may have been infected with a disease that's enabled us at the same time that it's disenabled us, but we have to remember that we live in the same world as everyone else. That's the biggest danger I see to the Society charter. The fact that we need blood to survive, that's going to be a huge psychological hurdle for non-Vyral people to clear, but the psychological impact of that need on the Vyrally impaired is as big an obstacle. I see it all the time, the drinking of blood, the fact that it comes from uninfected humans makes it very easy to begin seeing the uninfected as somehow less real than us. We can't afford that kind of, *elitism* isn't the word, but that kind of superiority to creep into our thinking. Smoking, just freely spewing your secondhand smoke around to kill people, that's political, Joe, whether you want to accept the fact or not.

I offer the pack to Lydia again.

—So you want one or not?

She slumps back in her seat.

—Just keep your window down, OK, I hate the smell of the fucking things and I don't want their stink all over the van.

I light up.

—Sure, window down, of course. I mean, where the hell am I gonna throw the butts if the window's not down?

She looks out her own window.

—Karma, Joe, it's gonna shit all over you one day.

—And it's been so good to me up till now.

—Without you even knowing it.

—Whatever.

I park the Econoline and open the door.

Lydia looks at the sign on the storefront and shakes her head.

—No. No, you will not be drinking and driving.

I step out of the van.

—Keep your panties on, it's not for me.

At Beth Israel, I find my orderly and give him his pint of Gilbey's and he uses his passkey in the elevator and takes me up to Evie's floor. The night nurse rises behind her desk as we approach, a hand reaching for the phone, but the orderly goes to her and slips her the twenty bucks I gave him and she turns down the hall and walks into the bathroom.

The orderly takes a hit off his pint.

—Five minutes.

I go into Evie's room. Curtains are drawn around her bed and the old lady's. I duck under hers.

She looks like hell.

I look at the bags in her IV stand. Straight fluids in one. And a morphine drip. She must have cramped badly after the chemo. She must have dry heaved for a couple hours and been unable to sleep. A trache tube juts from her throat. That's new.

I think about the night we met.

I think about putting a hand over the end of the tube.

I touch the scabs that have grown over the part of my ear the Count didn't rip off my head and think about peeling them away and leaning over the bed and pressing the wound to Evie's lips and finding out what kind of girl she really is.

What kind of man I am.

I take the chart from the foot of her bed and look at it. It means nothing to me. I put it back. I put a hand in my jacket pocket and take out the candy necklace from Solomon's store. I put it on the bedside table and leave, not having the guts to do anything that might help her.

The night nurse is at her station. I stop in front of her. She smells like a different brand of disinfectant than the one they use to clean everything in here.

—Why the trache tube?

She doesn't take her eyes from the screen of her computer, just raises her hand and rubs her fingers against her thumb. I grab her wrist. With a squeeze and a twist and a pull I could mash her radius and ulna and tear her hand from her arm and drop it in her lap and walk out with her screams as a sound track.

She looks at my fingers wrapped around her wrist.

—You'll have to let go of me, sir.

This isn't her fault. Evie being sick has nothing to do with her. She's just trying to get by.

I squeeze.

She gasps.

I haul her up out of her chair.

—The fucking hole in her neck, why's it there?

She puts her hand over mine, plucks at my fingers, stops, pats my wrist as if to calm me.

—The herpes lesions have spread into her throat. There was severe esophagitis and swelling.

I let her go and she drops into her chair, cradling her left wrist, staring at the dark ring of bruises around it.

I drop a fifty on her desk. Think about it. Pick it up and put it back in my pocket and leave.

Lydia looks up from the map she's spread over the dashboard as I climb in the van.

I point at it.

—I want to get there fast.

She traces a line with her fingernail.

—FDR to the BQE.

I grind the ignition and the engine catches.

She raps a knuckle on the plywood wall that seals off the windowless rear of the van.

—If there's an emergency, don't try to race back for me. Just park and wait out the sun in the back.

I look out the windshield up at the hospital, and turn in my seat and punch a hole in the plywood and heave and it crashes into the back of the van, leaving it wide open to any light that might pour in through the windshield.

Lydia picks up a scrap of wood, looks at it, sticks it in my face.

—What the fuck, Pitt? What the fuck?

I put the van in gear.

—Incentive to get this shit done before sunrise.

I pull from the curb, running a red light, speeding toward the FDR.

—What are you looking for?

We've cleared the eastern end of the Manhattan Bridge and I'm taking us through the insane series of ramps and loops that will put us on the BQE.

—I'm looking for signs.

Lydia takes her foot off the dash, leans over and looks at my face.

—No you're not.

I point out the windshield.

—The assholes that designed this shit wanted to kill us. I'm trying to find the signs that'll keep us from plowing into something made of concrete.

She leans back and puts her feet up.

—You're looking for an ambush.

I tighten my fingers on the wheel.

—No, I'm not.

She crosses her ankles.

—You're looking for a bunch of savage infecteds in loincloths. You're looking for zombie parachutists. You're looking for dragons. You're in the wilderness and you're scared the lions, tigers and bears are going to eat you.

I stop scanning the edges of the road and overhanging tree branches and overpasses and cars that pull up alongside us. I stop looking at any of the places I've been looking at, searching for ambushes.

—I'm just driving.

She taps the toe of her Doc Martens on the windshield.

—You ever been off of the Island? Before, I mean.

—I was born in the Bronx.

—You're such a New Yorker, never been anywhere. I traveled. I did a semester in Europe, in Italy. Went everywhere. And I'm from the West Coast. When I came out here I took a whole month to drive crosscountry. Been to Canada. Costa Rica. Mexico. Hawaii when I was a kid. Been to fucking Disney World. Most disgusting place on earth. Consumerism at its worst.

I chain another smoke.

—That radio work?

—Sure.

I toss the spent butt out the window.

—Mind playing something on it?

—What do you want to hear?

—Something that isn't you.

She flips the bird at me and clicks the radio and settles the dial on some college station that's playing some chick with an acoustic guitar.

Pet the Cat music, Evie calls it.

—This OK?

—If it includes you shutting up, it's OK.

She nods, draws a little spiral in the dust on the dash.

—How's she doing, your friend?

I reach over and spin the dial and put it on a jazz station and turn it up. Coltrane plays "Stardust."

Lydia ruffles her short hair.

—Just that you never asked about HIV again after that one time and I didn't know if you'd been able to get her some new meds. And stopping at the hospital just made me wonder?

—She's fine.

—If she's in the hospital, she isn't fine. I told you before, I know people in the treatment community. One of the Lesbian Gay and Other Gendered Alliance members was a hospice worker. If she needs care, we could arrange something.

—She doesn't need care.

—Hospital's not the place for someone who's really sick. They don't give a shit. Fucking HMOs, it's all about the bottom line. Get them in and get them out. Free up the beds for another pile of dollars. She could be at home, if she's that bad.

We grind into traffic merging from the Brooklyn Battery Tunnel and start crawling through Red Hook.

—She's not staying in the hospital. She's gonna be fine.

Lydia tugs on her rainbow-enameled ear cuff.

—You're not thinking about doing something to *make* her fine, are you, Joe?

I lean on the horn, cut the wheel and drive up on the shoulder, peel around a line of cars and jump back in the lane beyond the jam and put the pedal down.

Lydia adjusts the strap of her seat belt.

—Just as a reminder, infecting someone, on purpose, that's a severe abuse of the Society charter. An execution offense. You get the sun for that.

Greenwood Cemetery appears on our left. I know its name the same way I know the names of anything off the Island; I've read about it. It's a hell of a lot bigger than on the map.

Lydia looks at it as we drive past.

—And there's the moral issue. Do you have the right to infect anyone? Even if you think it might save their life, do you have the right to make that choice for them? Personally, I don't think anyone has the right to make any decision for anyone.

The cemetery disappears behind us. The road is open. We bend right onto the Belt Parkway toward the bay, the decommissioned docks on one side, Owl's Head Park on the other.

—And, of course, you never even know if it will work. I mean, I've never tried to infect anyone, but I know the survival rate is below fifty percent. And it's a horrible death.

On the POW/MIA Memorial Parkway, long span and towers of the Verrazano-Narrows Bridge ahead, a right turn and we'd be heading west.

Solomon's hogleg digs into my back. The Docks Boss' .44 weighs my left jacket pocket. A round from that in Lydia's side, lean over and open her door and push her out and take the ramp onto the bridge. See something else.

Lydia puts a finger on the radio dial, takes it off.

—Just acting like you don't care, Joe, that doesn't change anything. And it won't change how you feel if you fuck up and do something cruel and stupid. Something irrevocable.

Kill Lydia and drive away and see something else. Something new.

The first part has its appeal.

The rest of it? Ask me, there's probably nothing out there worth seeing. Nothing better than a dying girl with no hair.

The bridge slips away and we're on Leif Erikson Drive. The ocean on our right. I look at it. I've never seen it from this close.

Lydia stares.

—I flew over it. I flew over the whole damn thing. Twice. Imagine. And I'll never do it again.

She leans her forehead against her window.

—Fucking Vyrus.

I glance at her.

—Still talking to Sela?

The muscles in the back of her neck jump.

—Sometimes. She's Coalition now, but she's still a friend.

I look at the road, arcing onto Shore Parkway, away from the water.

—She's fucking the girl.

She turns from the window.

—I know.

I fish a smoke from my pocket.

She looks at the map in her lap, points.

—Cropsey Ave.

I take the exit. Neither of us talks. We hit a red at Neptune and watch the people draining away from the boardwalk where the rides are dark and the arcades are shutting down and the drunks are puking on the sidewalk outside Nathan's.

She points again and I take a right on Surf.

She starts folding the map.

—Love doesn't have a reason.

I ignore that nonsense.

She doesn't.

—Sela and the girl feel something. You can't do anything about that. And it's none of your business anyway.

I roll down toward Seagate and pull to a stop and park on Mermaid Ave., around the corner from 37th and the ragged-ass end of the Riegelmann Boardwalk.

—Yeah, funny you should say that about it being none of my business.

I take out the big .44 and flip the cylinder and make sure I filled it with big hollow-point bullets. I did.

—Because I've been thinking just those words for the last half a fucking hour.

Lydia points at the gun.

—Planning to use that, Joe?

I drop the revolver in my pocket and take out the hogleg and break it open.

—No plans, just hopes.

She opens her door and swings down.

—Do me a favor, keep it in your pants.

We walk down the sidewalk, windblown sand crunching under our feet. We make for the lights flickering on the far side of the boardwalk.

She inhales sea air.

—Smells good.

I inhale smoke.

—Sure does.

We walk out on the boardwalk.

Lydia stops.

—She could change everything.

I stop.

She's looking out at the water, a big moon rippling on the waves.

—The girl, Joe. Sela says. Joe. She could change everything.

I drop my smoke and grind it under my heel.

—Don't talk crazy, Lydia. You're smarter than that.

And I walk away from her and look down at the canvas tent, painted black and speckled with red gloss, that juts from beneath the edge of the boardwalk, pennants flapping from the center pole, torches burning at the entrance, a big banner cracking in the wind as a tall guy in a top hat and a tailcoat spiels in front of it.

—FREAKS! That's rightytighty, ladeez and gentilemans! Real! Live! Freaks! Not the cut-rate varietals one finds down the shore! But the Real McCoy! Bearded ladies and tattooed men and wild Borneo savages are best left to the amateurs! Within the folds of this modest tent we will reveal to you actual FREAKS of nature! Creatures that spurn the light of day! Fearful, unnatural sports of fate that were never meant to be! Step up and step in, ladeez and gentilemans! A show unlike any other! A spectacle! A horror show! A festival of disgust and blood! Step! Right! Up!

Lydia comes alongside me.

I look at her.

—Can we leave now, or do we have to sit through this shit?

Apparently we have to sit through this shit.

—Ladeez and gentilemans!

I spill the last unpopped kernels from the red and white striped popcorn box into my mouth and crunch them.

—Know what would make this better?

—Never before on any stage at any time have you witnessed an appetite like the appetite of . . . The Glasseater!

Lydia is staring through the torch-lit gloom to the tiny stage where the MC gives the tails of his shabby coat a flip and bows as the curtain parts and reveals a scrawny dude in a loincloth sitting at a dinner table with dull silver candelabra and chipped china.

—If it wasn't utterly exploitive?

Two chubby chicks in thigh-high leather boots, ripped lace corsets, snake tattoos and black lipstick come on stage. One ties a napkin around the Glasseater's neck while the other places a tray covered by a dented silver dome in front of him. She pulls the dome away with a lackluster flourish, revealing a huge soup bowl piled high with rusty nails, shattered glass, twists of broken spring, bottle caps, chips of razor blades and bent sewing needles.

He takes the soupspoon from his setting, breathes onto it and wipes it in his bare armpit, dips up a helping of the scrap, smiles with broken teeth, shovels it in his mouth and begins to chew with his mouth open as the audience groans and squeals. Blood and bits of torn flesh dribble from his mouth along with shards of steel and glass as he swallows hard and snorts and a fine spray of blood fans from his nostrils.

I toss the empty popcorn box on top of the pile of beer cups, beer cans, beer bottles and corndog wrappers erupting from a rancid trash barrel.

—If I didn't know he was gonna stop bleeding before he got off stage, and be as good as new tomorrow morning, that would make this better.

The small crowd of Brooklyn hipsters, old-school Coney Islanders, roughnecks and shorties does a collective gross-out and flinches as he spits blood at them and it splashes against the sheet of transparent plastic draped between them and the stage.

The frown on Lydia's face carves itself a little deeper.

—Waste. Immoral waste.

I poke a finger in the opening of my rapidly thinning last pack of Luckys and count the remainders.

—Not your blood.

She glances at me, shakes her head.

—Is that what you think? Well it is, Joe. It's mine and it's yours. And more than that, it's the blood of the uninfected people watching this spectacle without a notion of what's going on.

The act comes to an end as the Glasseater autoregurgitates the wreckage, along with a fair amount of blood and fleshy bits, and the curtain drops.

Lydia turns on the bleacher and whispers at me over the hubbub of the crowd waiting for the next act.

—That blood? Someone could have used that to stay healthy another day. And someone, someone completely ignorant of the Vyrus is going to be replacing the blood that asshole just wasted. It's like watching a Hummer drive by with the windows rolled down and the AC on full blast. Makes me want to puke.

The sound system cranks and Motorhead blisters the speakers with "Jailbait."

The chubby girls, topless other than crosses of black electric tape over their nipples, sporting ripped satin pantaloons, one carrying twin beds of nails and the other carrying a sledgehammer, come from behind the curtain.

I point an unlit cigarette at the stage.

—Then I'm guessing this act is gonna really piss you off.

The MC raises his arms.

—Ladeez and gentilemans! The esoteric and erotic mysteries of the Far East as revealed by Vendetta and Harm!

Lydia jumps from the bleachers, puts her head down, storms across the stained and threadbare carpets laid over the sand and ducks out of the tent.

I put my last cigarette in my mouth and watch the first girl sandwich herself between the nail beds and the second girl start tap-dancing on top of her, wielding the hammer like a cane. More blood flows.

Having seen enough to know that the point of the act isn't to demonstrate how one lays on nails *without* being harmed, I follow Lydia.

The torches planted in the sand outside the entrance whip in the breeze off the ocean, streams of greasy smoke tail up the beach and under the rotting wood of the boardwalk that half the tent hides beneath.

Lydia is stomping over the sand, kicking up little plumes with her Docs, headed for the tide line.

—Come get me when it's over. If I stay, I'm going to make a scene.

I peek through a gap in the entrance, see what the chicks are up to, and figure she's right.

My Zippo won't hold a flame in the wind so I take a light from one of the torches and lean against a piling, listening to the rock 'n' roll and the gasps and screeches of the audience, smoking and looking at the ocean in the moonlight. Counting seconds till the show is over and I can collect the Freaks Boss and get back to my life. Such as it is.

—Bum one of those?

It takes me a second to smell him, another second to see him. The first because he comes at me from downwind, the second because he's a fucking midget.

I squeeze the pack between my fingers, feel three left, give him one.

He takes the smoke and pats the pockets of the denim overalls he wears over his bare, blue-tattooed torso and arms.

—Light?

I offer him my smoke and he lights his own and gives mine back.

—Thanks.

I take a drag.

—So what's it like?

He scratches a wrinkled bald head.

—What's that?

I hold my hand three feet over the sand.

—Midget Vampyre? How's that work? Find it a bitch getting to someone's neck?

He smiles, flashing full sets of steel dentures, canines every tooth, and points at my upper thigh.

—Usually find something I can get to in a pinch.

I think about kicking him down the beach. Wonder if I could get him to the water. Wonder if he would float.

He takes a silver flask from the side pocket of the overalls, swigs from it and holds it up.

—You the guy from Manhattan?

I wave the flask off.

—I'm the driver. One you want is by the water.

He takes another slug of the thick dark rum I smell in the flask and slips it away in his pocket.

—Whatsay you come in and take a look at the finale?

—Whatsay we skip the donkey fucking, or whatever you close with and you grab your boss so we can do the swap and I can get back where I belong.

He looks up at me, blows a stream of smoke that just reaches my face.

—Buddy, I am the boss. And till the show is over, no one goes anywhere.

He drops the half-finished smoke at my feet.

—You can finish that if you want.

He turns and heads for the back of the tent.

—Me, I got an entrance to make.

It's a showstopper.

People cover their eyes, howl, run from the tent, one or two start crying, a couple who's been here before laugh and shake their heads, still not believing what they're seeing.

The midget is standing in the middle of the stage, tugging lengths of intestine from the hole he's chewed in his own belly and draping them over the shoulders of Vendetta and Harm, who admire them like mink stoles, giving them the occasional lick.

Lydia watches, nothing about her moves except her discontent. That's all over the fucking place.

The midget brings a loop of intestine up to his mouth, shows the steel teeth, the music crescendos, a full-fledged Guitar Wolf freak-out, he opens his jaws wide, the torches flutter suddenly, his teeth glitter and snap down and the torches go out and red and blue strobes pulse and everyone screams as the midget collapses and the girls fall on him and tear his flesh and stuff their mouths full of it and the guy who did a strongman act at the beginning of the show appears in his executioner's hood and swings a broadsword and hacks at the girls as they continue to feed.

The strobes stop. The tent goes black. The screams kick up a notch.

I smell the midget's infected blood, whiffs of his bowels, the kerosene the torches were dipped in, seaweed, salt air, stale beer and corndogs from the trash barrel, cigarette and pot smoke and the blush of uninfected blood freshly drawn.

I grab Lydia and push her behind me and put my hand on the butt of Solomon's hogleg.

Lights come on, strings of red Christmas lights looped among the rigging wires and poles of the tent.

The people on the bleachers stop shrieking.

The midget is standing center stage, dripping gore, he steps forward, does a pratfall over his own intestines, gets up and takes a bow.

The place goes nuts.

The Strongman lifts the girls, placing one on either shoulder, and they wave at the audience with fake severed arms and legs.

Lydia wrenches free of me.

—Fuck are you thinking, Pitt? There's trouble, stay out of my way so you don't get hurt.

I raise my hands.

—Yeah, my bad, forgot who's wearing the trousers.

—Fuck you.

The Freaks wrap their curtain call. The audience laughs and claps and hoots and hollers and throws crumpled bills and loose change and the performers clear the stage and Tom Waits sings "Singapore," their exit music, and the show is over.

I count heads as the audience files out of the tent, try to figure who's missing and how many.

—Unconscionable! Immoral! And fantastically idiotic!

—Oh! Oh sweet Jesus! Oh my Lord in Heaven, fuck me now!

The midget has tucked the last of his intestine where it belongs; gritting his fake teeth, he pinches the edges of the wound together as Vendetta pulls a glowing iron rod from the brazier where it's been heating in a pile of white coals and presses it against the torn flesh.

The midget drops his head back and laughs and screams like a little kid on a roller coaster.

—Hooooo! Whhooohoooo! Oh my! Oh my God! Sheeeeit!

Vendetta pulls the rod away and the Glasseater pours cold water over the steaming cauterization.

The midget brings his face down, tears running from the corners of his eyes, and exhales. He leers at Lydia.

—Sorry about the language, just that hurts like a motherfucker.

He peels one of the Pabst Blue Ribbons from the six at his feet and cracks it open.

—So now, *unconscionable,* you were saying? I'm not sure about that part, not knowing what the word means and all, but *fantastically idiotic* is a phrase I could learn to love. That right there, that just about sums up the whole Freak, whatyacallit, value system in two words. Hatter, what's a good word for *value system*?

The MC takes a coverless pocket dictionary from inside his tailcoat and looks at a page.

—*Ethos.*

Lydia has her hands on her hips.

—Make a joke out of it, make a joke out of it, but this is not the way we do things. If you plan on joining the Society, there's going to be a whole new set of behaviors to learn. Because behavior like that?

She points at the corpse flopped across the table they used in the Glasseater's act, the chump they snatched and slashed during the finale blackout. The Strongman, still in his hood, pumps the dead guy's chest, the last of his blood sputtering from the hole gnawed in his neck and filling the mason jar Harm holds against it.

—Behavior like that will not be tolerated. A random act of violence, an outright murder that begs for attention, that will not be condoned in any way, shape or form by any Clan in Manhattan, let alone by the Society. The waste of blood aside, the moral issues aside, there's just the practical question of exposure. A display like that? In public? You can make it look as fake as you like, but it's going to draw attention. And what about the legal implications? This is an unlicensed operation. You're only a half mile from the amusement park. What about the police?

He drains his beer and grabs another.

—Cops we got no problem with. Coney cops, you pitch them a C-note they couldn't give a shit what you do. As for attention, well, that's the whole point isn't it? No attention, no audience. We do things the freak show up on the boardwalk can only dream about. Funny thing is, they get up on their high horse 'bout what we do. Talk 'bout how faking is *counter to the freak way of life.* They only knew, they'd shit little purple HoHos.

—Uh-huh, and what about other kinds of attention? You know we have a Van Helsing in Lower Manhattan right now? What happens if a Van Helsing hears about your act? Do you think he or she will have trouble telling the difference between pig intestine, Karo syrup and red food coloring, and the real thing? What you're doing, it puts all infecteds at risk. Utterly without sanction. With no mandate at all. With no aim at all. Simple willfulness. Unconscionable.

—Sister, ain't no such thing as a Van Helsing.

Her eyes bug.

—No such thing?

—You ever seen one? I never seen one. Urban legend. Stuff to scare kiddies with. Trust me, work in this game long as I have, you know a fake when you hear 'bout it.

Lydia looks at me.

—Joe?

I look at my watch, the second hand sweeps around, shaving another sliver from the edge of the night.

I look at the midget.

—Got a guy on Rivington, in chunks.

He looks down at his beer.

—Cut up? How many pieces?

—Fuck do I know, didn't bother counting.

He swirls the beer in his can and takes a swig.

—Didn't count 'em, or don't know how?

I look to Lydia.

—These guys are assholes. We should go before they waste any more of our time.

The midget points at me.

—Watch who you're calling asshole, shorty.

I tap my watch.

—Terry said there were supposed to be a couple dozen of them. What have we seen? Six assholes. There ain't no more. They're carneys. Professional liars. And they're spastic. C'mon, we both know we're not taking any of these losers to Manhattan. Let's blow.

He looks at Lydia.

—Best put a muzzle on your hound, lady.

—Joe's not a dog, he's a person. And I am not a *lady*, I am a woman.

The midget runs a fingertip over the fresh seam of blisters that crosses his stomach. The white tips are already fading, pinking, healing; the Vyrus is putting the blood he sucked from the dead guy to good use.

He sips some beer.

—Hatter, look up *woman* in that dictionary, tell me if that's some other way of saying girl.

Lydia folds her arms and looks at the ground.

—*Girl?*

The midget purses his lips and covers his mouth with a finger.

—Oopsy. Did I say a no-no? Did I let slip with a term that doesn't fit with your lifestyle choices? Honey.

A little snicker runs around the tent. Only the Strongman doesn't laugh.

A thin stream of air slides between Lydia's lips. She looks at the midget.

—What did you say your name was?

The midget points at one of the faded blue tattoos on his neck.

—Like it says right here. *Stretch.* Name's Stretch.

She squints at the tattoo.

—Yeah. *Stretch.* OK, clearly I'm not going to be able to make my point with you the way I'd like to. Let me put it another way.

She pauses, looks at the top of the tent's center-pole, where smoke from the torches and the brazier slips out through a large hole, and looks back at him.

—You are fucked.

He raises his eyebrows.

—*Fucked?*

She nods.

—Raw. You had a chance not to be, but you are now officially fucked raw.

He blows out his lips, reaches back and rubs a buttock.

—Hell, fucked raw and I didn't even get a reach-around.

The snicker goes around the tent again, but not as far.

Lydia nods again.

—Yeah, no reach-around. See, here you are, you and your *Clan,* and you need something. You need something so bad, you have to go outside of your inbred little comfort zone and look for help.

—Help? Ain't no one asking for help around here. We're the ones making offers.

She gives him a look up and another back down.

—Like. Hell.

He stands, grimaces as skin around his wound stretches.

—You want to start watching your lip, *woman.*

Lydia looks at me.

—Finally, he calls me what I am, and he thinks it's an insult.

She looks at Vendetta and Harm.

—How can the two of you put up with being exploited by this piece of crap?

Vendetta grabs her crotch.

—Exploit this, cunt.

Lydia waves a hand.

—You're not my type.

Stretch puts himself in front of Lydia.

—You leave them girls out of this.

Lydia squats slowly, puts herself on eye level with him.

—Gladly.

His lips peel from his gleaming teeth, a bit of pink gristle caught between two of them.

—You best start treading softly.

Lydia purses her lips and covers them with a finger.

—Oh, did I say something out of line? Pardon me, let me be clear so I can make that up to you.

She shows her own teeth.

—You are on the ass end of the world. You are all alone out here and someone has your back against it. And you are so fucking terrified you call us for help to get out. Joe's right, isn't he? This is it, just a half dozen of you? The way you pathetic, self-destructive dysfunctions live out here, you couldn't sustain more than six members. And now, now you get a chance, a shot at getting off this sandbar and joining with a real Clan, having some stability, being a part of something real, and all you can do is swing your dick around and try to act like you don't need the help you're screaming for.

She shakes her head.

—Honestly, I don't know whether to laugh or cry.

She straightens.

—You're right, Joe, they're assholes. Let's go.

She starts for the exit.

Stretch takes a step after her.

—Hey! Hey, now! Now wait a second.

Lydia stops and turns.

—What?

Stretch licks his lips.

—You got a mouth on you, lady. Some mouth. Come on a man's turf and talk that way. Some mouth. Takes, know what that takes, takes balls. You got some balls on you. I like that. That's OK by me. You come back in here and let's have a beer and we'll do the swap and get rolling. We're all introduced now, so let's do some business.

Lydia creases her forehead.

—Asshole, you missed the point. We don't want you. You people are a mess. You're going to have to stay out here where you belong. Until you get kicked into the ocean.

She turns again.

Stretch snaps his fingers.

The Strongman's eyes narrow behind the headman's hood.

Harm sets the mason jar aside and rests her hand on her sledgehammer. Vendetta's fingers tighten on the iron poker. Hatter opens his dictionary wide and a derringer drops from the hollowed pages into his hand. Glasseater licks his lips.

Stretch folds his arms over his little barrel chest.

—Tell me, you uptight Manhattan snobs think you can talk to me like that and walk out of here in one piece?

I pull the hogleg from my belt and put it against his forehead.

—Tell me, do you think you clowns can stop me if I decide to blow your stomach open, rip your guts back out, *stretch* them across the boardwalk, and run my van over them a few times?

Lydia raises both her hands, opens her mouth to chill the situation, and something slaps the stiff canvas of the tent, whispers through the air and imbeds itself in her neck.

I blink.

—Jesus fuck, is that an arrow?

A heavy rain hits the tent, sharp reports followed by chorused sighs.

Fletched steel shafts sprout in the sand. Pepper the table and the corpse. Bristle from the Strongman's back as he scoops Vendetta and Harm together and bends his body over theirs. Glasseater gnashes his broken teeth on the one that springs out of his mouth, and finds it inedible. They chase Stretch as he crawls under the stage. Hatter pulls one from his foot, turns and runs into a flock of them that pelt his chest and face.

I drop to the ground. One passes through my right biceps and into my side, pinning my arm to my torso.

The storm stops.

Something black flutters at the entrance of the tent. I see the Wraith in my memory, stop breathing, roll onto my left side, fire both barrels of the hogleg, the recoil jerking my arm back, the shaft of the arrow tearing flesh, the barbed tip twisting between two ribs.

The black shape in the entrance sprays a cloud of blood and explodes back into the night.

A man, a man in a cape. Only a man.

I breathe. Smell the Vyrus thick in the fresh blood.

Not a Wraith, but not a man. More are out there.

I get up. Lydia has the arrow in her neck, more in her legs and abdomen. I grab her and drag her toward the rear of the tent, kicking the brazier from its stand as I pass it, spilling flaming coals over the grease-stained carpets and under the dry boards of the stage and the bleachers.

Fire wastes no time, begins to eat the tent and its contents.

I reach the back of the tent, drop Lydia, grab the canvas at its base and heave it up, tearing long iron stakes from the sand. I look back, see more black shapes beating at the entrance, leaping across the flames, the trailing wings of one catching fire.

The Strongman rises, porcupined in steel, and takes his broadsword from the edge of the stage as Vendetta and Harm worm beneath the platform, over the coals scattered there. Two of the caped silhouettes jump, the broadsword arcs, dividing one of the shapes into two bleeding halves and imbedding in the other before it slams into him and drives him onto his back. The heads of the arrows burst from his chest and stomach and he grabs the wounded attacker and pulls him close and fire is reflected everywhere in blood.

I wrap my fingers in Lydia's hair and duck under the edge of the burning tent, hauling her through the sand, jerking to a stop as something grabs her and she's torn from me; dropping the fistful of her hair, snagging her wrist and digging my heel into the sand as she's pulled back into the tent.

—Pitt.

Lydia, rasping over the arrow in her throat, reaching to me with her other hand.

—Gun. Gun.

I drop the hogleg, force my right hand across my body, ripping the hole in my biceps wider, twisting the barbs deeper. I tug the Docks Boss' gun from my jacket pocket and toss it into the sand as the things holding her legs heave and we're both pulled toward the flaming canvas.

She scoops up the huge revolver.

—Let me go. Go.

Three arrows pierce the tent and fly into the darkness behind me.

Lydia twists her arm to free herself.

—Go. Just fucking come back.

I let her go and she's dragged screaming into the tent and I snag the hogleg and I run into the darkness below the boardwalk, trailing blood, the sound of the revolver crashing behind me.

Lydia, filling the blazing night with lead.

Burrowed deep in sand where it piles up high under the boardwalk, I break the hogleg, drop the spent shells and replace them. I face back on my trail and wait for something that I can blow in half.

Nothing comes.

I watch the tent burn. I watch the fluttering silhouettes hack the lines, tumbling it down so that it burns faster. I watch them gather bodies and parts of bodies. Three of them carry the Strongman and the smaller corpse pinned to him.

I listen.

—Don't leave anything.

—I'm not leaving anything, Axler.

—We need it all.

—I never buried anyone? I never sat Shiva? I don't know we need it all?

—Just don't leave any of Chaim on the ground.

—It's too late. He was sprayed all over the tent. And half of Fletcher burned before we could get to him.

—Burned. Fuck. Will the Chevra Kadisha be able to do anything?

—Ask your papa.

—Shit.

One of the silhouettes stands at the edge of the firelight, peering under the boardwalk.

—Selig, come away, we have to go.

—Some got away.

—Too late. We have to go. The fire.

—They got away. The one that shot Chaim got away. The midget got away. One of his whores got away.

A siren whines, coming closer.

—We have to go.

—They killed Chaim. They killed Fletcher. They killed Elias. We have to find them. We have to kill them.

More sirens join the first.

—We have to go, Selig.

—Chaim. They killed my brother. Chaim. I have to kill them.

He starts to scramble under the boardwalk.

I train both barrels on his shadow.

He stops, scents, his head turns toward my hiding place. Two of the others come after him and grab him.

—Selig. *Ha-Makom yenahem ethem b'tokh sha'ar aveilei Tzion v'Yerushalayim, Selig*. We have to go.

They pull him from under the boardwalk, dragging him away from the flames, away from my gun that killed his brother.

Lucky fucker.

I pinch the hollow shaft just below the plastic fletching and flatten it between my fingers. Sitting on the floor of the van, arm tight to my side and braced against the paneled interior wall, I grip the arrow just above the pinched alloy and begin to bend it back and forth, stressing the metal. The tip wiggles between my ribs.

When the metal bends with ease, I wrap my fist around it, take a few shallow breaths, feeling the point dig at the side of my lung, and give a single sharp yank that tears the tail of the arrow away and hurts like a motherfucker. I drop the scrap on the floor and lift my right arm and pull it free, fresh blood running from the hole that had sealed itself around the shaft that juts from my side.

I press my fingers into the hole in my side, feeling for the sharp-edged barbs, finding them. I'm lucky that they haven't slipped in past the ribs. I won't have to break my own bones to dig the fucker out. That would have sucked.

I take my switchblade from my boot top and it snaps open. I have to use my left hand to cut short twin seams through the skin and muscle on either side of the shaft, then drop the knife, twist the shaft so that the broad surface of the arrowhead is parallel to the ribs and jerk it and find out that it has two shorter barbs right at the tip that snag on the bone and only come free when I curse and twist my right arm around and get a two-handed grip and pull the fucking thing out along with a hunk of meat and cartilage and muscle and slivers of bone.

I pick up one of the strips I've already torn my undershirt into and start wrapping it around my torso. The Vyrus will seal the wounds soon, but the more blood I can keep inside, the better this will go for me. I've already dribbled a fair amount. And I'm likely to lose more by the time I've killed all the people I want to see dead right now.

Someone puts a hand on the outer handle of the rear door and tests to see if it's locked. It is.

Out the windshield I can see the whirling lights on the cop cars and fire engines and ambulances reflected on the apartment fronts at the intersection of Mermaid and 37th. No cops have poked around over here yet, just one cruiser that drifted down the street playing its searchlight over the garbage cans and row houses. That doesn't mean they won't be going car to car soon.

They tug a little harder on the handle. Someone says something. Someone answers. I try to smell something other than my own blood. Catch the scent.

I edge to the door, picking up the pointy end of the broken arrow, ease the lock button up and the door swings suddenly open and I grab the midget and haul him in and throw him down and push the arrow into his ear farther than it should go and point at Vendetta still crouched outside the van.

—Get the fuck in here and sit in the corner and don't move.

She climbs into the van and pulls the door closed.

Stretch starts to open his mouth and I twist the arrow and blood runs freely from his ear.

—Close your mouth.

He closes his mouth.

—Show me those teeth again and I'll clean both your ears at the same time.

Vendetta shifts.

—The cops.

I keep my eyes on Stretch.

—I know.

She moves.

I give Stretch a little more of the arrow.

—He's already gonna be deaf in this ear, honey, move again and I'll take the short route to making him deaf in the other.

She stays where she is.

—The cops. They're looking in cars. Coming down Thirty-seventh.

I look out front. Bobbing flashlight beams are working toward the intersection.

Fuck.

I can shove the arrow through Stretch's ear and jump the girl and probably break her neck before she screams, and start the van and roll with the lights off and circle around Seagate.

I lick my lips, shift, my left hand tenses on the arrow.

Stretch is looking in my eyes.

—She's alive.

I poke the arrow deeper.

—Told you to keep those teeth hid.

He winces.

—They got her. But she's alive. Get us out. I'll tell you where.

The flashlights are coming closer. Once the cops are at the intersection I'm fucked. They see the van rolling, they'll be after me. High-speed pursuit in a crap van. Busted. Dead.

I put my knee on his chest, pull the arrow out of his ear, shove it in his mouth, push the barbs into his inner cheek, fishhook him and pull.

He strains his neck, trying to keep his face in one piece.

I tug.

—Where?

He gurgles.

—Fuggckgyooog.

The lights are bright at the end of the street.

I drop the arrow and pick up the hogleg and rise and kick him in the crotch three times with my steel toes and whip the barrels of the gun across Vendetta's forehead and give her the boot.

—Don't fuck with me or I'll kill you bad.

I get in the front seat and start the engine and pull out, lights dark.

—Where?

He turns his head.

—Sorry? That was my bad ear.

—Where, fucking where?

His smile shines bloody as he works the arrow out of his mouth.

—Gravesend.

He's a talker.

—Pisses me off is that it's Friday night. Supposed to be safe night. Why it's the only night we do the act.

He picks at the dry blood crusted around his right ear.

—Don't suppose you know if eardrums grow back?

I ignore him. Trying to think. Trying to figure how far I can take this. The cost of returning without Lydia.

He points at my own mutilated right ear.

—Just askin' cuz it looks like you have some recent experience with this kind of thing.

Trying to figure if I can just dump him and Vendetta and haul ass back to Manhattan and tell Terry I did everything I could, but Lydia is gone.

—'Course, yours look to be more of the external variety.

He snaps his fingers next to his bad ear.

—Damn. Fucker's dead as dead. Pisser. Years of mutilatin' myself, never did a stitch of permanent damage. Mind you, there was a period of trial and error where it was more from luck than anything else that I didn't ever bite off nothing that couldn't grow back.

I think about the solid Lydia once did for me. How I never paid it off. How it was too fucking big to be paid off in one installment. Till now.

Vendetta looks at him from her spot on the floor between our seats.

—Don't forget the toe.

He holds up his hands.

—Well sure, the toe. Just the pinkie toe, mind. But that was pure experimentation. Tell you, got no regrets about that toe. I hadn't tested it out first, I might have bit off a finger or something like that. As it is, I've sliced and diced and gnawed my flesh just about every which way you can and kept myself in one piece all the while. Traveled my act far and wide. 'Course that was when this was an open city. That's when the borough of Brooklyn on Long Island was a free place, where a man could go where he pleased and do as he pleased.

He waves his arms at the avenues reeling past us as we roll down Stillwell.

—Toured from Greenpoint to Brighton to Cobble Hill to Canarsie to Bay Ridge. Wintering in Coney, of course. No *turf* in Brooklyn then. That's a Manhattan thing. Here, you just pay a mind to where you are, be respectful to whoever the big dog happens to be on the block. Nothing formal. Just a matter of using your head and slipping a dollar or a pint in the right hand. I'm out Red Hook, pitching my tent, taking a bum or two off the streets, I know I gotta throw something to the Docks.

He looks my way.

—Least that's how it was. Till the Docks up and went to Manhattan and ain't come back not a one.

I drive, half listening with my half ear, thinking, figuring, looking for an angle that will send me home before I do something stupid. Stupider than usual.

He talks.

—Not that I give a damn. Bastards always had their fingers in one too many pies far as I'm concerned. And they got damn grabby with the ladies when they came around to see the show. A little touching ya got to expect, but Docks boys tended to ride their flippers a bit high up the thigh for my liking.

Vendetta folds her arms on the dash and rests her chin on them.

—Docks stink. All of them. Of tar. Think because a girl's in show business she's naturally a whore. Had to take the burlesque out of the act when we went out there. Would have raped me and Harm to death they'd seen that.

She puts her forehead down.

Stretch touches the back of her head.

—We'll get her back, darlin'.

Her voice is muted by her arms.

—What they gonna do with her?

Stretch clacks his teeth.

—Gonna do nothin' to her. Lay a hand on her, gonna find it's a stump when I come through their turf.

I touch the smoke tucked behind my whole ear. My last smoke.

He shifts his ass and adjusts the pieces of 2×4 he dug out of the back of the van and put on the seat to use as a booster.

—Turf. *They* started that shit out here. First thing was, they sealed themselves up. Few years back, five or six, you wanted to get from Sheepshead Bay to Sunset Park, suddenly you had to circle through Dyker Heights. Then they started pushing out, clearing blocks for just themselves. Not a matter of talkin' to the right fella to pass, just no damn passage at all. Try to go straight across Bensonhurst like you used to, a freakin' boat comes cruising up and a bunch of guys with beards and fedoras come piling out, beat the crap out of you, toss you outside their turf. If you're lucky. You're not lucky, you never see the outside of Gravesend again.

I've got my fingers on that smoke, I start to tug it from behind my ear, stop, look at him.

—A boat?

He spreads his arms.

—Car. Bigass Caddies and Lincolns an' suchlike. You know, Jew Canoes.

I put the cigarette in my mouth and put it to work and I get a little less stupid, for the moment.

They don't go out on Friday nights. *Chaim. Shiva.* Trying to save the bodies of their friends from the fire. The lingo they were talking.

—Jesus, they're Jews.

He scratches his chest.

—Well, that's one way of putting it.

—Thing I can't figure out, how a man comes all the way out here and doesn't bring an extra pack of smokes.

—I was planning on going straight back over the bridge.

—Sure you don't have a spare hiding somewhere?

—I had a spare it'd be sticking out of my face right now.

Vendetta points out the windshield.

—There. There.

We come forward from the back of the van, me crawling, Stretch walking.

I try to see something, but we're on the far side of McDonald Avenue with all of Friends Field between us and Washington Cemetery.

—What?

She jabs her finger at the playground on the edge of the Field.

—In there. Someone was walking around in there.

—What about in the cemetery?

She points again.

—No, just there in the park. I can't see shit in the cemetery.

I edge back and sit on the floor.

—This is bullshit.

Stretch comes back.

—Tellin' you, they got to bury their dead within twenty-four hours. It's like a rule they have.

Vendetta turns.

—Like not working on the Sabbath.

He kicks one of the pieces of wood littering the van.

—That was pure bullshit that was. Ain't no confusion about that. Everyone knows they don't do nothin' from sundown Friday to sundown Saturday. Don't work, don't drive, don't answer the phone, don't turn on a fuckin' light. Only way anyone gets around anymore in Brooklyn is Friday night. Only time safe to go out and do some foraging. We couldn't do the act at all anymore they didn't lie low Friday night.

I pick up one of the wood scraps and pop my switchblade and start whittling.

—Based on the way they fucked your shit up, I'd say that rule's become pretty fucking optional.

He sticks a thumb in his own chest.

—All I know is, they have to bury their dead, and they got to do it in one of their own cemeteries, and this is the cemetery they use.

Long shavings of wood curl from the stick I'm working on.

—And what if they do it tomorrow night?

He hooks his thumbs in the straps of his overalls.

—They won't.

—We know that because?

—Because they won't.

He looks at the stick I'm honing.

—Is that a stake you're making?

I run my blade along it.

—Yeah.

He lets his arms hang at his sides.

—That like supposed to be humorous or something?

I hold the safe end of the stake to my eye and sight down it.

—Not to me.

—Why you making it, then?

I test the point with my thumb.

—Because I may need to kill more people than I have shells for if your shitty plan gets us that far.

He grunts and turns and goes back front with Vendetta.

—Telling you, this is the place.

I flick the blade across the tip of the stake, wondering if this is the worst play I've ever made. The competition is stiff. Sitting, waiting to get lucky. Lucky enough to throw down on guys that favor bows and arrows and fuck knows what else. Hoping to get lucky that they have Lydia with them or know where she is. Lucky enough to cruise over their turf to wherever she may be and get her out. Because I owe her.

But I owe Evie more. For what, I don't know. But there it is.

I owe her.

I stop carving. I fold the knife away and tuck it in my boot. I feel in my coat pocket for the keys. Finally getting smart.

—Fuck this.

I come forward, drop the stake on the dash and get behind the wheel.

Stretch puts out a hand.

—Whoa, whoa. We drive in there, someone's gonna see us. We gotta wait till they come and start the service. They start chantin' and rockin' back and forth and sayin' kaddish, we can get the jump on them, take a couple hostages.

I turn in the seat.

—We aren't going in there. We're getting the hell to Manhattan.

Way to handle this is, we let Terry Bird handle it. He's a fucking politician. Lydia's with them, he'll get her out.

Vendetta rises a little.

—Papa.

He touches her.

—Don't worry, pumpkin.

I start the van.

—You guys, you can hop out and get killed here or you can ride with me as originally planned.

Vendetta takes his hand.

—Get her back, Papa, we got to get Harm back.

I put the van in gear.

—Bird'll do what he can. He loves that stuff. Helping out. He can get Lydia back, he can get your chick back.

Stretch puts a hand on my arm.

—You're not thinkin' straight. Harm is with them. I'm getting my girl back. *Your* woman? Who knows she's even alive?

I look at his hand.

—*You* know she's alive.

He moves the hand.

—Well, yeah.

I put my hand on the hogleg.

—You said you *saw* her alive.

He wipes his mouth, smiles.

—Well, it was awful chaotic with the blood and the fire and the killin' and all that was goin' on. Could be I confused things a bit.

Vendetta jumps and flops her body across my lap and hits my gun hand and the hogleg falls into the step well and she starts flailing her hands and flicking the headlights on and off and slapping the horn. I put my left elbow in the back of her neck and reach for the stake on the dash and Stretch's teeth go into my right thigh. I kick and grab his head with both hands and wrench it to the side and he comes off with a mouthful of my leg, spitting it and hissing and vomiting from the taste of the Vyrus and I throw him in the back of the van as headlights shoot through the windshield and something huge and heavy barrels into us and the door next to me crumples and Vendetta is tossed from my lap across the cab into the other door. I reach down into the step well and Stretch slams into the back of my seat and crawls over the top of it and drops on my bent back. People are piling out of the big cars that have us boxed at the curb. I stand and the hole in my leg is jammed into the steering wheel and I pound Stretch into the roof and reach and my fingers find the stake on the dash and I shove it into the meat between Vendetta's shoulder and neck as she flies back across the cab at me. Her velocity carries her into me and I fall back into the crushed door and Stretch is slashed on the shards of glass that are all that's left of the driver's side window. I still have hold of the stake and I twist it and wrench it down and Vendetta's collarbone snaps and the ends tear through her skin as I pull the stake out and her blood sprays the windshield red, the headlights glowing through it.

Then they're in the van. In through the rear. In through the passenger door. Pulling Stretch out the window behind me and dragging the ruined door open. Piling on top of me, cutting, pulling, hammering.

Then leather straps go around my arms, keeping me from punching; and around my legs, keeping me from kicking; more around my head and between my teeth, keeping me from biting.

One of them runs at me, screaming, waving a small axe.

—Chaim! Chaim!

Others grab him and take him to the ground, all of them losing their fedoras in the struggle, but not the yarmulkes pinned to the tops of their heads.

Stretch pulls free and runs to where Vendetta is sprawled on the curb trying to push her bones back inside her skin.

—I got you, pumpkin.

A tall one gets up, dusts his fedora, returns it to his head, straightens his vest and the long threads that dangle from beneath it.

—Someone get him away from the girl.

Stretch cradles bleeding Vendetta, my flesh still on his lips.

—To hell with you, Axler. Your cousin is bleeding-out here and you fuck with her father. Now take me to your dad. I want my other daughter back.

I miss the rest of the reunion when the lid of a car trunk slams shut on me.

—Kill them.

—We will, Selig.

—Kill them now.

—Your brother, Selig, think of your brother.

—I am. What else is there to think of? Kill them.

The tall skinny one puts his hands on the little fat one's shoulders.

—Selig, to talk about killing them here, now, it doesn't do. It won't do Chaim any good.

Selig pulls free and turns, his arms spread wide between the tombstones.

—I don't know, I don't know what is best for my brother? To have his murder avenged is best. To have his whole body would be best. Not to have parts of him scattered and burned would be best. To have a proper burial would be best. To say the prayers and take the time would be best. None of this is right, Axler. None of it. I didn't want it. Chaim wanted it. I only came for him. To protect him. Too late. So what if we kill them now? Here? So what? Nothing else is right. Nothing is right in the world.

Axler walks to him and grabs the lapels of his long black coat and shakes him.

—Shut up. Coward. Shut up. Your brother is a hero. A warrior. You are a coward. Shut up. Stop saying his name. You want them dead? You should have been with your brother when he was the first in the tent. You could have killed them then. After, only after it was over, did you become brave. Coward. Help bury your brother and leave vengeance to men.

He pushes the little one and he stumbles back and falls over a low headstone, scattering the rocks piled on top of it.

He gets up on his hands and knees and crawls around, crying, gathering the rocks while the others dig the grave for his brother and mutter hurried prayers.

He places the rocks back on the headstone, one by one, eyes turned from the blood-soaked shroud that wraps his brother's corpse.

—It was wrong, Chaim. A sin. All of it. On the Sabbath. Working. Making a plan. Driving. On the Sabbath. Small sins leading to greater. Killing on the Sabbath. Killing in the name of God on the Sabbath. I told you you'd be punished, brother.

Axler turns from his digging and spears the point of his shovel in the ground.

—Shut up. There were no sins. This was not work. This was service to God. We didn't even drive ourselves. And we didn't use guns. Guns are machines, yes. A bow and arrow is not. An axe is not.

Selig clenches his fist around a rock.

—It's a tool. A knife, an axe, a bow. They are tools.

Axler picks up the shovel.

—This is a tool. Should I wait to bury your brother if it means I must dig? If we sinned, God will let us know.

They lower the dead body into the grave. They put his long knife and his bow and his little axe in with him. And they put their shovels aside and begin to pray.

Selig joins them.

They pray a long time.

Then they turn to the Strongman and start working to pull their other friend free of the arrows that pierce them both.

That takes much longer.

Deep inside Washington Cemetery, they've left us bound at the edge of one of the roads that wanders back and forth between the fenced burial plots. Off blessed earth. Or whatever the fuck they call it.

Now, all the stiffs six feet under and on their way to wherever, they come for us.

Axler and Selig, a half dozen others in black coats and wide-brimmed hats. Some limping or cradling limbs that took shells from Lydia's gun. A couple others waiting in the cars, the headlights dark.

Time for Selig to get his wish.

Axler bends and rips the leather strap that winds over Stretch's face.

Stretch snaps his bare gums.

Axler reaches into a pocket and pulls out the steel dentures.

—Looking for something, old man?

—Fuck you, punk.

Axler puts the teeth back.

—You, old man, you should have known better than to keep what's ours from us.

—They ain't yours.

—They are. And they know it. That's why she came back.

—Vendetta doesn't want to be here. She wants her sister and her own life.

—She wants her home and family, her own kind. That's why she betrayed you and signaled for us.

Stretch tries to spit, can't without his teeth and it dribbles on his chin.

—Fuck, *we* signaled you. *We* came to you. *We* came for Harm.

Axler reaches inside his vest and brings out a long sheathed knife.

—Don't lie now, old man, of all times.

—We signaled you for a swap. For Harm.

Axler draws the blade from its sheath.

—You have nothing to trade. And we don't deal in flesh.

Stretch's eyes shoot at me.

—I have *him*.

Axler sets the sheath aside and lays the long blade at Stretch's throat.

—No, we have him. And he'll die just like you. Easier, actually. He'll simply die for having killed Chaim. You, we'll divide you together with your bones in twelve pieces, and we'll send you into all the neighborhoods of Brooklyn. So they'll know we're coming.

—Asshole, *he's* not from Brooklyn.

Axler's fingers shift on the handle of the knife.

He looks at me.

He looks back at Stretch and presses the knife into his skin and draws blood.

—Where?

—Kid, what do you think you can cut on me that will make me tell you shit if I don't want to?

Selig steps up.

—We have to kill them, Axler. Now.

—Shut up.

Stretch bares his neck further.

—Yeah, kill us. Kill me, the one guy who can tell you who he is and where he's from and what he wants. Then kill him, the guy from *Manhattan*. And see what kind of hell comes down. Your papa will be so proud. 'Course he's gonna be pretty pissed as it is if I know the man at all. But I might be able to put a spin on the deal that'll make things shine a bit brighter for you.

Selig touches Axler's shoulder.

—Don't listen to him, we have to do it now. And we can't lie about it. We have to accept the punishment we have earned. We've sinned, Axler.

Axler pulls the knife back.

—Put them in the cars.

—Axler!

He sticks the long knife in Selig's throat just below the chin and pushes and the point rips out the back of his neck at the base of the skull and he holds him in the air while his legs dance for a moment and then he drops him from the blade to the ground.

A couple of the others take a step back. None step up.

He wipes the knife.

—And we must dig another grave. For Selig, who died bravely with his brother Chaim.

And they do as he says.

But his mom is pissed.

—Axler, Axler, what did you do to the car?

—It's nothing, it's some Bondo.

—Look at it, it's a cavern. It's a crevasse. That dent, it's an abyss in the fender. You can't fill that with Bondo.

—You pull it out, you put some Bondo in there, you sand it and you primer it and paint it and it's as good as new.

—What are you talking about, new? It's not like new. It's ruined. Look at it, look at it. How did this happen?

—We hit his van.

—*You hit his van?* This is what comes of driving on Sabbath. Accidents. God's judgment on you.

—It wasn't God. We drove into him on purpose.

—*On purpose?* You did this to my Cadillac on purpose?

—And I wasn't driving. Rachel was driving.

—*Rachel drove the car?* You steal my car and you give it to Rachel and you tell her to drive it into a van?

—I didn't steal it.

—*Didn't steal it?* You call it what, when you don't ask to take my car and you take it and you let someone else drive it and you wreck it? You call that *borrowing*?

—Ma, please.

The big old lady raises her hands, turns and walks into the house.

—Yes, of course, you have things to do. What business of mine is it what you do in my house or how you stole my car and what you did to smash it up? Do what you have to do.

Axler watches her with his hands on his hips.

—Fuck.

He kicks the crumpled fender of his mom's car.

—Fuck.

He looks at me lying between the two cars on the concrete garage floor.

—Are you smiling at something?

I don't say anything, my mouth still being gagged by leather straps.

He points.

—Get that off him.

Someone cuts the straps around my head.

I work my jaw, but I don't bite anyone.

Axler looks at me again.

—I asked were you smiling at something?

I tongue a thick scab at the corner of my mouth.

—Naw, I wasn't smiling at nothing.

—Good.

—Just kind of surprised.

He pushes his hat to the back of his head.

—About what?

I look at the door into the house where his mom disappeared.

—About how all those Jewish mothers jokes are so dead-on.

He starts kicking my face.

OK, figure talking about someone's mama is never a good idea.

—Axler!

He stops kicking my face.

—Papa.

Through the blood in my eyes I see the man in shirtsleeves who has come out of the house, a wreath of dark curly hair around the bald spot not quite covered by his yarmulke, a book in his hand, index finger tucked between pages to mark his place.

He looks at me and Stretch on the floor. He looks at the blood-spattered young men shifting from foot to foot. He looks at the ruined fender of his wife's car. He looks at his son and rubs his forehead with the back of his wrist.

Axler opens his mouth.

His father holds his hand out.

—No. Not now.

He points at Stretch and me.

—Cover their heads and bring them to the temple.

He looks at the fender again and shakes his head.

—Your mother's car, of all things.

Harm is already in the temple in an ankle-length skirt, loose blouse and headscarf, sitting erect on a bench. Vendetta's head is in her lap, the healing bones back inside her skin.

Across the aisle with the other men, I shake my head, trying to do something about the itch under the small circle of black felt they pinned to my hair.

I look at one of the young men that bracket me.

—Buddy, could you scratch my head?

He looks at his partner. His partner shrugs. He looks to the altar where Axler and his father stand in front of the arc, whispering.

—Rebbe?

Axler's father turns.

—Yes?

—He wants me to scratch his head.

The Rebbe pats the top of his own head.

—A man with his hands tied has an itch on top of his head and asks you to scratch it for him. This needs a Rebbe to tell you what to do?

The kid raises his hand toward my head, hesitates, looks again at the Rebbe.

The Rebbe throws his arms up.

—Scratch. Scratch. Give the man some relief.

The kid scratches my head.

The Rebbe watches.

—You're from Manhattan?

My head stops itching. I move it out from under the kid's hand.
—Yeah.

Axler steps to his father and starts whispering again and his father waves him off.

—Axler, I'm talking to the man. Where in Manhattan?
—He's from the Coalition.

The Rebbe looks at Stretch.

—Did I ask you?
—You don't gotta ask me, I'm telling. I'm the only one in this room knows the guy's story.
—Except the guy himself, of course.

Stretch snorts.

—Like he's gonna tell you. Like the guy's from the Coalition and he's gonna tell you what he's doing here.

The Rebbe comes down the aisle, stops next to my bench.

—The Coalition, is that right?

I don't say anything.

—You didn't hear the question?

I shift, try to find a way of sitting on the bench with my wrists and ankles bound that doesn't make the hole in my thigh throb or my ribs grate or my face ache.

—Sorry, got lost in a little déjà vu there.
—This seems familiar to you? The temple? Us?
—No, being beaten and tied up and listening to some asshole try to frame my ass seems familiar. Swear I've gone through this shit before.

He taps one of my escorts on the shoulder and the kid gets up and the Rebbe takes his place.

—You're not from the Coalition, then?
—Fuck is he gonna say?

The Rebbe shakes a finger at Stretch.

—You want me to have them gag you again? Yes? No? No. So be quiet for a moment. What my sister saw in you, all the talking without ever listening. A midget, I could almost be proud she was blind to such a thing, loved you despite your infirmity, but the talking and the cursing and never waiting to listen to anyone else, it's a frustration.

—Fuck you, Moishe.

The Rebbe looks at me.

—See the mouth on him. With or without those grotesque teeth, the mouth. My sister, God love her and comfort her, she thought he was funny. She thought he was clever. To say *fuck* is clever? This is wit?

I look at Stretch, look back at the Rebbe.

—Fuck do I care.

He purses his lips, covers them with his fist, nods.

—Yes, you're from Manhattan. It's in your voice, your accent. And in your attitude. And an attitude like that, I would not be surprised if you are from the Coalition.

—He is, man, that's what I'm telling you.

The Rebbe bangs his fist on the back of Stretch's pew.

—Abe! If I have to ask you again to be quiet in the temple while I am speaking. I will be very upset if I have to do that. I did not tell these boys to do what they did.

He looks at his son, still by the Torah and the arc.

—I did not tell my son to abuse the Sabbath in this way.

—Dad!

—Shht! The things they've done, they raise grave questions. But they are done. Too late to change them. You are here. The girls are here. This man is here. Now there is nothing but to determine how best to proceed. And when you talk out of turn, you cloud the matter. And when you speak, Abe, it makes me think that perhaps you wish to cloud the matter. And that makes me regard you with doubt. So be quiet, Abe. For the sake of whatever passed between you and my sister. For the sake of my nieces. Be quiet.

The kid who scratched my head holds up a finger.

—There's also the other girl.

The Rebbe looks at him.

—What?

Axler comes down the aisle.

—It's nothing, Dad, a shiksa. She was there.

The Rebbe stands.

—Where is she?

Axler looks at the guy who opened his mouth and slits his eyes.

—She's at my place. With the Lucys.

—What have I told you about that word? I raised you to use that word?

—No.

—Name them with respect.

—She's with Rachel and Leah of the Tribe of Benjamin of the Chosen.

—Get her, bring her here.

Axler points at one of the other guys.

—Go on, get her.

The Rebbe steps to his son, looks up at him.

—No, you. You go and get this woman and cover her head and bring her here. You.

Axler bites the inside of his lip, nods, walks around his father and leaves the little temple built just behind his father's house.

The Rebbe comes and sits next to me again and sighs.

—It won't be long. *His place* he calls it. A room above our garage and he calls it *his place*.

He looks up at the ceiling, talks to whatever lives up there.

—No hurry, but he could move out soon, God? Anytime you see fit, but soon perhaps?

He drops his face, looks at me, smiles.

—The prayers of a father.

I've seen worse, but Lydia looks bad.

Someone's removed the arrows from her abdomen and legs and done a shit job of it. They left the one in her throat, afraid they'd take her esophagus out with it, I suppose. Or maybe they like the way it looks there.

The Rebbe watches as they lay her on the pew behind Harm and Vendetta, a scarf tied round her head. He gets up and walks over and bends and inspects the raggedly bandaged wounds and the arrow in her neck.

—This was poorly done.

Axler rubs the back of his neck.

—She's dangerous, Papa. She shot Matthew and David and Hesch.

Three of the boys touch holes in their black garments.

Axler takes his hand from the back of his neck.

—And she killed Selig.

He points at me.

—This one killed Chaim. And she killed Selig.

The Rebbe puts his index finger on the notched end of the arrow.

—Chaim and Selig. Selig was with you?

—Yes.

—Selig. His brother, I am not surprised, but Selig is a scholar.

He looks at me.

—A smart and a gentle boy. Promising. More than promising. A Rebbe born.

I glance at Axler.

—Not my problem, I killed the other one.

The Rebbe walks to a cabinet on the far wall.

—Always you are like this when you have killed? Lighthearted? Making jokes?

I ignore him, not having made a joke.

He comes back to Lydia with a small black doctor's bag, sets it on the bench next to her head and opens it.

—I'll need a cutter.

He opens and closes his hand as if squeezing something.

—In the garage, with the garden tools, there should be something.

One of the boys hurries out.

Axler puts a hand on his father's shoulder.

—Papa, you shouldn't. Let me do it. I've already broken the Sabbath.

The Rebbe pats his son's hand.

—Yes, you have. Good of you to say so. And you think it will make it better now if you spare me the same? I have never broken Sabbath? Talked on the phone? Turned on a light? God will understand this. Will he understand what you have done, my son? Without studying the Moed, I cannot say. But this, helping a girl, he will understand.

The boy comes back with the bolt cutters.

Rebbe Moishe takes them, looks again at the arrow, holds it steady where it sticks from Lydia's skin, fits the cutter around the shaft and firmly snips off the tip.

He takes two large paper-wrapped pads of gauze from his bag and rips them open.

—Some blood?

Axler shakes his head, points at Vendetta.

—We gave it to Hannah.

Harm turns in her seat and looks at him.

—Her name is Vendetta, dickface.

—Fuck off, slut.

—Better a slut than a mama's boy.

—Whore, if it wasn't for you, none of this would have happened!

—Sure, fucking blame us for wanting to have our own lives instead of being little baby factories for you small-dicked godmonkeys.

—The temple!

They look at the Rebbe.

—A little peace in the temple? Yes? Please? And if not peace, the imitation of it? And less of this language? A little respect.

Harm turns away.

—Fuck you too, Uncle Moishe.

Axler points at her.

—See, see, that's how she is. I don't even want her, Papa, I don't even want to marry her, let alone have a child with her.

Harm gives a bark.

—Not to worry, cousin, you won't be marrying me. And you sure as fuck won't be doing anything with me to make a baby.

—Enough! Yes? Enough? Now. Enough. Axler, you said Leah and Rachel are here, yes?

—Yes, Papa.

—Can either give blood?

—Leah is on her period. Rachel gave some to David and to Matthew.

—How much?

—A pint.

—She is a healthy girl. She can give more. Bring her here.

One of the boys leaves and Axler goes to the altar for a small wood box with a bit of cloth wrapped around it.

Moishe presses one gauze pad around the shaft of the arrow where it emerges from Lydia's neck, takes the other end of the arrow in his right hand, and draws it out in a long, smooth motion and drops it and claps another pad at the opposite end of the wound. Both pads are quickly stained red.

He cranes his neck and looks at me.

—She is something to you?

—Not much.

—Too bad for you. A beautiful girl. And strong. As much as she has bled out, she should be dead. But a little fresh blood, she will be heartened. She'll be weak, but well enough.

He looks back at Lydia.

—That you should care so little for this woman. A shame. They are everything to us, our women. Everything comes from them. Our blood. Our faith. The Tribe of Benjamin would have died long ago. The women in our tribe, they can trace back to Benjamin, one of the sons of Jacob. Grandfather of the twelve tribes. Without the women, none of this is passed on.

Axler comes down the aisle with the box.

The Rebbe peels the gauze from the wounds on Lydia's neck.

—See how strong she is? Wounds closed. So little blood, still strong enough to heal that much.

He takes the box from his son, unwraps the piece of cloth, drapes it over his shoulders, kisses the top of the box, says a prayer, opens it and takes out a small single-edged knife with a silver handle.

—This is why Hannah and Sarah are so important to us, yes?

Harm looks at the ceiling.

—Our names are Vendetta and Harm.

Moishe shakes the knife.

—Call yourself what you like, young lady, your names are Hannah and Sarah.

—What*ever*.

He sets the little box aside.

—My sister's girls. Is it a surprise they are as willful as she was? No.

He presses the knife to his forehead, mumbles another prayer, takes it away.

—My sister, running off to join the circus, of all things.

—It ain't a circus, Moishe, it's a freak show.

He faces Stretch.

—What did I say, Abe? About being quiet and listening, what did I say? Did I say to try doing that? I did. I'm certain I did.

Stretch lets out a long sigh and leans his head against the back of the pew and closes his eyes.

—Fine, I'm listening. Tell me when you want to stop fucking around and let me and my girls out of here.

The kid comes back with one of the Lucys that drove them around. A big girl, dark complexion, dark hair mostly hidden by a scarf, a plain long skirt and a blouse that matches the ones they put on Harm and Vendetta. She smells fresh, alive, the only thing I've smelled here that doesn't carry the Vyrus. All the blood I've lost, my mouth starts to water.

She goes to Moishe.

—Rebbe.

He cradles her cheek in his palm.

—Rachel.

He looks at me.

—This girl, a treasure. Pure faith in God.

—And in you, Rebbe.

—Shht, nonsense. A sin to even say it.

—I'm sorry, Rebbe.

He smiles.

—Don't be sorry. I tease, I'm teasing. See, a good girl. She understands. Rachel. A wife of Jacob. And Leah, another wife, yes? Mothers of the twelve tribes.

He bares the girl's forearm, revealing a long series of scars, white slash marks down the length of her arm.

—The word my son used, *Lucy,* a disrespectful word. These girls are of our tribe. A sacrifice, a great sacrifice they make to keep their blood sanguine. And kosher?

He grins.

—These girls have never seen a pig, let alone eaten any part of one.

He kisses her forehead.

—Blessed and washed and dieted as proper Jewesses. Blood like this, it is all that will do for us. She is not the only one, of course. But still, there are not enough like her. We're forced to hunt in Bensonhurst and Borough Park and Bay Ridge. But these girls are the only way to be certain the blood is truly kosher. From one who keeps kosher. We've tried buying. Of course we have. But the market is an unsure thing, yes? One is never certain of what one is getting, yes? And not all merchants understand the importance of this to us. Rachel, she is a blessing. A true daughter of Benjamin.

He sits her on the bench with Lydia.

—The Tribe of Benjamin, the tribe we descend from, was cursed, yes? You know this?

I scoot so I face him.

—Christ, no.

He drops his head.

—About being a smartass, what can I say? Other than it is rude, what can I say? It is rude, yes?

—Sure, yes. Doesn't mean I'm gonna stop.

—Yes, I'm not surprised. Yes. Benjamin. Cursed. The whole tribe. It's a story from the Bible. Well known.

He places the knife to Rachel's skin and slices deep and she gasps and he presses the open wound to Lydia's mouth and Lydia's lips wrap around it and she begins to nurse; a baby at her mother's tit.

I flinch when the scent of the blood hits the air. Sweat on my brow, a small erection in my pants, I watch Lydia feed and think about ripping free of the straps binding me and tearing her from the girl and clawing the wound in her arm wider and filling my belly till I vomit blood.

The Rebbe places a hand on Lydia's throat, feeling the contractions as she swallows.

—Not too much, Rachel. Just what she needs.

Rachel has her eyes closed.

—Whatever I can give is yours, Rebbe.

He looks at me, and then at his son and the boys and Stretch and Vendetta and Harm.

—See, this is instructive, what she says. The story I mentioned, from *Judges* nineteen and twenty and twenty-one: a man travels with his concubine. Coming to Gibeah in the land of the Benjaminites they could find no lodging. No one would take them in, you see? All doors were closed. Windows sealed. No welcome as night came. None would even speak to them. None but one old man. He took them in, yes? And that night, men of Gibeah, they came to the old man's house and demanded the stranger. The old man, fearing for the stranger's life pleaded for them to leave. They refused. And the old man he offered them his daughter to do with as they pleased if they would leave the traveler in peace. But the men would not harken to this. Then the traveler offered to the men of Gibeah his concubine, and the men of Gibeah *knew her and abused her all night until the morning*. Our tribe, the Tribe of Benjamin did this.

He looks in Rachel's eyes.

—And she died of it, the concubine. But she did not complain. Sacrificing herself. And because of this sacrifice, the traveler took the body of his concubine, a woman who, it must be noted, had been infamously unfaithful to him, and he *divided her, together with her bones, into twelve pieces, and sent her into all the coasts of Israel.*

He looks away from the girl's eyes.

—And the message was not lost on the other tribes.

He looks down, takes a firm grip on Lydia's jaw and on Rachel's wrist and pries them apart, Lydia's throat continuing to work, her tongue swiping blood from her own lips.

—Four hundred thousand men they sent to Gibeah. A city whose men numbered seven hundred. *Seven hundred chosen men left-handed; every one could sling stones at hair breadth, and not miss.* And beside these seven hundred stood twenty-six thousand other men of the Tribe of Benjamin.

He's gone back into his bag for more gauze, and begins to bandage Rachel's wrist.

—So, twenty-six thousand, seven hundred against four hundred thousand, yes? Not good odds. Roughly, it's what, sixteen to one, yes? Not good odds.

He ties off the ends of the bandage.

—In the first battle, just the first, the men of Benjamin killed twenty-two thousand of their enemies.

He pulls the sleeve of Rachel's blouse back into place.

—Somewhat better odds, now, but still not good. Not a betting man's odd, I think. Not at all. And, on the second battle, after the men of Israel had prayed to God for guidance and *drew the sword,* the men of Benjamin *destroyed down to the ground of the children of Israel again eighteen thousand.*

He rises.

—And the children of Israel, not surprisingly, were troubled. But they went up to the house of the Lord and they fasted and they burnt offerings and they prayed for what they should do and God said, *Go up into battle; for tomorrow I will deliver them into thine hands.*

He steps into the aisle.

—And God kept his promise, yes? Of course he did. *And the children of Israel destroyed twenty and five thousand of the Benjaminites that day and a hundred men more.*

He walks toward the arc.

—*All these drew the sword.*

He reaches the arc, opens it, touches the scrolls of the Torah.

—There was more killing, of course. No surprise again, yes? The children of Israel chased the Benjaminites to the walls of Gibeah and trod them down. And they entered the city and put it to the sword and burned it.

He turns, his hand still on the Torah.

—In the end, six hundred men fled to the rock of Rimmon in the wilderness. And that was all that remained of the tribe. And it would have died, the Tribe of Benjamin. Except that the children of Israel knew this would have been a great sin. An unpardonable sin, yes? There is such a thing. So, they were driven out, they had no kingdom, but four hundred virgins were taken from the slaughtered tribe of Jabesh-Gilead and given to the Benjaminites as wives. And more were taken dancing in the fields from the daughters of Shiloh. To keep their tribe alive, yes? You see it, yes, the women? The women. How precious. Some few were descended from Benjamin, children of mothers who had married into other tribes. And so the Benjaminites survived.

He looks at me.

—But none of the men of Gibeah.

He comes toward me.

—The men who at *night* encircled the old man's home and demanded the stranger. The men who *knew and abused* all *night* the two innocent girls and went away with the dawn, yes? The *seven hundred chosen men left-handed; and everyone could sling stones at an hairbreadth, and not miss.* The seven hundred men of Gibeah who led the Benjaminites against the four hundred thousand children of all the rest of Israel and killed in two battles forty thousand men.

He spreads arms to take in his son and the other boys.

—But the men of Gibeah are here. Their blood is here in our veins. You see that, yes? The blood of Gibeah is in you. Not the blood of Benjamin, but, yes, Gibeah is even in you.

He waves Rachel over and she comes to him.

—A child of Benjamin, the blood of Gibeah is owed to her, for her fathers came to our assistance when we needed them. But she forgoes having Gibeah in her. To sacrifice her blood *to* Gibeah. To keep our tribe alive. The lost Tribe of Gibeah.

He comes to my pew and looks down at me.

—The descendents of the seven hundred.

He puts a hand on my shoulder.

—So if you are from the Coalition, yes? If you are truly one of the spies we have seen at the edges of our land, one of the skulkers hiding in Queens? Yes, if you are one of them?

He takes the freshly healed skin on my mangled ear between his fingers and rips it off.

—You would do best to remember we were defeated only once.

He drops the bit of skin in my lap and wipes his fingers on my shirt.

—And only then when God intervened.

—Holy hell, will you can it with all that superstition?

We all look at Lydia, sitting up on her pew, a hand massaging her throat.

—It's like I'm with my dad talking all that crap at Seder all over again.

—The little person is lying. We're from the Society.

—*Little person? Little person?* Bitch, I get my hands free and drop trow, you'll see how little I am. Keep that politically correct shit, I'm a midget.

He leans forward.

—And you're the one who's lying. Telling you, Moishe, these are Coalition whaddayacallims? Fascists!

Lydia looks up from inspecting the puncture wounds in her stomach.

—*Fascists?* Are you? Alright, this is too much. This is just. Me? A fascist?

She looks at the Rebbe.

—We're from the Society. I am a serving member on the Society's directorate council.

She points at me.

—Joe is the head of Society security. We're pledged members to a Clan devoted to unity and equality among all rational living things and. *Fascists?* We're, I don't want to make a big deal out of this, but we're freedom fighters. We're fighting for your freedom and you. We're trying to create an atmosphere in which this woman.

She points at Rachel.

—Won't have to be indentured and used like a hamster feeder. Which is not to say I don't appreciate what you did giving me your blood, but believe me, you shouldn't let yourself be used like that by these men. And.

Her jaw drops.

—*Fascists?* Forgive me for harping on this, but I'm just dumbfounded that you could even try to. Do you know?

She looks at the Rebbe.

—Do you know we're here at his request? Did you know that? He and his *Clan* made contact with us and requested a meeting because they wanted safe passage into Manhattan. An alliance. And now he's. I just. I'm, OK, I'm not making much sense here so I better be quiet for a moment and gather my thoughts because I am just at a loss for words as to how I should respond to that kind of ignorance and blatant disregard for the facts and. Well, I just have nothing to say.

She pulls up her sleeve and points at the upside-down pink triangle on her shoulder.

—Do you even know what this means?

Stretch nods.

—Means you're another bitch doesn't know how to keep her mouth shut.

She gets to her feet and lurches in Stretch's direction.

—Motherfucker, I'm going to fucking kill you, you fucking half-wit half-pint half-man, say one more word like that and I'm going to fucking kill you and kill you!

Moishe puts a hand on her arm.

She looks at it.

—Get it off me.

He removes his hand.

—Of course, this is not meant in disrespect, yes? Is it? No. Just that you are injured. Better to sit, yes? Sit. Please.

She sits, looks at me.

—You planning to join in, Joe?

—Hey, you're the diplomat.

Stretch opens his mouth and the Rebbe puts a finger to his lips.

—No. No, Abe, no more. You've made your case, yes? They are from the Coalition, you say. You know why they are here, you say. You will tell me what they are here for if I turn Hannah and Sarah over to you. This is what you have to say. I do not need to hear it again. These two, they say what? They say you are a liar. They say they are from the Society. Like that should mean something to me they say it. What does it mean? If they are telling me the truth this should make me feel better? Safer? To know more outsiders are involving themselves in our concerns should make me at ease? No. This is what I know.

He closes his eyes and puts fingers to his temples.

—The Coalition, they have been here.

He opens his eyes and looks at Lydia.

—You did not know this? Yes? No? They have been here. Offering alliances. Assurances. Promising Brooklyn to us. As if it were theirs to give. If you are one of theirs you may know this. Or not. What can I tell them? Brooklyn is already ours. This is our land. The land of the Benjaminites. The city of New Gibeah. This is ours. And they say yes, OK, yes. They leave. Very civilized. But they have been seen. Just north. In Queens. The Coalition. Many of them in Queens. What does this mean?

He folds his arms.

—If you are Coalition, I would like to know this. And if you are not? And if you are? Does it matter?

Axler puts a hand over the knife sheathed inside his vest.

—We should kill them, Papa.

—Did I ask you, Axler? Did I ask you anything but to be quiet?

—Wherever they're from, they're here to make trouble. We have to make a lesson of them. The people, Papa, the rest of the tribe, we told them we would keep them safe. This is how we do it.

He takes the knife out and points it at Vendetta and Harm.

—We keep the women of the tribe for increase.

He points it at Stretch.

—We kill the enemies of the tribe for safety.

He points it at me and Lydia.

—And we kill invaders to protect the borders of the tribe's land.

He points the knife at himself.

—You may not like the way I did this tonight, Papa, but it had to be done. The rest of the tribe will not want to know it was done this way, but it had to be done. They can sleep safely in Gravesend only if we make these choices. I sinned. I broke the Sabbath. But someone has to.

Rebbe Moishe pulls down the corners of his mouth, raises his eyebrows, unfolds his arms and hoists his shoulders.

—Sometimes, not always, but sometimes my son can talk sense.

I clear my throat.

He drops his shoulders.

—Yes?

—Would it be possible for me to ask a question?

—These manners, where have they come from? Yes, of course, a question, ask it.

I look at Axler.

—I was wondering if that's the knife you used to kill Selig?

No one says anything. So I carry the conversation for the moment.

—In the cemetery? It was just a little while ago? You stuck it through his throat and cut his brain stem with it. Was that the one you're waving around there?

He comes in my direction.

—Axler!

He stops and looks at his father.

—A filthy lie! Do you need any more proof, Papa?

I lean into the aisle.

—Hey, I'm not asking anyone to take my word for this, Rebbe. Try grilling one of his lameass posse here. Based on the spine they showed when he was waxing their friend, I'm guessing they'll spill the beans in about a second.

I look at the kid who scratched my head.

—What about it, buddy, you and Selig close? Got any regrets about not stepping up when junior lost his cool and killed the promising young rabbinical student?

The head scratcher opens his mouth, stands, sits, closes his mouth, looks at the Rebbe, looks away.

—He's lying, Rebbe.

I shrug.

—Well, that's it, looks like I'm screwed. Testimony like that, how can I not be lying?

Axler's fingers are white on the handle of the knife when he waves it at me.

—He's lying. He killed Chaim.

He waves it at Lydia.

—And she killed Selig. She killed Selig.

Lydia straightens.

—Hold on, hold on. I admit I fired indiscriminately and can't account for every round, but I didn't stab anyone. I'm certainly not prepared to accept the blame for a death I can't say for certain I had any involvement in.

Stretch goes red faced.

—Will someone please shut that cunt's mouth before I go crazy?

Lydia comes off the bench.

She careens across the aisle and throws her shoulder into Stretch and knocks him to the floor and grabs him by his bound ankles and lifts him and swings him high in an arc over her head and brings him down and his skull shatters three of the large white tiles that cover the floor, sending a spiderweb of cracks across them and gouts of blood and shards of bone through the air.

She falls to her knees and drops his ankles and watches him jerk twice and stiffen and we all smell his bowels go and the blood stops pumping and the one eye that still has a socket to hold it in rolls around and stops and glasses over.

Lydia looks at the dead midget, looks up at us all.

—I told him I'd kill him if he talked like that again.

Harm goes berserk.

Vendetta goes berserk too, but all she does is grab her dad and howl and shake. Harm wants to make Lydia dead. And she makes a living doing the nail act with her sister. And the rest of the crowd is trying to get her down without killing her.

Fucking fiasco.

I do the smart thing and roll off my pew and squirm under it and watch. Lydia just sits on the floor and stares at Vendetta with her dead father in her arms.

Harm gets close, but Axler's boys keep wrestling her down. They have to break a few bones to do it, Rebbe Moishe all the time telling them to be gentle.

When they try to get Stretch from Vendetta's embrace, she bites someone's thumb off. They get smart and let her hold the dead guy and just lift them both from the floor and carry them out to wherever they took Harm and Rachel. Axler's place, I guess.

And in the middle of all this, Axler comes for me.

Knife out, chaos behind him, he reaches under the pew and pulls me out and I twist my wrists and the straps hold and I kick my legs and the straps hold and he pulls my hair and stretches my throat and when his father hauls him off me and throws him to the other side of the temple he takes hair and scalp with him.

And soon after that, it's pretty quiet. The girls are gone with the escort of boys, which leaves me bound on the floor, and the Rebbe sighing deep, and his son dragging himself to his feet and looking for his knife, and Lydia, still staring at the door where they took the dead father and his crazed daughters.

Lydia looks at Moishe.

—I did warn him.

He crouches next to her.

—Yes, you did. No one said otherwise.

—I've never done anything like that before.

—Of course not, why would you have? He tasked you. You are wounded and exhausted and in danger and he tasked you.

—I mean, I've, I've, I've killed before. But in self defense. I. I've never. In anger. I've never done that before.

—You were raised well, then. You said your father kept Seder? You were raised in a proper house? He was Jewish? Yes?

She looks at the cracked tiles.

—What? Yes. Jewish. All that nonsense. All of us. Yeah, yeah, but California Jewish is different from New York Jewish.

—Shht. Nonsense. There is only Jewish. Look at us, yes? I came from Poland. Do you believe this? It is true. Deep in the dark holds of ships. Smuggled out. From Poland. Over the sea. Are we different from New York Jews? Perverse as we are, are we not Jewish? Yes, we are. Your father raised you Jewish, you are Jewish. And your mother?

—Yeah, like I said, all Jewish. Bat mitzvah, the whole thing. Till I was old enough to think for myself.

—Well, they must have raised you well and loving. You've been blessed. In this our life, only to have killed in self defense. Never until now in anger. Never from greed or hunger. That I could say the same.

He stands, he stands and takes a step and puts himself in the path of his son, who has recovered his knife and has crossed the temple and is coming for me.

—Axler.

—Move, Papa.

—Boy.

—Move.

Axler sweeps his arm at his father to knock him aside.

And the Rebbe grabs his son's wrist and twists it and cranks it down and behind his back and pushes it up and kicks him once behind each knee and Axler goes down and throws his free hand out to catch himself and the knife flies from his fingers and his father forces the arm high and his son bends until his forehead touches the ground, his face rubbed in the pooled blood of his uncle.

—Boy, you have done enough. Enough. And is there no length you will not go to cover your sins? Laying hands on your father? Your Rebbe? Piling bodies on bodies to hide the ones beneath? Invoke the safety of the tribe to excuse your shame? Shht.

He releases the arm and straightens. But Axler stays as he is.

—My son.

He walks to the fallen knife and picks it up.

—My pride and joy.

He comes to me with the knife.

—Do you know how many older brothers he had, this one?

He slips the blade between the straps on my ankles and parts them.

—Six. Six boys older. And perhaps wiser, yes? How could they not have been?

He slips the blade between the straps on my wrists and parts them.

—But only this one survives. When he reached the age when I could pass the blood of Gibeah, only he had the strength for it. Of seven, only this one of my sons.

He tucks the knife in his belt, crosses to Lydia, puts a hand under her arm, helps her to her feet, leads her to a pew and seats her.

—It's not carried in birth, the blood of Gibeah. Even though his mother and I both have it, our children were born without it. The act of love, it will not carry this warrior's blood.

He finds a handkerchief in his trouser pocket and wipes spots of Stretch's blood from Lydia's hands.

—But the ones who have the strength, they take the blood young. After the bris, of course.

He tucks the handkerchief away and looks at me as I sit up on the floor.

—Imagine, if we put the blood in them before the bris? The mohel's dismay. *Wait, didn't I just cut that off?*

He smiles with half his face.

He gets up again, goes to his son, rests a hand on his back.

—Get up, Axler. Get up. There is shame in what you have done, but there is also pride. You are my son, yes? Nothing you do, nothing I do changes this. We cannot change this.

Axler lifts his face from the blood, looks up, raises his hands, holds his arms to his father.

—Papa.

—It's OK, boy.

—Papa.

The Rebbe takes a step forward and presses Axler's face to his stomach and Axler wraps his arms around him.

—Papa, I killed Selig. And Chaim. Chaim died. And their bodies. Chaim was burned and. Fletcher. Fletcher was also killed. Pieces of him were lost. And Elias, his body. And another. We didn't know what was his and. And the others, they came because I told them it was alright. That if the girls drove and we didn't use guns, the sins would be less and. I killed Selig, Papa.

—Shht. Shh.

He holds his son's head and looks at me and Lydia.

—This is what war does to us, yes? Our principles, our love, everything is tested. We find out everything there is to know about ourselves in two things only. In war. And in love.

He puts a hand under his son's chin and lifts his face and looks at him, tear tracks cut through the blood on the boy's cheeks.

—My son has just learned that he is not so strong as he thinks.

He glances at Lydia.

—As have you.

Axler sobs, coughs.

—I'm sorry, Papa.

Moishe shakes his head.

—No, no, don't be sorry to me, be sorry to God. To God you owe your apologies. Apologize now to God.

Axler nods and closes his eyes and begins to whisper.

The Rebbe looks down at him.

—And, you see, tonight you find out more than that you are weak in war. You find out you are strong in love. The love for your friends. It was too strong for you to lie. When the time came, your love was too strong not to do what you had to. Not to face the truth, yes?

He runs his fingers through his son's hair, straightens his yarmulke.

—This is the nature of love, to shine a light. To show us all what we really feel and want.

He looks at the ceiling.

—We have only to open our eyes and look, to see what love demands of us.

He slides the knife from his belt, pulls his son's head back, baring his throat, and he pushes the knife through his neck, much as Axler did to murder his friend; a killing stroke he must have learned from his father.

I'm about to come off the floor and grab the Rebbe's head and twist his neck and drag Lydia the hell out of this madhouse when the boys come back in and I have to put that particular plan on hold.

* * *

—And so we are diminished. Four sons of Benjamin. All with the blood of Gibeah in their veins. All killed in one night. And Abe as well. We must not forget Abe, yes? Not a Benjaminite, true, but he carried Gibeah in him. And he fathered two girls both strong enough to carry Gibeah themselves. A rare thing. Here, lift him.

He tucks the tail of the shroud around his son's body and gestures to two of the boys and they lift Axler and carry him to the front of the temple and lay him at the foot of the altar.

Another boy comes back from the errand he was sent on and places a large bucket of soapy water and a pile of rags where the Rebbe points.

—There. No, leave them. All of you. Just. Sit please, yes? And be quiet for a moment. If this is not too much to ask? Yes? Thank you.

The boys take seats in the last row of the temple.

Rebbe Moishe takes one of the rags and dunks it in the water and starts to wipe up the blood of his son and his sister's husband.

—And now the girls are of more importance than ever, yes? Daughters of their mother and of Abe. We'll need them not only because they can produce true sons and daughters of Benjamin, but because they come of such strong stock. With luck, perhaps one or both of them will give us a boy who can carry the blood of Gibeah.

He twists the rag over the bucket and it rains red.

—But, this doesn't matter to you, yes? You have heard enough of our problems. This our life, to sustain a history and a people that we trace back before Christ and Moses. What is that to you? Nothing. To you there is one question, yes? Coalition or Society, *What is to be done with us now?* is your only question.

He scrubs the temple floor.

—What is happening here, here in our land, in New Gibeah, this is for us, not for anyone else. If some others here who carry the blood of Gibeah do not wish to remain in the city, they may do as they please. They may leave. Provided, this is no surprise by now I think, provided that like Abe they do not try to take our daughters with them. But to leave is one thing, yes? To bring outsiders here is another. It invites misunderstanding and chaos.

He holds out his arms, the rag dripping.

—Chaos. War. Death.

He wrings the rag and bends to clean.

—We do not want these things brought here to our doorstep. Nor do you, I think, want them brought to yours. The Gibeahans, the seven hundred left-handed warriors we can muster, brought to your house, would not suit you.

He looks at us.

—Yes?

He cleans.

—Shht. Of course not. So a message must be sent. A message clear and without ambiguity must be sent.

He drops the rag in the bucket and comes to his feet.

—You remember the message that was sent, yes? When Gibeah was destroyed by the children of Israel, you remember? The concubine, *divided together with her bones into twelve pieces and sent into all the coasts of Israel.*

Lydia and I are on our feet, the boys are on theirs.

The Rebbe raises his hands.

—No. No. That will not be the message tonight. No. There has been enough. No. Not tonight. If you come again, if any of you come again across the river, yes, that is the message we will send. That is the warning we will send, the promise we will make and keep.

He looks at the body at the altar.

—But not tonight. For love's sake we are done with that tonight.

He walks to me and holds out his hands.

—Come.

I don't move.

He takes my hands and squeezes them both.

—Go to your home, tell your people this is our land, our home. Ours to defend and do with as we wish. No one else's to give. We don't ask for permission to do the things we do. We do them. For our protection, for God, we do them. Tell them the strength of our resolve, yes?

He looks over his shoulder to his dead son.

—The lengths we will go to here. Tell them the story of what we do here to be certain the tribe is safe. The sacrifices we make. Our willingness to cull our own herd of the weak to make the strong stronger.

He squeezes tighter.

—Yes?

I nod.

—Sure.

The boys start down the aisle.

—They'll take you to the edge of Gibeah. From there you find your own way home.

I nod.

Still he holds my hands.

—The lecture on war was wasted on you, yes? You know what war is already. But perhaps not the one on love? I think not.

He squeezes tighter.

—Know what you love best before you sacrifice on its behalf.

He looks at the boys, and they are on Lydia, one on each limb, another to bind her while they hold her down and she screams.

I jerk my arms back and the Rebbe turns them under and lifts them and I freeze.

—Think what you love best.

Lydia is on the floor.

Screaming.

—Joe! Joe!

I relax my arms.

Moishe eases his grip.

—Good, yes? Think, yes? You know this is as it must be. Her mother was Jewish, she said, yes?

—Joe! Don't you let these fucking lunatics keep me!

—Her mother was Jewish. Perhaps not of Benjamin, but a woman of Jewish blood, descended of a woman of Jewish blood. And she has the blood of Gibeah. She is ours. You know this, yes. Even if she does not, you know this.

—Fucking, Joe! Joe!

—Her children will make the tribe stronger. Her children will be clean. Can carry blood for the sons and daughters of Gibeah.

—Oh no, fuck no!

Her arms and legs are bound. One holds her head, another gags her. She twists and struggles and keens through the gag.

The Rebbe raises a finger.

—Know what you love best, and what you are willing to sacrifice for it.

I look at all the blood smeared in this temple. I look at Lydia.

And I know what I love best. The only thing I love. And what I will do for her. And how little time I have left to do it.

I stop looking at Lydia and look at him instead.

—Hey, man, I barely know the chick. All I'm interested in is a ride home.

The boys hoist her high and bear her out of the room.

They keep my blade and my works and my guns, but they give back my money and my keys, and they let me ride in the backseat instead of the trunk.

One of the boys on either side, two more up front, they drive me in Axler's mom's beaten Caddy.

Out Ocean Parkway to the Prospect expressway and the BQE, we trace back the route I took with Lydia through Red Hook. No one says anything. The car smells like the blood we've all spilled. Dry and crusted to our clothes. It burns the nostrils, as if someone had spilled a can of paint thinner in the car. One of the boys keeps his window down and rides with his face tilted into the wind.

At Hicks, the driver swings off the expressway and pulls to a corner and one of the boys gets out and holds the door for me as I climb out. It's the head scratcher. He avoids my eyes, but I'm not looking at him. I'm looking at the ramp of the Brooklyn Bridge, the walkway that spans its length, the dark sky above it, starless.

He gets back in the car.

I rap a knuckle on the door before he can close it.

—Got any idea what time it is?

He looks at me, looks away.

—Just go around to the other side of the ramp. Some stairs are there. You have plenty of time to walk back.

—Sure, but do you know what time it is?

He closes the door and they drive away, the right front tire grinding against the crumpled fender when they turn at the corner.

The ice air off the river burrows into the wound in my ribs and the holes in my leg and arm. I pull my coat closer around me and walk a block to Cadman Plaza West and limp across it in front of some traffic and follow a path around a little park and hit the sidewalk on the other side and walk down it and find the staircase cut into the stone footing of the bridge and I go up and stand on the wood planks of the walk and look at downtown Manhattan about twenty minutes away. At the other end of the bridge somewhere is a yellow cab waiting for a fare, waiting to take me the fuck home.

I turn around and go back down the stairs.

Jesus loves me and I find a 24-hour deli on Henry Street.

A crackhead skips from foot to foot in front of the door. He skips a little farther to make room for me.

—Pennynickledimequarterdollarmilliondollars?

I walk inside.

—Catch me on my way out.

He skips and smiles toothless.

The beer cooler is locked. I look for the clerk, see that no one is in the store. I think about breaking the glass, remember the precinct house we passed as we came off the expressway just down the street. I smell something and walk to the counter and lean over it and see the guy on his knees, curled over, his forehead touching the prayer mat that covers the floor. I wait a minute while he chants.

He stands, rolling the mat and putting it and a copy of the Q'uran on a shelf above the condoms and hangover cures.

—Sorry. These hours. I have to sneak it in when I can. My imam would shit.

He looks up and sees my scab-crusted face and the blood-soaked shirt stuck to my chest and his eyes drift down and he sees the hole in my pants and the bloody denim.

—Uh.

—The cooler's locked.

He looks up.

—Uh.

—It's not mine. The blood.

—Uh.

—In an accident. Driver got messed up bad. Most of it's his.

—Uh.

—I could use a beer.

He nods.

—Right.

He comes from around the counter.

—Sorry. Have to lock it while I'm at prayer.

He unlocks the cooler.

—Chester out there would come in and try to clear out every forty in the place if I didn't.

I reach in the cooler and grab a six of Bud and a 40 of Old English 800.

At the counter he bags the beer and tosses in the two packs of Luckys I ask for.

—That it?

There are some odds and ends hanging on wire hooks above the candy racks. Scotch tape, blunted scissors, notepads, sewing kits, playing cards, a spatula, toilet plunger, screwdriver. I take down a sewing kit and a serrated kitchen knife shrink-wrapped to a piece of cardboard and he rings it up.

—Thirty-seven, eighty-nine.

I dig the crumpled bills from my pocket and give him two twenties and he gives me the change.

—You OK?

I pick up the bag.

—I'm gonna be.

—You live around here?

—I live around.

—You need a ride, there's a car service up the street.

—Thanks.

I go out.

—Pennynickledimequarterdollarmilliondollars?

I pull the 40 out of the bag and show it to Chester and tilt my head up the street and he follows me away from the storefront. I hand him the 40 and watch while he unscrews the cap, gives the mouth of the bottle a wipe with the greasy XXL sweatshirt that hangs off his skin and bones, puts it to his mouth and watercoolers half of it.

I put one of my beers down my throat.

Chester swirls the beer at the bottom of his bottle.

—Lookin' fera rock?

I nod.

He tilts his head back, goes at the bottle, his Adam's apple bobbing, drops the empty on a littered patch of dirt at the foot of a sick tree and skips toward the corner.

—C'mon.

I follow him onto Orange Street and in the middle of the block I punch him in the back of the neck just at the base of the skull and his head snaps forward and he takes another step and then his feet stop moving and I fist a wad of his sweatshirt before he can faceplant on the pavement and drag him to an iron fence and hoist him up and throw him over into the small churchyard it encloses.

I drop the plastic bag between the bars and climb over and jump to the ground, the holes in my body bitching at me. I grab Chester and my bag and drag them into the darkness at the foot of a statue of someone who was probably really important once, but now he's just dead.

I crack a beer and take a sip and set it aside and get the kitchen knife from the bag and tear it from the plastic and cardboard and thumb the serrated edge. It's dull. Sharp enough for bread, but little else. I pull up the sleeve of Chester's shirt and spill a little beer on his wrist and mop it away with the paper napkins the clerk tossed in the bag. I open the sewing kit and thread a needle and set it close by.

And I pick up the knife and put it to his skin and cut quick and deep, the blade sharp enough for this.

My mouth is over the wound, and Chester's diseased and ravaged blood is pumping into me and the Vyrus goes into it and feeds on it and I don't feel the cold anymore and I don't feel my wounds and the hairs on my stomach and chest stand up and my eyes roll up in my head and I almost laugh at myself for buying the sewing kit.

He's not empty when I'm done. Not for lack of trying. But after I start gagging up blood for the third time I drop his arm and find more of the napkins and wipe my mouth and rinse my face with beer.

I look at Chester. There's still blood in there, but none of it's coming out, his heart having stopped pumping after the first three or four pints ran down my gullet.

I pick up the knife and hack his arm with it a couple times, creating something that might look enough like stress cuts to make the cops shrug and say *junkie suicide* and not give a fuck. I wipe the knife handle and wrap his fingers around it.

I squat there and drink another beer and smoke and try and remember if there was a video camera in the deli. If there was, I should go back and make the clerk show me where the recorder is and take the tapes and kill him. But I don't think there was.

I collect my empties and butts and the sewing kit and stand and look at Chester again and put my foot on his chest and pump it a few times to force more blood from his wound so there will be some pooled on the grass when he's found.

It looks like shit. Looks like a shit kill by an asshole who doesn't know what he's doing.

Fuck do I care? I'm a new fucking man.

The holes in my body are sealed tight and they flush warm and tingle as they heal. I can smell the crisp night in every detail. I can see the stars that were invisible before. I can hear the tics and fleas that infest Chester's clothes start to suck at the blood I've left for them. I can feel the vibrations of the cars climbing the ramp to the bridge blocks away.

I leap to the top of the fence and perch there.

I'm a monster in the city at night. And I can do what I fucking please.

It's Brooklyn. Burn it to the ground and see if anyone pisses on the fire.

Two drivers and the dispatcher at the car service sit behind a Plexiglas partition playing dominoes on a card table with a crooked leg, filling the office with smoke.

The dispatcher looks at me and the mess I am and shakes his head.

—No cars.

I go in my pocket and come out with more of the Society's cash and put four twenties on the counter and slide them under the partition.

He shakes his head again.

One of the drivers calls domino and slaps down and they total their points and the other driver curses and looks at my money.

—Where?

I tell him and he takes the eighty bucks and gives sixty to the guy who just skunked him and pulls on a parka and the dispatcher buzzes him out of the booth and we walk into the cold and he unlocks his Lincoln.

I start to get in and he holds up a hand and gets a blanket from the trunk, spreads it across the backseat so I don't get blood on his cracked and faded leather.

I get in and pull a beer from the bag and put a fresh smoke in my mouth.

He turns in his seat and looks at me.

—No smoking. No drinking.

I hand him my last twenty and a beer and he pockets the money and opens the beer and drives.

He drops me off next to the Field and I walk across it drinking my last beer and toss the empty can at the bottom of the fence and jump it and hit to the ground on the other side and weave through the headstones.

I find the freshly dug graves of Chaim and Selig and Fletcher and Elias and whatever parts of the Strongman that made it into the ground here. I have to dig with my hands, but the dirt is loose and I'm strong and it doesn't take long. I get to the corpse I want and I take his long knife and his little axe. I brush dirt from them and test their edges and find them honed.

Cypress Ave. cuts through the cemetery. I walk along it and settle into some bushes at the base of a tree where I can see the end of 57th Street and the lighted upper windows at the rear of the house with the small temple in its backyard, and the young man in a long black coat and a wide-brimmed hat walking back and forth next to the fence that separates it from the cemetery.

I think about Lydia and what a pain in my ass she is.

I think about Predo and Terry and the way it feels when they jerk my strings and my arms and legs jump and I dance dance dance to their tune.

I think about Daniel and things he's said to me over the years about what Enclave is and what they want and how I'm one of them.

I think about Rebbe Moishe and what he had to say about love.

I think about love and what you sacrifice for it and what you do to keep it in your life.

I think about Evie.

I think about the only way you can stay with the person you love forever. How you have to die to do that. I think about how close Evie is to death. And what it will be like when she's gone.

I think about what's expected of me. How little.

I think about seven hundred left-handed warriors.

And I walk out of the bushes and use the long knife and the axe to kill one.

He fights quiet.

Mostly he fights quiet because I come at him from behind and he smells me too late and when he turns the axe cuts through his windpipe. After that his screams don't do much except whistle and spray blood. He reaches for something riding on his hip and I stab the long knife through the back of his hand and into his gut. His right hand comes at my throat, but I'm bringing the axe back around and I imbed it in his shoulder and I know I cut something important because his fingers won't squeeze when he gets them on me. I push him up against the fence and he gurgles and leaks all over the place. He jerks his left hand free of the knife, losing his thumb as he does it, and goes for my eyes. I pull the axe and the knife from his body and looks like I was the only thing holding him up because he slides down the fence and onto his back and his limbs pedal at the air like a dying bug.

I leave him where he is, close to all the other dead people in the cemetery, and go over the fence and the guy on the other side is waiting for me and I find out what the Rebbe was talking about when he said they can *sling stones at a hair breadth, and not miss.*

The half-inch steel bearing this guy whips from his sling hits me in the left kneecap and the bone turns to a fistful of gravel and I swing the leg out in front of me and step on it and it makes me want to scream but I won't do that and I walk on the fucking thing and it makes me pay for it, and it looks to me like the problem with a sling is that after you fire your first shot you have to get another stone or whatever cradled in that little pocket and spin the thing up to speed and if the asshole you just nailed keeps coming at you and chops your arm off before you can do all that, you're fucked.

So that's what I do.

This one makes some noise, until I put him on the ground and stomp on his head a couple times.

My knee hurts like something my dad did to me once when I was too young to know that pain stops. But I'm older now. And one way or another I won't have to worry about the knee much longer.

Two more boys come out of the house.

One has a spear. The other one is in his underwear and his yarmulke and doesn't have shit.

I worry about the one with the spear.

He rushes me and plants his feet and thrusts just like someone has trained him to do and I drop the long knife and grab the spear shaft behind the point and it slips through my fingers and about three inches of steel slips into my stomach and I bring the axe down and the shaft splinters and the guy who had a spear now has a stick and I have the axe and the business end of a spear and I pull it out of my belly and flip it in the air and catch it and hold it out and the guy in his underwear has already leapt into the air and is coming down at me and can't do shit about it and the shock of the impact tears the spear from my hand and he hits the ground and starts trying to pull it out of his chest but it's in deep and lodged tight in his breastbone and he rolls around and dies and the guy with the stick turns to go back in the house and trips over the arm of the boy who had the sling and I limp over and swing the axe once and swing it a second time and the second time does the trick and I go inside the house with the axe in one hand and a head in the other.

The door leads into the kitchen. The boy in the kitchen is the head scratcher.

And he has a bow.

His hands shake as he tries to knock an arrow into the bowstring.

I hold up the head.

—Hey.

He flinches and the arrow slips loose and the string twangs into his forearm.

—Uh.

I point the axe at the head.

—Where's the girl?

He points at the floor.

—Uh.

—Basement?

He nods.

I lower the head.

—You can run if you want.

He drops the bow and turns and runs through the doorway into the livingroom and I throw the head at his legs and he goes down and I walk over with the axe and put my foot in his back and raise the axe to get my second head.

—A message is meant to be heeded, yes?

The Rebbe stands halfway down the stairway in his trousers and slippers and untucked shirt, a prayer shawl draped over his shoulders, a Colt Defender in his hand. I notice a black cloth draped half over a mirror on the wall next to him. A basin of water at the end of the hall near the front door.

The Rebbe tugs the cloth over the mirror, but it falls away again.

—For my son.

He looks at the head scratcher.

—Coward.

He shoots the head scratcher and I throw myself up the stairs and swing the axe in a high arc and I crash into the stairs and the blade rakes his leg and hooks in the meat of his thigh and I heave and the leg folds under him and he's falling backward, two rounds punching through the ceiling, and I pull the axe from his leg and put it in his stomach and pull him down the stairs toward me and the gun comes at my face and the barrel smashes my cheekbone and it goes off and the muzzle flash sears my eye and the bullet splinters the banister and I pull the axe free and put it in his chest and pull him closer and I'm on top of him now and his face is in front of me and I know what I love and what I'll sacrifice for it and I don't care when he fires again and the bullet tears my neck open and I pull the axe free and I bring it down and I bring it down and I bring it down.

—Moishe.

His wife stands at the top of the stairs.

Covered in her husband's blood, I pick up his gun and shoot her dead.

I pull off the Rebbe's shawl and wrap it around my neck. The wound is growing hot as the Vyrus clots the blood. My left eye is blind and blistered. I sit on the stair and smoke, my head listing to the side where the bullet ripped a hole in the thick muscle that connects it to my body.

When the cigarette is finished I go to work, dividing the Rebbe together with his bones into twelve pieces.

I don't bother to send the pieces into any place. I'm pretty sure his people will get the fucking message.

—Where is that fucker?

Lydia takes the long knife from me and cuts the bindings from her feet and sits up on the cot in her basement cell.

—Where's the fucker that thought he was gonna turn me into a rape slave?

I pick some dead skin from my blind eye.

—I got him.

She stands, totters, puts out a hand to brace herself and grabs my shoulder.

—I want to see.

I flick the skin from my fingers.

—No, you don't.

She looks me over, standing crooked on my one good leg, dressed in one of Axler's too-tight black suits and my sticky leather jacket, the rest of my clothes up in the house, soaked in half the blood of Brooklyn.

She grits her teeth.

—He deserved it.

I cough up some blood. I don't know whose.

—No doubt.

She looks at the hand on my shoulder, pulls it away.

—You OK?

—No.

She nods.

—OK. Let's get going.

I push off the wall and we both limp out the door and she stops and looks at the other cell across the basement.

She steps that way.

I don't.

—Lydia, I need to get out of here.

She looks me over.

—You'll hold up a little longer.

She walks, holding her belly.

—Fucking arrows. Who uses arrows, Joe? Savages, that's who. I mean, no disrespect to any native peoples intended, but arrows are for savages. These people are savages. They have the same superstitions as savages. And they treat women like savages. And I'm not leaving these women here to be baby incubators for savages.

—Open that door and untie them and they're just gonna try and kill you.

I come up behind her.

—You killed their father, Lydia.

She looks at the lock.

—All the more reason that I won't leave them here, Joe. If that means we carry them out of here hog-tied, then that's what we'll do.

She looks at me.

—Do you have anything to get the lock off?

I hand her the axe.

—Try this.

She brings it down on the lock and it tears loose and she pushes the door open and light hits Vendetta and Harm, hanging from the water pipe that runs across the ceiling, nooses tied from their headscarves knotted around their swollen necks.

Lydia stares at them.

I make for the stairs, glad that something was easy for a change.

—I don't know how they did it.

I steer Axler's mom's Caddy up onto the bridge.

She rubs her forehead.

—They must have hung there forever.

I push the dash lighter in and put a cigarette in my mouth.

—They were tough little tarts. And they knew what they wanted. Want it bad enough and you'll do anything.

She watches me take the lighter from the dash and use it.

—Fuck you, Joe.

I push the lighter back in its socket and drive.

—Yeah, fuck me.

Over on the horizon, something a little like dawn shows upriver.

I pull to the curb, back on Society turf.

—Where's this?

—I got things to do. You can keep the car.

Lydia looks out the window.

—No. Absolutely not.

I open my door.

She grabs my arm.

—I thought we talked about this. I thought I was clear about where I stand with this kind of thing.

I pull loose and step out of the car, leaving the keys in the ignition.

She comes around from her side and stands in front of me.

—This is not OK. You are not thinking straight. And it's not even remotely the time to have a debate on the subject. We have to go to Terry and tell him what happened. Regardless of who was to blame, what happened out there was a fiasco and there will be consequences, and we have to begin to prepare for them right now.

I jam the Rebbe's Defender into her stomach.

—Lydia, get out of my fucking way.

She looks down at the gun.

—Don't be ridiculous, Joe.

I shoot her.

She goes down on the sidewalk and I scoop her up and stumble into the emergency entrance screaming and we're mobbed and they pull her from me and I cling to her and someone tells someone to get rid of me and I let them drag me to a little room down the hall past the security desk and a guy tells me I have to be calm and I punch him and he goes down and I limp out of the little room and to the elevators and go up and the night nurse is behind the desk with her wrist in a brace and she looks at me and I look at her and she looks back down at her computer and I walk into the room and there's my girl.

She comes out of the drugs a little when I'm detaching all the wires and hoses, and looks at me and touches my face.

I put a finger over the end of her trache tube and she smiles and her voice scratches its way out of her throat.

—Hello, handsome.

—Hello.

—You don't look good.

—Yeah.

—You should go to a hospital.

—I should.

I pull the blankets and sheets away and she winces as I pull out her catheter and air whistles from the trache.

I help her to sit up.

—Sorry.

She covers the end of the tube.

—I'm gonna make a mess now.

—That's OK.

I go to the closet and find her big leather jacket and tuck her into it.

—We going somewhere?

—Yeah.

She points at the bed table.

—My present, my present. I want to wear it.

I pick up the candy necklace and rip the package open with my teeth and stretch it and put it over her head and around her skinny neck.

She cocks her head and touches it with her fingertips.

—Am I beautiful?

—Hell yeah, baby.

I pick her up and put her in the wheelchair at the foot of the bed.

And the night nurse is gone from her desk, hiding. And the intern in the elevator ignores us and leans his head against the wall and closes his eyes. And the security guards on the ground floor are all outside looking for the gutshot woman who climbed off her gurney and threw one of them into a wall and ran out the door and drove off in an old Cadillac and must be on more PCP than the devil. And the cabby that stops for us doesn't know how to fold the wheelchair and neither do I so we leave it at the curb and when he drops us off on Little West 12th Street I carry Evie in my arms to the door and kick it until someone slides it open and I stagger in on a ruined leg and someone catches me and takes my girl from me and I try to take her back and Daniel cradles her gently and smiles.

—Simon, you made it.

—L'chaim.

I take the Dixie cup of blood from Daniel.

—Is that supposed to be funny?

He hands the small pitcher of blood back to the Enclave who gave it to him.

—Sorry. Was that in bad taste? After your story, I couldn't quite resist.

I drink the blood and tear the cup in half and run my finger over the insides and stick it in my mouth and suck it clean.

—Glad I could lighten your load.

He blows out his sunken cheeks.

—*Lighten my load.*

He holds a hand to the candle that sits between us on the floor and his skin goes translucent.

—My load is amply light these days.

I crumple the cup and drop it.

He points at my knee.

—Any better?

I give it a poke with my index finger and the pain jumps up my spine.

—Feels like a hot-water bottle stuffed full of broken seashells.

His eyebrows rise.

—Oddly, I have no idea what that would feel like. May I?

I shrug.

—It's your place.

He pokes my knee. I flinch. He smiles.

—You know, I think you're right. *A hot-water bottle full of broken seashells*. You're showing a touch of the poet this morning, Simon.

—Want me to stick a finger in the hole in my neck and come up with a nice simile for that sensation?

—No, no. I've had my hands in plenty of open wounds. I know well enough what they feel like. But let's take a look in any case.

He picks up the candle and holds it close to the crusted bullet hole. He hums and taps the side of my head and I tilt it away from the wound and the scabs crack and ooze.

—Well, I won't say I envy you, but it will heal.

He points at the knee.

—This could be more of a problem. The bone will knit, but it won't reform itself. You'll have a nasty limp.

I look at the swollen purple mass.

—Care to take a crack at it?

He sets the candle down and places his hands on the knee and probes it, and waves of pain and nausea roll over me and he digs his fingers in and shoves and presses, and chips and flakes of bone scrape and snap into a new arrangement and he takes his hands away.

—Not as designed, I'm sure, but a little better. Maybe.

We sit.

Around us the Enclave are moving about. The blood is being passed up and down a seated line of them. Some taking a slight drink, others fasting. A few push big brooms across the floor. I pick up my crumpled cup and toss it into the heap of dust one of them is moving down the length of the warehouse. A couple of them descend the steps from the loft that runs the back of the building.

Somewhere up there, that's where they took Evie.

—So how about it, Daniel?

He's picking at an old spot of dry paint on the concrete floor.

—Hm?

I dig a finger into the wound on my neck. Feel it hurt me.

—How about we go take a look at my girl?

He drops his head far back and stares up into the darkness above us.

—There are skylights up there. We painted them black, of course. But we never covered them over. It was discussed. Common sense suggested we should lay some sheets of plywood over them. Tarps at the very least. But someone, it may have been me, argued against it. Our home is so ordered. Disciplined. By necessity. We starve ourselves to the edge of reason. Beyond. Without structure, rigidity of manner, it would devolve to chaos and bloodshed here. Very quickly. But it's not natural. Proper, yes. But not natural. An element of the random, danger, no matter how remote, seemed like a nice touch.

He rises, still looking up.

—So every once in a while, a bird dies in midflight. An owl, of all things, once shattered two panes and landed at my feet just a few yards from this spot. Snow and ice built up another time and brought down an entire skylight. A bullet someone had fired into the air. The wind. A flaw in the glass suddenly exposed. All these have happened. Each time we've repaired or replaced the broken glass, painted it black, and left it uncovered. Each time it causes great excitement. Most every other physical aspect of our lives being all but utterly predictable.

He looks at me.

—And you know, not once, never, have any of the accidents occurred by the light of day.

He looks up again.

—I don't know what that means. But I find it a bit of a disappointment.

He bends at the waist and puts a hand alongside his mouth and whispers.

—There have been more than a few Enclave over the years who I would have given my eyeteeth to see hit with a sudden blast of sunlight.

He straightens and looks around at the white figures bustling about.

—Prigs most of them. Unseasoned. So little sense of proportion. That's one of the dangers of the cloistered life. An expansive sense of the universe, sure, but try having a conversation about art or music or a woman's legs and they have nothing to contribute at all. *You've* been around. *You've* seen a thing or two.

A strand of tendon in his neck starts to jump and he claps a hand over it.

—Hm. Yes. Seen. Things.

He takes the hand away. The tendon is still.

—Do you remember, do you remember the Wraith, Simon?

I look elsewhere.

—I was out of my skull, man. I don't know what I remember.

—Don't lie. It's beneath you.

I almost laugh at that one.

He does laugh.

—Alright, yes, lying is far from beneath you. Little is beneath you except the floor. I surrender. But. The Wraith. Something for you to think about. It came from somewhere.

—If you say so.

—I do. It came from somewhere. I know. We asked it here. From somewhere else. But, Simon, that doesn't mean I know what it is. I do have a theory.

I get my good leg under me and lever myself to my feet.

—Daniel.

—Yes? What?

—You're acting kind of weird. I mean, even for you. Are you OK?

He spreads his arms wide, lets them drop to his sides.

—Simon, if only I had the time to answer a question like that.

—Well, if you're done spacing out here, how about we go look at Evie?

An Enclave comes near, hovers just off Daniel's shoulder.

Daniel looks at him, holds up a finger. The Enclave stays there.

Daniel brushes at him with the finger. The Enclave takes a step back, but doesn't leave.

Daniel nods, looks at me.

—I'm sorry, you asked what?

—Evie. My girl, Daniel. I need to know.

He raises a hand.

—Right, yes. The girl. You want to know who she is.

—No, I know who she is, man, I want to-

He lays a hand on my chest. It burns.

—Simon, you want to know who she is. Not her name. Not where she was born. Not what her parents do or where she went to school or if she ever wore braces. You want to know who she is. What she is.

He raises his hand and cups my chin, the heat from his skin is intolerable.

—You want to know if she's like you.

The Enclave shuffles his feet.

Daniel moves his hand to my cheek.

—What will you do, Simon? What the hell will you do?

I swallow some spit and the muscles contracting in my neck pull at the wound.

—I. If she. I'll, I'll save her, Daniel. She's dying and I want to. So.

He drops his hand.

—That's not what I meant.

The Enclave moves closer again and Daniel nods. He tugs my sleeve.

—Come on, I'll help you.

He moves next to me and I put a hand on his shoulder and we walk.

—Thank you for coming by and telling me what you've been up to, Simon. Your stories always serve as a reminder. Of how pitifully banal most of the world's concerns are. And how hilarious the contortions most people go through to make themselves believe any of it matters.

—Sure. My pleasure.

More Enclave are coming near, clustering, walking behind and around us.

The door is in front of us.

We stop.

I take my hand from Daniel's shoulder.

—Daniel, I'm not leaving, man. I'm not going anywhere until you look at Evie and tell me.

He takes a step toward the door, places a hand on it, runs his fingers across the even white paint that covers the steel.

—You, you are well seasoned. You I could talk to about a woman's leg. But I wish you had some little of the other, a concern for things larger than yourself. It would have made our conversations more fruitful. You might have learned something. You might have. Well. Who cares, really? Not you. Not even me. Not anymore.

I look at the Enclave arrayed around us. All of them.

I tug at the waist of Axler's pants.

—Daniel, I'm not going out there without her.

He puts his other hand on the door, lays both palms flat and leans his forehead between them.

—If you'd ever listened once. If you'd ever observed for the slightest moment what happens here, you'd know what an ass you're making of yourself.

I reach for him and I am pinned suddenly to the door and it takes a moment to realize that Daniel has taken me by the throat and snatched me to his side.

—Look, Simon, look around and what do you see? What do you ever see here?

I look. I see Daniel. I see Enclave.

I try to move. His grip tightens, threatens to tear off my head.

—Yes. You see always one thing. Enclave. In here. Always the same. Enclave. Nothing else comes in. Nothing else leaves. Only Enclave.

His fingers loosen.

—And you ask if the girl is like you. She is as much like you as I am or any of us here.

He takes his hand away.

—You are Enclave.

Tears, viscous and white are filling his eyes.

—As she is here, as I let her in, so she is Enclave too.

I break for the stairs.

And am in the grip of Enclave. Held fast.

Daniel wipes the back of his hand over a cheek, smearing the tears. He shakes and his teeth chatter and he clenches his fists and a bone breaks in the back of his hand and juts from his skin and he exhales slow and stops shaking. But the tears keep coming.

—As for leaving. She'll have the chance to make that decision for herself.

He looks up at the black skylight.

—For the moment, I'm the only one going out.

He turns to the southward-facing door and takes the handle and pulls and it slides open on well-greased tracks and the light washes in and the Enclave rustle back from it and Daniel walks out onto the loading dock and steps off and drops to the street and walks across the cobbles that peek through the worn tarmac of Little West 12th and the sun crests the tops of the tenements at the east end of the street and hammers him and he turns into it and lets the thin white robe fall off his shoulder and to the ground and the light reflects off his white skin and he smiles and his head turns our way.

And watching him there, smiling in the sun, for a moment I believe.

Then purple blossoms like the ones that cover Evie climb over his face.

Cancers boil out of his nostrils and his ears.

His eyes swell and puss drains from them and steams.

The Enclave release me as they scuttle farther from the sunlight and I tear a white shawl from one's shoulders and the bones Daniel shifted in my knee come loose and I drag my leg outside and into the street and wrap the shawl around my head and when I grab Daniel's wrist the skin slips off the bone and I get my arms under him and scoop him off the cobbles and for the second time I lurch into the darkness with a diseased and wasted thing in my arms.

But no one takes this one from me.

Noises come from the misshapen clot of tumors that used to be his face and I put my ear to a bloody and bone-rimmed hole and he reeks poison.

A mass that used to be a hand touches my face.

—*Be seeing you, Joe.*

And he laughs and coughs his throat out on the floor and he dies.

The room is quiet except for the sound of the door rolling shut. As the light is cut off, glass breaks, and a large black bird falls dead a few yards from us, pinned to the ground by a shaft of morning sunlight.

—OK, man, now that was just plain freaky.

I look up and watch as the Count comes down the stairs, dressed all in white.

—I don't know about you, but I have had one weird fucking night. I mean, no shock there, right? Not in this place. I'm guessing nothing that passes even remotely as unweird has happened in this joint for a loooongass time. But look who I'm telling. Oh, oh, man, do they always do that?

I watch as the Enclave that has placed the bucket under Daniel's hanging corpse slits its throat. Nothing comes out of the gash.

I pat my pockets. Find my cigarettes. I put one in my mouth and try to find my lighter. Stop looking. Watch as the Enclave begins to cut Daniel open from crotch to neck.

The Count leans over and snaps a Bic in front of my face.

I flinch. Blink. Lean in and light my smoke.

He takes the lighter away.

—Are your hands shaking, Joe?

I put the cigarette in my mouth and tuck my hands into my armpits.

—I'm cold.

He feels his own skin.

—Tell me about it. Like an icebox in here.

The Enclave begins pulling viscera from the corpse.

The Count turns his head and whistles.

—Oh, man, that is rude. I mean, who needs to see that shit? Nasty.

He takes a seat on the floor next to me.

—But that's the way they rock it here. One of them dies, doesn't matter what they were before they went out, they get gutted and nailed to the wall. Some kind of lesson thing. That's what the guy told me when I asked.

—They'll boil his bones and eat the marrow.

He looks at me.

—No shit?

I pull a hand from my armpit. It's stopped shaking. I take the smoke from my mouth.

—Yeah. That's the deal.

—Whoa. Man. Can't say I'm looking forward to that.

He nudges me with his shoulder.

—Then again, check this out. You know the bones, that's where blood gets made. In the marrow. Like, by the time we're adults, it's only made in a few places. Your spine, sternum, pelvis, some little patches in your upper arms and legs. That's where you get your good old, controversial pluripotential hematopoietic stem cells. Try saying that shit five times fast. Stem cells manufacture blood cells, determine that they will be blood cells. So think about this. Drink another Vampyre's blood and get sick as hell. Unless it's super freshly infected and has been made into anathema. In which case you get high as hell. So what happens when you eat a dead Vampyre's marrow, man? His stem-cell factories?

He licks his lips.

—I'm guessing you get some weird deep Amazonian Carlos Castaneda shaman fungus high.

He shakes his head.

—I'm not saying I'm gonna be thinking about where that shit came from, but I'm dying to try me some of that soup.

The Enclave pulls a wad of tumors from Daniel's body.

The Count turns his head again.

—What say we move this conversation?

He stands.

I watch pieces of Daniel hit the floor.

I stand. The Count reaches to help me and I pull away and stumble, but I keep my feet.

He raises his hands.

—As you wish, man. Just trying to help.

I follow him.

He limps on that foot I ruined for him. I limp on the knee Daniel tried to fix for me.

—Wanted to thank you, by the way. I don't remember too much about what went down at my place. But from what I can put together, probably would have been easiest thing just to waste me.

He grins.

—'Course, knowing I still hold the purse strings on my trust fund, that was unlikely. I mean, experience has taught me you can knock me around if it amuses you, but Terry would be steamed if you ever kacked my ass before he can get his hands on those accounts.

He stops, blinks a few times, takes a couple deep breaths.

—Sorry. Whew. Shit I went through the last twelve hours, wrung me out, man. Going cold turkey on the anathema. Bleeding the Vyrus dry. That was some extreme shit. I mean, I knew I was asking for trouble, but damn.

He snaps his head from side to side.

—Whammywhammywhammy! Shit had me on the ropes. Oh, check this out.

Ahead of us two Enclave are sparring.

A whirl of blurred white limbs.

Crack of bone on bone.

The Count makes karate hands and chops the air.

—That's the shit I'm really looking forward to. Getting my kung fu on. I know I'm not the kind of guy you expect extreme patience and discipline from, but if it means coming out the other side with moves like these guys, I will meditate until my ass bleeds. I mean, whoa that shit is badass.

The stairs are close by. I turn and look at them.

The Count comes over.

—Me, I'm a little surprised they can get it up to do that shit. Losing Daniel, way I gather it, that's like a major setback, yeah?

—I guess.

—Guess nothing, man. You've been hanging out at this place for a few years now, right?

—I come by sometimes.

—Sure. So he was the man. I mean, I only spent a couple hours with the guy while he was helping me get straight last night, but even I could see he was righteous beyond the ken of normal men. If you follow.

—I follow.

—So now, the way he laid it out, one of them is always on point, leading the way toward what he tried to do. Toward the whole transmutation thing they're into.

—Something like that.

—And he was way ahead of the pack. He was, like, the best hope they'd have for, like, forever. Now, man, it's like they are at square one or something. Got to pick up with whoever's been fasting the longest. What I hear, the dude in second place is way back from where Daniel was. But here they are, carrying on, doing their thing. And on top of that, they're getting ready to eat their Dalai Lama's marrow. Telling you, these are some well-adjusted citizens.

—Count.

—Yeah.

—You're talking a lot.

—Well, I do do that, don't I?

I face him.

—I have something I need to do. So get to the point.

He scratches his head.

—The girl. Right.

He points at the stairs.

—Come on, I'll show you where.

He starts. I don't move. He looks back.

—C'mon, man. Not like it's a secret or anything. Place isn't that huge. There's a sick girl in the house. Everyone knows it. So come on up.

He leads me up.

—Daniel kind of filled me in. Not that he was gossiping or anything, but he was just talking. He always spacey like that?

—No. He wasn't.

—Was last night. Don't get me wrong, man was like a fucking magician with me. Like, I don't know what, like Zoltan the Mind Master or something.

He stops on the stairs and looks into my eyes.

—Dude locked eyes with me, put a hand on me, was like he, man, went into me. Which I know is just the gayest thing you've ever heard, but that's what it was like. The Vyrus, it was tearing me apart. Eating me. Was like he told it to chill. Got me to balance with it. And I did. A-fucking-mazing. Only lasted for a couple seconds maybe. But I was there. This perfect point where the Vyrus was kind of at its most pure and raging, and I was, I don't know what, riding it or something. Talk about a high? That is something I *will* feel again.

He moves his eyes from mine.

—After that, he gave me a little blood. Knew I couldn't contain that shit. Vyrus settled. I mean, I am starving here, but it settled. Best thing? It worked.

He inhales deep, lets it out.

—Like, all my thinking about anathema, and how you hooked me on the bad dose, and the way that . . . man. The way that felt. Wanting to get out from under that more than anything. And the reading I was doing for Terry. Learning about regular viruses and shit. I knew there had to be a way to burn that shit out of your system. I knew it.

He taps my chest.

—And, Joe, I knew you were the guy to turn to.

He starts back up the stairs.

—Not that I thought you'd nurse me through if I asked or anything. I just figured me and my money are too valuable to lose. Which isn't to say I wasn't ready to die, man. Was I ever.

We reach the top of the stairs and he puts a hand on the wall and closes his eyes.

—Hang on a sec, man. Still rocked. You see things, Joe. When you dose like that, you see things. I'm not saying they're real, but you see them.

He opens his eyes.

—I saw shit. All that stuff on the walls and the floor. I mean, that was no act. I started flippin'. I thought something was coming for me. Started reading Crowley and shit online. Wicca.com. I mean, lame. But I was scared. Once I stopped feeding. Once I poured out the last load of anathema Terry sent by, I went somewhere else. I was ready, man. I was ready to die.

He takes his hand from the wall.

—Then you came. Well, you had to. You and Phil are the only ones who *ever* came over. Phil to drop off blood and anathema. You to tell me how much money Terry wanted transferred into the Society account. Knew Phil would call you if he found me first. Only real risk far as that went was if I would drink him.

He makes a face.

—Still can't believe you put some of his blood in me. Nasty.

He bites his lip.

—Anyway, thing is, none of it, none of it was an act. Want you to know that. I definitely made a play to put you in a position where you had to help me, but none of it was an act. So. Thank you, I guess.

I don't say anything.

He nods.

—Yeah, fuck me. I know.

He starts down the hall that runs between the cubicles where the Enclave sleep.

—Will say, I never figured I'd end up here. Heard about these guys. But never thought for a second you'd bring me here. Never had this in mind. Did you know?

—What?

—That they only allow Enclave inside?

I put my hand to the wall, taking some weight off my knee as we go down toward the end of the hall.

—Never thought about it.

—Just brought me over here. Didn't even know what it meant when they let me inside. Just random.

—Or something.

—Yeah, think about that. *Or something*. Like, is anything random, right?

He stops again, turns and faces me, the last door beyond him.

Her scent in the air.

—Like, how about this? You dose me on anathema. I mean, hook me on the bad dose. And I see things. And I can't take it. And I, just on instinct and whatever I've learned from what I've been reading, I try to burn it out by starving the Vyrus. And you bring me here. And I *happen* to be Enclave. Daniel looks at me and knows. Which is part of what being him was all about, I guess. And he lays the whammy on me. And I trance out. And he brings me back. And here I am. Up and about. And, like, I was up almost right away. And he was impressed. I mean, they were all impressed. The dose I was on, the way I went head-to-head with it, the way Daniel got me to do that dance with the Vyrus and then I just snapped to, turns out that's some heavy shit. I mean, Joe, it's not just that you brought me here. I got *potential.* Real potential. How's that for *or something*?

I push him to the side and walk.

—Fuck do I care.

I walk into the room and she's there. On a mat on the floor, a thin blanket over her, face sweaty, shivering. An Enclave seated at her feet, one hand holding her toes, whispering.

The Count comes in behind me.

—Tell you, Joe, I can see it. Even all fucked up as she is, I can see what you got there.

I walk over to her and kneel on the floor and run a hand over her head and come away with sweat and hair.

I touch my pockets. I don't have a blade. Only Rebbe Moishe's Defender.

The Count crouches at my back.

—A girl like that, what's a man to do? How can you have a girl like that and not try everything to save her?

Her eyes open. She looks at me. She smiles. A hand comes out from under the blanket and touches the candy necklace and her lips move and she's asking me a question but can't speak past the hole in her throat.

*Am I pretty?*

I nod.

Her eyes close again.

I put my fingers at the clog of scab and new flesh that has grown over the wound in my neck.

A girl like this, how can I not try everything to save her? How can I keep myself from trying every last cruel and desperate trick to keep her with me?

Simple.

I can't.

I tear open the wound in my neck and lean close and place it against her mouth and the Count grabs me and pulls me away and my hand goes to the Defender and the Enclave has it and I am across the room and more Enclave are there between me and Evie and I try to go through them and I cannot.

The Count leans over her and mops at her mouth with the cuff of his white shirt.

—Hey, man, what's up, you trying to kill the girl? I mean, dude, imagine if her throat wasn't swollen shut. She'd be spewing foam all over the place right now.

I try to get to her.

They stop me again.

The Count stretches his arms, hands pushed out at me.

—Joe, man, cool it. You're gonna get all fucked up by these guys if you don't cool it. I can only do so much here. Sure I got potential. But potential only gets you a little ways. You got to deliver if you want your shit to stick.

He opens his shirt.

—Now, I know Daniel told you the girl's like you, but he just meant that she's Enclave. Or Enclave potential, I guess. Enclave enough to get in here. That doesn't mean *you* can infect her. That takes a special touch.

He peels his shirt from his skinny torso.

—Check it. The Vyrus changes when it comes into us. That's what Daniel said. That's common sense. That's why one Vampyre's blood can infect some people, but kills most others.

An Enclave hands him a short silver tube, one end cut on a bias and honed to a point.

—Thanks. But then, it reasons, some can't infect *anyone*. And some, they can infect *lots* of others. Like carriers. Daniel, he was a carrier. Know what he did? Part of what made him who he was? This is so cool, he told me about this last night, right up here. He infected new Enclave.

He sits down next to Evie.

—Like, if they saw the potential in someone out there, they brought them here. No questions asked. No choice. And Daniel bled into them. And it didn't always work. Mostly it didn't, but it worked more than for most Vampyres. Or infecteds. Or whatever you like.

He's handed a small hammer.

—So we're talking, me and him. He's impressed with the way I handled that shit last night. He's also whacked as hell, you saw him at the end there. Who knows where he was on the inside? But he wanted to talk. Lots of things. Mostly Enclave, but wanted to talk about music too. All kinds of stuff. Women. Kept asking about how high the hemlines are this year. Trippy. And I told him about my girls. Remember my girls?

He raps the hammer against the floor.

—Sure you do. Three sweet little things, wanted nothing but to party, have a good time, give a man some comfort. Well, how could you forget, what with the way you shot them down?

He puts one end of the tube at his eye and looks down it at me.

—That was not cool.

He takes the tube away.

—But I'm off topic. Check it. Daniel was even more impressed that I'd infected all three on my own. Hey, granted I broke a few eggs before I had my girls. There were definitely some that didn't make it on the way to that ideal three, but it was still pretty unusual. The fact that I could infect three out of a pretty small fucking sample was beating the hell out of the odds.

He taps his temple with the tube.

—And here I am, dropped on Daniel the night before he's going to try and take the next big step in his evolution? Well, he was a man who believed in signs and that kind of shit.

He looks at Evie.

—And then there's her.

He holds up his index and middle fingers.

—Two new Enclave. Coming in, just like that. Bang and bang. I don't need Daniel to tell me that's got to be some kind of record. That's got to mean something. That's got to be an *opportunity* for something. To *learn* something.

He pulls Evie's blanket down.

—'Cause a man can have all the potential in the world.

He places the pointed end of the tube at his heart.

—But that's just meaningless.

He hefts the hammer.

—Unless he does something with it.

He strikes the end of the tube and it pierces his chest and blood shoots from the end and he bends and places it over Evie's trache and the blood fills it and it spills over her neck and face and her heels bang against the floor and her arms tremor and her throat works.

And she's swallowing.

And she doesn't die.

She doesn't die.

And I try to get past the Enclave to kill the man doing what only I ever should have done. But I can't. I'm too weak.

So I fail.

—That was doing it old school.

He's balled his shirt and uses it to mop blood from his chest, carefully circling the hole he's tucked a finger into.

—Mean, you don't *have* to do it that way, but from what I gather it's something they respect around here.

He drops the bloody shirt and puts his back against the wall and shakes his head.

—Which stands to reason, right? I mean, if punching a hole in your own heart doesn't say something about who you are, I don't know what will. Shit hurts, I can tell you that.

I sit across the room from him, watching the place on the floor where Evie was before they took her away.

—Heart's blood. No reason why it should make a difference, but Daniel mentioned it a few times. Said it made for a closer bond between whoever was spilling their blood and whoever was drinking it. What do you think? Me, I can't see why that'd be. But who knows. Mothers say they can tell when their kids are in trouble and shit, even when they're hundreds of miles away. Maybe it'll be like that. Maybe I'll know when she's in trouble. Or happy. Or sad. Maybe I'll just kind of always know what she's feeling. What about that?

I touch the finger I've stuck in the wound I reopened in my neck, the scabs have sealed tight against it. I ease it out and some blood leaks and then stops.

The Count pokes at his own wound.

—About that time, huh? Well, let's see.

He draws his finger free and the clean edges of his unscarred flesh suck closed.

He looks around the empty room, hushes his voice.

—Truth, I didn't hit my heart. Fuck that. Sometimes a little medical training comes in handy, let me tell you. Hey, would I have been surprised if my aim was off and I stuck myself in the fucking aorta? No. But there was no way I wasn't gonna try and miss. We can theorize all we want about what the Vyrus will heal and what it won't, but that was a chance I wasn't interested in taking.

I put my hands on the floor and push myself up and work my back up the wall until I'm standing on my good leg.

The Count gets himself up.

—Yeah, getting late here, isn't it? Probably time to call it a day. Things are gonna be plenty interesting for me. Should be getting my beauty sleep. Sure you don't want to stay and see how this is all gonna work out?

I head for the door.

He walks behind me.

—Yeah, kind of what I thought. You got places to go, things to do, people, no doubt, to fuck up. Too bad. Things are gonna be getting very interesting around here, Joe. I mean, they got no one. I mean, no one on deck to take Daniel's place. And here am I. Just arrived out of the cold dark. Overcoming terrible struggles in my first night. Representing by sticking a fucking pipe in my heart and successfully bringing a new Enclave to the Vyrus. Got the inside track, man. Got influence already. Like, the king is dead, long live the king, right?

At the landing we look down. The Enclave at meditation, arrayed on the floor below, seated and silent, the most withered at the front, the robust at the rear.

The Count points.

—I'll have to start in the back with the guys who are still kind of getting the hang of fasting and all, but that won't last. There's no seniority here. Just willpower. Whoever can take the most, push the Vyrus the furthest, and live, they go to the front row. After that last year riding the bad dose, I can take a lot.

He places a hand on my shoulder.

—Thanks for that, Joe.

I ignore his hand.

I inhale. Smell her. Her new smell.

Knocking his hand away, I go past him. I smell her again. There's a door between us. I make it go away.

She's in there. Sitting, back against the wall, legs sprawled in front of her. She's pulled the trache tube from her throat and holds it and stares at it, as she fingers the already healed incision just above the candy necklace that is speckled with blood. She looks up at me and shows me the tube.

—It itched.

—Sure it did.

She drops it and touches her head.

—My hair feels weird. It feels like it's growing.

The sores on her face have started to fade. Purple to pink.

It hurts lowering myself to the floor, but I do it.

She wrinkles her nose.

—You smell funny, Joe.

She sniffs.

—Everything smells funny. It all smells bad here.

I look at her neck.

Thinking.

You don't change things by wanting them changed. You change them by knowing what to do and when to do it. And by doing it.

I never seem to know what to do until it's too fucking late.

She pinches her nostrils closed.

—I don't like it here. I want to go home. Can you take me home?

I nod. But I'm lying.

I'll never get her out of here. I'll never get her past the maniacs down there. I'll never get her away from the psycho setting up to take over this madhouse.

I touch her neck.

—Hey, baby, know what?

She covers my hand with hers.

—What?

—I love you crazy.

She smiles at me and opens her mouth to say something and I start to squeeze and this is what I know how to do and this is what I have to do and it is not too late to make this better and she looks at me like she suddenly doesn't know who I am and grabs my fingers and I can do this I can do this and she looks at me and I can do this and Enclave come into the room and pull me from her and my fingers hook the strand of candies around her neck and it snaps and they scatter over the floor and she screams at me.

And I'm gone.

The Count looks down at me.

—Know much history, Joe?

I sit in two feet of dirty water at the bottom of the sewer shaft where they threw me and look up at him.

He points at himself.

—Not my best subject, but there's stuff you connect with, right? Like even in the lamest class, there's bound to be something you get a rise out of. History of Western Civilization was like that for me. That class was like nap time.

There is no ladder. No way back up.

—Monday, Wednesday and Friday, one to two-fifty for an entire year, man. Professor Hocker would start droning and, like, fifty undergrads would simultaneously nod off. You could sell that guy's lectures on CD and make a fortune from insomniacs.

A feeder runs through here, washing the cold water around me, the occasional clump of waste getting lodged against my back.

—Only time I perked up and took notice? When he started getting into the Roman emperors.

I sit in the water, it soaks my clothes and makes my knee hurt worse.

—Those guys, once they got rid of the senate, know how they ruled? They ruled by caveat. Know what that means? Means they ruled by fear. Means they did whatever the fuck they wanted to.

The water is dirty. Does that mean it's on its way to the river, or away from it? I don't know.

—Hey, you know that fear rules the brain? Seriously. Our brains, this is amazing, they devote more space to dealing with fear than to any other emotion. Because, hey, fear is what makes us learn shit and survive. It's fucking key. Know where it lives? Fear lives in this little thing, 'bout the size of an almond, called the amygdala. Fear in the brain. Something bad happens to you, you got no choice but to be afraid of it happening again. Until it happens so many times that you get used to it.

Iron grates on concrete as he drags the shaft cover to the edge of the hole.

—So tell me, how many people who you love do you think you have to have taken away from you, before you stop being afraid that it'll happen again?

He looks over his shoulder, looks back down at me.

—Oh, hey, and can you guess which of the emperors was my favorite? No? Give up? OK, I'll tell you.

He sticks his head into the shaft.

—Caligula.

He laughs through his nose and shakes his head.

—Yeah, sick but true. I am so fucking predictable, right? But I tell ya, once I get my thing going up in here, that's gonna be the scene. I'm gonna introduce a whole new way of doing things around here. I mean, everybody is scared shitless of these dudes, how can I not find a way to make use of that?

He pulls his head back.

—So anyway, one last thing about fear in the brain. When you fuck up around here, like say you maybe try and strangle a fellow Enclave or something? They don't kill you. No beheadings or getting put out in the sun. Instead they drop you down this shaft into the sewers. Maybe it's symbolic. I don't know. Doesn't happen often. I mean, really rare. What I gather, mostly when they get cast out they just kill themselves.

I hear something splash in the water. Rats.

—But the story is, at least one of them is hanging on down there. Has been for years. Lone ex-Enclave looney wandering the sewers and living off God knows what. Could be like that alligators being flushed down toilets thing. Urban Vampyre legend. If you get me.

He starts to move the cover over the mouth of the shaft, stops and puts his face into the last remaining gap of candlelight above me.

—Still, pretty fucking scary, huh?

The cover slides and drops into place.

Whatever moves in the water isn't a rat.

It's fast and it's strong and as soon as the darkness is total it's on me and I'm being dragged through the water, banging off the tunnel walls, hauled up black shafts and flung across chasms I know are there only by the echoes of my screams.

—Hey, buddy, hey, buddy, hey. Got a smoke? Man. Got a smoke?

I can't see anything. My eyes are open, but I can't see a fucking thing.

But Jesus I can smell.

Stench. A river of sewage flowing somewhere below where I'm

huddled. The stink of the city. Raw. Crackling taint of electricity from the subway train that rumbles past somewhere behind thick concrete. A puff of warm air carried out of the MTA tunnel brings oil and diesel fumes from a service train. Wet, meaty rat fur. Rot in too many hues to separate. And the Vyrus. Boiling and thin as steam.

—Asked do you have a smoke, buddy? A cigarette? *Parlez vous?*

I don't say anything. I don't move.

—Buddy. Buddy. I know you're alive, buddy. You tryin' to possum me? Huh? Want me to come over there so you can get a bead on me and grab me by the balls and rip them off, buddy? That what you got goin' through your head? That's it, ain't it, buddy? Don't bother to deny it, nah, don't bother. I know that's what you're thinking. I know it is. Cuz, buddy, I can see it, I can see just exactly what you're thinking. And you're 'bout as interesting as last month's fucking *Post.*

Something moves.

—Here, let me make it easy on you, buddy. Let me get up close.

He comes close. I feel him first. The heat. He smells like the sewer. And the Vyrus. Burning.

—How's that, buddy? Better? Want to take a shot?

Water dribbles out of my hair and into my eyes. I wipe it away.

—No.

He shifts.

—Yeah, right. Good thinking. Sharp. You're a sharp one, buddy. So?

—What?

—You got a smoke or what?

I reach in my pocket and find the Luckys.

—They're soaked.

—That's OK, buddy. I forgive you. Pass 'em here.

—I can't see.

—*Can't see. Can't see.* 'Course you can't fucking see, buddy, it's darker than a nun's virgin anus down here. Just hold the fucking things out.

I hold out the pack.

—Filterless? Hell, buddy, what you trying to do, kill yourself?

He gurgles.

—That's a joke, buddy. Ah, never mind. These'll do. These'll do.

He shuffles.

—*Can't see*. Right, right. Well, we'll see if we can do something about that.

Light explodes.

I cover my eyes, a purple burst on the inside of my lids.

—Whoops. Got you by surprise there. Sorry 'bout that, buddy.

I take my hands away, crack my lids.

He's across from me on the shelf of brick that juts from the mouth of a dry spill tunnel over the river of shit below us. Hunkered on spider legs, white to the point of transparency, bald and huge-eyed, he thrusts his face into the beam shooting from his flashlight and bares his teeth.

—*Gollum*.

He gurgles.

—That's another joke, buddy. Another joke. Read that in a book. That one kills 'em. Kills 'em every time, buddy.

He tucks the wet pack of Luckys into one of the pockets of the vest that hangs open over his withered torso and waves the light down the tunnel.

—C'mon, buddy, I ain't carrying you this time.

I keep close to the jet of hot air blowing from the louvered slats at the bottom of the switch-room door.

—Cold? Sure you're cold, cold as hell down here, ain't it? Not that I feel it. Not that I feel it a'tall, buddy.

He reaches over and moves the cigarettes around, rotating them in the hot air, helping the tobacco to dry.

—Yeah, just about right, yeah. Just about there.

I rotate myself, straightening my bad knee in front of the vent. The bone is knitting, it grinds when I move it.

He plucks at my damp slacks.

—What's with the getup?

—Dead guy's clothes.

He strokes his neck, his skin reflecting the blue of the light above the switch room.

—Didn't ask from who, asked what's up. Where's your whites, buddy?

I look at his own clothes, the soiled cargo vest and painter's pants. Both were once white, I suppose.

I rub my knee.

—Never wore whites.

—Never, huh?

His arm snaps out and he lays a finger along my chin and turns my head.

I don't flinch.

He looks me over.

—Yeah, but you're Enclave. Way you're looking at me, you're too fucking mean to be anything else.

He drops his hand.

—Didn't take to the warehouse, huh, buddy?

—Never tried.

He fingers the cigarettes.

—Good call, that. Yeah, sure, sure, good call, buddy. This one's done. That thing working?

He points at the open Zippo next to the smokes.

I pick it up and flick the wheel and sparks jump, but no flame.

—Still too wet.

He digs fingers into one of his pockets and comes out with a folder of matches.

—Hate to waste these things. But the need is urgent, buddy.

He tears out a match and lights it and brings the flame to the dirty, bent cigarette in his lips and inhales.

—There you go, that's it, sister, come to papa.

He drops the match and holds the smoke for a second and blows it out.

—Well, tastes like shit, but that comes as no surprise, buddy. Here.

He offers it to me and I take a drag. He's right, it tastes like shit. I take another drag and pass it back.

—Daniel went out in the sun this morning.

His hand freezes. He takes the smoke, looks at it.

—He make it?

—Fuck do you think?

He sucks smoke.

—I think he got burned and died, but a man can hope, buddy. Even down here, a man can hope.

A train blasts past just beyond the alcove that hides the door, and I watch the real people flick past inside.

—They got me off the street. Long time gone, long time, buddy. Know how long?

—Nope.

—Neither do I, buddy. Neither do I.

He puts a hand out and we drop back between girders and wait as an MTA service crew in orange vests and helmets crosses the tunnel dragging tool bags over the tracks and cursing and telling dirty stories.

He waves and we start walking again, following the line of the third rail.

—Saw I was Enclave one of them did, buddy. Saw me wandering out of a saloon down the Bowery and saw it in me. Well, Vyrus don't lie. So I was told.

He stops and points at the tunnel where the service crew disappeared.

—That's a dead tunnel. Probably, buddy, they're scrapping something down there. That or goin' off to get high. Bums live down there mostly. Couple of 'em will get scared out by the crew. Crew loves to shove the bums around. Bums, buddy, bums in all the dead tunnels. 'Cept mine. Nothing lives in my tunnel but me and the rats, buddy. Me and the rats.

He starts off again.

—Daniel was the one bled into me. That meant somethin'. Not to me. Did to him. Tried not to make a big deal of it he did, but it mattered to him, buddy. All us he put the Vyrus in, we were kind of special to him. Didn't make much difference. I never took to it.

He stops again and squats and I lean against a girder, not wanting to bend my leg.

—The quiet's what got to me, buddy. Ever notice how quiet it is in there?

—Yeah.

—Too fucking quiet. Everyone meditating. Pondering. Thinking on the Vyrus. Fuck. I wanted some chatter. Buddy, I tell you, it drove me just about out my fucking head.

He spreads his arms.

—Now look at me. Know how often I get to have a conversation, buddy? Just about never. Talk to the rats, buddy. Tell them everything on my mind. Know what's on my mind?

—No.

—What's on my mind is the fuckers finally drop someone down that hole doesn't kill himself first chance he gets, someone a man might expect to have a word with, and I end up with a monosyllabic son of a bitch like you, buddy. That's what's on my mind.

—Huh.

—Yeah.

—I was a discipline problem, buddy. Same way I was in the army. Know how many times I got the stockade? One time, buddy. Just the one time after I got drunk and cut my bunkmate's ear off with my bayonet. When I got out of the stockade it was just in time for me to get kicked out. Buddy, that warehouse, it's a fucking miracle I lasted a day. As it was, I made it a couple years. But only because of Daniel. You know the old man well, buddy?

He climbs up on a dead platform and reaches down to me.

I take his hand and he pulls me up.

—We talked some.

—Riddler he was, wasn't he?

—Yeah.

—The sun, huh?

—Yeah.

—Crap.

He leads me to a rusted gate and yanks on it and it scrapes open.

—Down this way.

I follow.

He looks back at me.

—You need the flashlight?

The blue and yellow and red lamps of the tunnels fade behind us.

—Yeah.

—Here.

He passes it to me and I point it straight down, the reflected light more than enough for my eyes.

He kicks a pile of rags from his path.

—If the old man hadn't had a feeling for me, I never would have lasted. Tell ya, buddy, sure seemed as though he liked the trouble cases. Seemed to have a taste for the ones that didn't fit right in there. What would he make of me now, huh? Tell ya, he wouldn't recognize me at all, buddy. Not at all.

He touches his stomach.

—I was fat. I mean, by Enclave standards, I was a damn pig. Fasting. I came from an ass-poor family. Why I went in the army the first place was to have all I wanted to eat. *They* wanted me to *not eat* on purpose. Know what kind of sense that made to me?

—None at all.

—Yeah, you got that one, buddy, none at all. But. Here I am.

He runs a fingertip down his ribs, like raking a washboard.

—I didn't grow up with any religion to speak of. But I got a feeling, if I had, it would have stuck deep. Would have been one of them people strays hard from the way, only to come back to it twice as hard in the end, buddy. 'Cause living down here, with no one and nothing to keep an eye on me, with hot and cold running bums wandering around ripe on the vine, with no reason to do anything but feedfeedfeed, I found faith. How's that for a pisser?

He stops.

—Yeah, you tell me that Daniel went out in the sun, my first thought is, *Shit, that sad sorry fuck finally went and did it and got himself burned.* But what I'm really thinking under that is, *Please let it be real. Please let him be the one who makes it. Please bring me home.* Buddy, I am one lonely fucking man.

He takes out the cigarettes I gave him and puts one in his mouth and I flip the Zippo open and it lights this time.

He blows the smoke down into the cone of light at our feet, watches it swirl.

—In the end, buddy, I'll do it too, ya know. When I can't hold it in anymore, when the Vyrus says, *Shit or get off the pot,* I'll climb up there and take a crack at it. Daniel, he probably thought he'd make it. Right till he cooked, that SOB probably thought he was gonna cross. Me, buddy, I'll do it knowing I'm gonna burn. So you tell me.

He offers me the smoke.

—Which of us is crazier, buddy, me or him?

I take the smoke, drag and give it back.

—Got me.

He taps ash.

—Yeah, it's a puzzler. Crap. Always had a hope I'd see the old man again. Show him that I turned out OK. Show him that I took it to heart in the end. That I believe. Even if I don't want to. Wish I could tell him I was sorry for the trouble I caused him. Buddy, I tell you, in the end, when I blew, I blew hard. Went spastic and grabbed a blade and started cutting. Killed half a dozen Enclave. Half a dozen of my own, buddy. Know how many killed half a dozen Enclave?

He taps his chest.

—Me. That's how many.

He smiles.

—Not that I'm proud of it or anything.

He loses the smile.

—And it made a pile of problems for Daniel. As he'd been nursing me along all the while.

He drops the butt and grinds it under a bare leathered foot.

—Bitch's bastard, I wish I could have a word with the fucker. I really do, buddy. Still. You never know.

He squints at me.

—Ever seen one of them things, buddy?

I play the light over the floor, don't say anything.

He nods.

—Yeah, you seen one. Scary as all hell, yeah? Know what's scarier? Nothing. Nothing in this world scarier than a Wraith, buddy.

He moves closer.

—I watched it happen once. Watched Daniel and a couple other of the old-timers sit and meditate for days, none of us allowed a drop of blood while it was goin' on. Watched a crack open. In the air. A crack in the air. Know what that looks like, buddy? Looks like nothin'. Looks like what nothin' looks like. Watched one of them things squirm out of it.

Closer.

—And then I stopped looking. 'Cause I didn't want to see anymore.

Closer, whispering.

—Know what they say? Say about them? What Daniel said they are, buddy? Know what they are?

He licks his lips.

—They're what happens. They're what happens when the Vyrus is done with us.

He points at himself.

—They're what's gonna happen to me.

He points at me.

—And they're what's gonna happen to you, buddy.

He leans his mouth close to my ear.

—They're what we become.

He puts a hand on my shoulder.

—So you never know, buddy, we both may get to see Daniel again.

He leans away and looks me in the eye.

—Boo!

I jump.

He laughs.

—Sorry, sorry, buddy, it's the prankster in me. I may be a true believer now, but I still got discipline problems.

I crack a knuckle.

—Yeah. I can see that.

He stops laughing.

—Buddy, they call it a sense of humor. Look into it.

—Sure, as soon as you show me how I get the hell out of this place.

He points up.

—There. Up the ladder, buddy.

I rake the light up the wall and see the rungs bolted into the concrete, leading to a trap.

—It's an alley up there. Might be a couple garbage cans on top of the trap, but no lock. That work for you?

I shine the light back at the floor.

—Yeah, that'll work.

He reaches out and takes the flash and switches it off and we're in darkness again.

—Well, up you go, then.

I climb.

At the top I put my shoulder against the trap and heave and some cans crash to the ground and it swings open and flickering Manhattan night light fills the narrow sky above the alley.

—Buddy, hey, buddy.

I look down into the black tunnel.

—Yeah?

—You sure about that, goin' up there, you sure? 'Cause think about it, what's gonna happen sooner or later?

—What's gonna happen?

—Buddy, what's gonna happen is that sooner or later they're gonna find us out. Shit, buddy, they may already know about us. Seems kind of far-fetched to think they don't, huh? And when they're ready, when they got things set up for us exactly how they want, they're gonna hunt us all down. Right, buddy, that sound about right? Sure it does. My religious zeal aside, I got no illusions. Why do you think I stay down here? Up there, what you got? Think. It's not even natural. Trying to live a life that isn't yours anymore, right? That's all it is, buddy. Down here, I'm safe as houses. No one hunting me down here. I hit a bum for some blood, no one cares. No one calls the cops. Buddy, down here, I'm the top of the food chain. Down here, I can last forever. If I want to. Think about it. Down here is where you belong. It's where we all belong, buddy.

I look up at the sky.

—I'm not saying you're wrong. But I got someone up here.

—Huh. Well, that's different, then.

I look back down into the hole.

—What's your name, old man?

—Joseph. Yours?

I blink.

—Simon.

I hear his feet padding away.

—Be seeing you, Simon.

I climb out into the alley and close the trap.

I make for home, my stink clearing the sidewalk ahead of me.

I make for home.

Where I have blood and guns.

I want them so bad, I want blood in my gut and a gun in my hand so bad that I don't even see Lydia's bulls coming for me. Just the tattoo across the biggest one's knuckles before her fist lands in my face.

FURY.

* * *

—I try, Joe. I try harder than most to take your smartass bullshit and not lose my cool. I try to understand that something made you the way you are, but there are limits to my compassion and my patience.

Lydia points at a chair and her bulls drop me in it.

—You push and you push and you push. You do just enough to make me think you might have an ounce of decency, and then you fuck it all up.

She leads the other women to the kitchen door and ushers them out. She closes the door behind them and turns to face me.

—What I really can't stand is that you insist on engaging in behavior that forces me into taking actions that aren't part of my nature. I end up doing the kind of things Tom would have done. Do you have any idea how that makes me feel? Unhealthy. That's how. I hate it. But let me tell you.

She crosses the room.

—Shooting me was the fucking limit!

She's spent a day getting straight. Drinking from some crazy stash of cage-free, no-hormone-injected, organic blood that she keeps around so her sensibilities won't be offended. She took too much hurt in Brooklyn and from my gun to be a hundred percent. But she's close enough. The fist she plants in my gut tears something in there. Something that hurts a lot. Her next punch might just put a hole in my stomach and go right out my back.

Fortunately Hurley comes in and pulls her off me.

Hey, I'm a lucky guy.

She jerks free of him.

—Don't, Hurley, don't ever touch me.

He rubs a hand over his whiskers.

—Sure, Lydia, don't mean nuttin' by it, I know I ain't yer type a feller an' all. Just dat Terry asked I should see ya don't kill him none. An' looked fer a moment dat der might be some danger of ya gettin' carried away some.

From the floor I look up at her.

—Hey, Lydia.

She looks at me.

—What?

—I could have swore you told me never to *threaten* you again. I didn't think actually *shooting* you would be such a big fucking deal.

Hurley shakes his head.

—Shut the fook up, Joe.

And his boot puts me out.

—This is getting a little old, isn't it, Joe?

—Don't know what you mean by that, Terry.

—Us sitting around the table. You with your back to the wall. Me and Lydia spelling out how things are. You finding a way to live with that and get a little of what you want from the situation. How many times we been through this?

—Put it that way, a few.

—More than a few, Joe. Many more than a few. And let me tell you, I am getting, man, I don't know, weary of the dynamic.

Lydia stops staring at her hands resting on the tabletop and looks at him.

—*Weary of the dynamic*, Terry? Come on. Can we cut through the crap?

Terry rubs his forehead.

—Yeah, yeah. I'm just trying to create a little context for the discussion. I just want us all to understand that we've been this way before and maybe we won't be able to sort things quite the same as we have in the past. Things change, you know, and it may be that there's a sea change happening here that won't allow us to deal with this situation in the same manner as we would have in the past.

—I said, *Cut through the crap,* Terry.

—I know what you said, Lydia.

—Well then?

He starts to raise a finger, drops it.

—OK. OK. The direct approach. That's really your style anyway, isn't it, Joe?

I'm on the floor in the corner of the kitchen, Hurley seated on a stool next to me. Not that he needs to keep an eye on me. Not that I'm gonna do anything. Not that I can do anything.

I touch the welt Hurley left on my forehead. I think I can feel the pattern of his boot tread impressed in torn skin.

—Sure. The direct approach.

I take my hand from my forehead.

—You sent me to Brooklyn and I got all fucked up and caught in the middle of some crazed holy war, and I killed a bunch of people and chopped a Rebbe into pieces so they'd know not to fuck with us. And if you didn't want it to turn out that way you should have sent someone else.

Terry clears his throat.

—Well, yeah, man, that's all, I don't know, good as far as it goes. Lydia covered that part for me already. Except, you know, the chopping into pieces stuff. But I can see that. I can see how that will be effective. But, you know, having done all that, and having, and this was impressive, having saved Lydia, you, well, man, you shot her.

I look at her.

—She got in my way.

Terry folds his arms.

—Thing is, Joe, it's not the first time you've shot a member of the Society council. And, sure there were extenuating circumstances the last time, but it's not the kind of thing we can let roll by. And then there's this other thing Lydia mentioned.

He looks at her.

She looks at me.

—Where is she, Joe?

I count heartbeats, get to twenty before Lydia gets tired of waiting.

—What did you do with your friend, Joe?

Terry has his elbows on the table, he leans his forehead into his hands.

—Did you infect her, man? Did you do that, Joe? Did you consciously and willfully go into the uninfected community and infect someone with the Vyrus?

I count fifteen this time.

Get tired of counting.

—I didn't infect her.

Lydia and Terry look at each other.

Terry rotates the little gold hoop in his earlobe.

—Tell me you didn't try, man. Just, please, man, tell me you didn't try.

I count one heartbeat.

—I did try.

—Ah, fuck.

Lydia stands.

—You killed her. You. You tried to infect her and you screwed up and you fucking killed an innocent woman, you stupid little. Joe. You. Damnit. Damnit.

Terry takes off his glasses, rubs his eyes, slips them back on.

—Did you do it? Is that how it happened?

I don't count anything this time. But I don't say anything either.

Lydia comes around the table and makes for me.

—What are you? What are you? We're trying to change things. We're trying to change and you. You.

Hurley is in front of her.

She stops. Looks at the floor. Walks back to the table and sits.

Terry watches her. Waves Hurley to the side. He taps the tabletop.

—This is a big deal, man. So, you know, I need you to tell me, Joe, is that what happened?

I think about what happened. I think about the Count's blood in Evie. Instead of mine. I try to think of a way of saying it out loud. But I don't have to. Because what happened is so very simple.

—I tried to infect her. And it didn't work.

He takes off his glasses again and covers his eyes.

—Ah, fuck.

Lydia walks to the door. Stops with her hand on the knob.

—The sun.

And walks out.

Terry takes his hands from his eyes and looks at Hurley.

—Hurley?

Hurley stretches his neck.

—Whativer you say i'tis, Terry, so i'tis.

—Not this time, man, you got to make the call for yourself.

Hurley looks at me, shrugs.

—Sun i'tis.

Terry nods.

—Yeah. The sun. Unanimous.

Hurley rises.

—Ya want I should lock him away till mornin'?

—No. That's cool. Leave us alone for a bit. We've got stuff to kick around.

—Sure.

He gets up and tips his hat at me.

—Too bad ya fooked up like dat, son. Fer a woman an' all. Still, nuttin' personal.

And he's out.

Terry stands.

—Joe. Man. What can I say? I mean, it's not like you gave me any choice. I make an exception on something like this, well, where's it gonna end? Lydia? How long do you think I can keep her loyal to the Society if we start bending on basic principles? No. It's greater-good time, here. Time to. Ah, shit.

He walks to the door and stands there for a moment with his ear against it and locks it and stuffs his hands deep in his pockets.

—When I found you, Joe. Man. You were. I don't know, you were an animal. You were.

He smiles.

—Such a classic punk. Like, you know, like you had invented attitude and had to show it off. Pure promise. Made for those days. All that rough and tumble. I never regretted bringing you in. Even after you left the Society. Even then I.

He comes away from the door and crosses toward me.

—Well. You know. And when I got you to come back in last year? That was, that was like a dream come true. But. Then. I guess you could say I was living in the past maybe. Well, no *maybe* about it. I *was* living in the past. You can't go back. That is the truth. It's a cliché, but it's the truth. All that stubbornness you had when you were a kid, all that attitude, I thought you'd outgrow it.

He laughs.

—Wow, was I wrong.

He's in front of me. He looks over at the door. Looks back at me.

—I want to do something for you here, man. But you got to tell me something.

He takes his hands from his pockets.

—Where's the Count, Joe?

I almost laugh. But it would hurt too much.

—Took you long enough, Terry.

He squats.

—Uh-huh, and now I'm asking. Where is he?

I look around the room.

—Notice you waited till we were alone to get into this.

—Joe.

—Still hiding the delicate inner workings of the ecosystem from your nearest and dearest.

—This is, man, this is very serious. So I'm, you know, clinging to my cool here and asking politely. Where?

—Hey, *man*, here's a question for you.

—Not now, man.

—What was it like when you were in the Coalition? What was it like being all cronied up with Dexter Predo, you fucking fraud?

He puts a hand to his temple and rubs.

—I'm wondering, Joe. I'm wondering if you can possibly be as stupid as so many people think you are. I'm wondering if I have been wrong about you all these years and you really are the idiot people talk about you being, you know, behind your back.

He picks me up and throws me across the kitchen and I smash into the cupboards and hit the floor and shattered dishes rain over me.

He comes for me.

—I mean, hey, man, do you really think anyone would give a shit about that crap?

He grabs me by the ankle of my bad leg and swings me around and my back hits the table and it explodes around me and I keep going and I put a dent in the refrigerator door and eight of my ribs break.

He comes for me.

—Think about it, man, you know, the Society, it was created by a revolution against the Coalition. You know who starts revolutions? Citizens! *Yes,* I was in the Coalition. *Everyone* was in the Coalition. You think that's a secret?

He takes me by the hair and punches me in the face twice and shakes his bloody fist.

—It's not a secret. Yeah, I was an enforcer for the Coalition. I don't, you know, go advertising it around or anything, but it's not a secret. How do you think I learned about power, Joe? How do you think I learned about corruption? And when I learned those lessons, know what I did? I, you know, matured and changed. Like a normal fucking person. You think Lydia doesn't know? She knows. But that's because she bothered to learn some history. That's because she knows something about Hegel and revolutionary dynamics. She knows that every thesis has an antithesis and that if you want to get anywhere you have to, man, you have to create a synthesis. And that, you know, that doesn't just, like, happen. That takes work. And you need tools to get it done. So I'm asking you, Joe, seriously now, to drop the crap before I lose my cool.

He jerks my head from side to side.

—Tell me where the Count is.

Somewhere inside the fridge a bottle broke and OJ is leaking out onto the floor. I watch it drip.

—Yeah. Alright, I get it. I get it. I'll tell you.

I look at my oldest friend through the blood in my good eye.

—He's gone Enclave on you, Terry. So, *you know,* all you got to do is run over there to their turf and grab him.

He lets go of my hair.

He rocks back on his heels and drops to his ass.

He looks at the floor between his legs.

—Joe. Oh, man. Oh, man. Man. Do you?

He looks up.

—Do you not get it at all? Has it all just gone over your head, man?

He waves a hand above his own head.

—Is it all just up here in the ether? Because let me break it down. There's a war. There's a war being fought and it's heating up, man. The new faces from Brooklyn, why are we trying to sort through all those rejects for the ones we can use? Because we're gonna need them. It's getting unstable. The Island is getting unstable. And it can't last like this. We have to have, man, this is the deal, we have to have something new. It can't go like it has forever. We have to try something new. And we need every resource. We need, God, I wish it were not so, but we need money. We need the Count's money. And. More than that.

He touches the blood on his knuckles. The Vyrus.

—They are trying to figure *this* out.

He shoves his hand at me.

—Predo and the Coalition. They are studying this. And they have resources that we don't have. The Count. We needed him to learn shit. We needed his, you know, expertise. Such as it was. We can't. If you want synthesis to happen, man, if you truly want two things to become one new stronger thing, the two have to be balanced and equal. Otherwise you just get one thing eating up the other. And shitting it out.

He lowers his hand.

—So please, man, please, tell me, you know, tell me you're fucking with me.

I look him over. This man. He took me in. He found me dying on the floor of a toilet and took me in and kept me alive. He taught me what I needed to know. Without him, I would have died that first night. Without him, I would have died a hundred times. Without him, I'd have been dead years ago and Evie would be in a hospital bed right now.

Like that's his fault or something.

I want it to be, but it's not.

Like it would change something about where we are now.

—I'm not fucking with you, Terry. He's in the warehouse. He's Enclave. They got him.

He flops on his back and stares at the ceiling.

—Shit. Shitshitshit.

—And Daniel is dead. So things are likely gonna get much more fucked up over there very soon.

He levers himself up on his elbows. Looks at me. Shakes his head. Gets to his feet and toes some of the wreckage from the table.

—OK, Joe. I guess that covers it.

He bends over and picks up the broken halves of his glasses.

—This, man, this is so perfect.

He drops them.

—Shit. Well. We're gonna put you in the sun in the morning.

He walks to the door.

—I'll see you, then.

Alone again. Which is actually nice. Because I am so fucking tired.

Naturally, I dream about Daniel.

Or a thing that used to be Daniel.

A black tendril of it worms from a split in the air and it shivers and peels its way from one world into this.

The old man of the subways points and laughs.

—See, buddy, see? Like I said. Looks like nothing, that rip in the air. Nothing a'tall, huh, buddy?

I study the rip. It's doesn't look like nothing. It looks like a rapidly healing scar in the throat of a sick girl.

Evie folds her arms on her chest.

—Why'd you lie to me, Joe? Why'd you lie about everything?

She cries a little and wipes the tears and puts a hand on my face.

—You didn't have to lie like that.

Purple sores rise across my face and over my scalp and my hair falls out and the Wraith shudders from the scar in Evie's throat and leaves her empty and it goes through me and freezes my blood and its passing whispers to me.

*Be seeing you, Joe.*

—You saved my life, you asshole. You saved my life and got me away from those animals and. I would have called it a wash. I would have said, *Yeah, the asshole shot me, but he also saved my life.* I would have said, *Let's just call it even.* Where's your humanity, Joe? Where is your damn humanity? You had to infect that poor woman? She wasn't sick enough? You had to try and do that?

I open my eyes and look at Lydia sitting in the dark kitchen on one of the chairs from the ruined table.

—You gave her no chance. No choice. Just made it for her. Just. Look how small it makes us. Look how small our lives are. Look what we're fighting over. The things we do to one another. You chose this for her? This little life, or an awful death. Awful.

I uncurl from the ball I've twisted into on the floor and my knee snaps loud twice and I wince and put my hands behind my head.

—Lydia. Do me a favor, go whine somewhere else.

She doesn't go.

—I already saved your life once, Joe.

—Sure. Why else would I come back for you?

—Right. Was there ever any question. So, debt's all paid up? All square up? The way you like it?
—Far as I'm concerned.
—Except maybe I owe you a bullet.
I shift, try to find a position where something on me doesn't hurt.
—You're gonna have to hurry if you want to get that in.
She stands over me.
—They would have used me. They would have raped me and made me have babies they could bleed.
—Yeah, so what?
—Never occurred to you?
—Just evening accounts.
—And now they're even.
—Yeah. You're doing nothing wrong. So stop wringing your hands and let me get some sleep.
I roll back onto my side.
She stands there for a minute, then I hear her walking to the door. Stopping. Turning back.
—I saved you once already. I don't owe you anything.
I tug my shit-stained jacket closer.
—Lydia.
—Yeah?
—You're an alright chick. Too bad about the whole dyke thing.
—Fuck off and die, Joe.
—Sure. In the morning, babe. In the morning.

When she's gone I think about getting up and going to the window over the sink. The nails she pulled out when I was smoking are still on the sill. I think about pushing it open and rattling the security gate accordioned across it.

Then I try to get up. And I can't. I try again. Terry did a new number on my knee when he threw me. And the ribs. And everything else.

I look at the door.

I drag myself over to it and try the knob. It's unlocked. I ease it open.

Hurley is on a chair in the hall, reading the funny pages.

—Joe.

—Hurl.

—Ya wanta be gettin' back in der?

—Not really.

He pulls a .45 from inside his jacket and points it at my hand.

—Bang.

I close the door a little.

—Got a smoke, Hurl?

—I said, *Bang*.

I close the door.

I look at the nails way up there on the sill. I get a grip on the counter and pull myself up and snatch the nails and fall back to the floor. I wrap my fingers around the nails. When they come for me I might get lucky. I might get to put someone's eye out before Hurley shoots me in the legs and drags me in the sun.

I think about the usual.

I sit in the dark kitchen and think about killing things.

Evie.

Oh, baby. I'm sorry.

An hour later there's gunfire and screaming in the hall and then silence and then Hurley backs through the door and drops his .45s on the floor and puts his hands in the air and looks over his shoulder at me.

—Someone ta see ya, I tink.

And Sela walks in with a machine gun.

I look at the machine gun.

—Jesus, where the hell did you get that?

—You coming?

I get to my feet. And I fall back down.

Sela waves the gun.

—I'm gonna pick him up, Hurley. Don't move.

I point at him.

—Fuck, just shoot him.

She looks at me, and Hurley makes his move, and she jerks the trigger and rakes him with bullets and sidesteps and he hits the floor bleeding from a dozen holes.

—Fook, ah fook. Not again.

Sela grabs my hand and hauls me up and I wrap an arm around her and she gets me in a hip carry and we make for the door.

Hurley writhes.

—Gah, shite. Mither. Ah, mither, does it got ta hurt so?

I drag my feet.

—You should kill him.

Sela looks out the door into the hall, looks back at Hurley.

—He'll die soon enough.

—No he won't.

But we're in the hall, passing the ripped-open bodies of three dead Society partisans, and Terry is stepping out of the room where we slaughtered the Docks Boss.

—Stop, Sela.

Sela doesn't stop.

—Get out of the way, Terry.

I try to pull free of her.

—Shoot him.

He holds up one hand, the other is hidden by the edge of the doorway.

—Let's just all, you know, cool it here before this goes too far.

Sela doesn't stop.

—Back off.

I point.

—His hand, what's he got in that hand? Shoot him!

He starts to bring the other hand out.

—It's all cool.

Sela shakes her head.

—Don't bring the hand out.

I wrap my fingers around her gun hand and squeeze and she mashes the trigger and bullets rip the hall to splinters as we fight over the gun and Terry dives back into the room and the door slams shut.

Sela pulls the gun away.

—Hell. Hell. Hell.

She drops me and ejects the empty clip and takes a full one from her pocket and snaps it home and opens up on the door and Terry comes through the wall next to the door in a cloud of plaster and lathe and Sela turns toward him, but it's too late as he brings up the fire axe Hurley used on the Boss and I'm still on the floor so I shove one nail in his inner thigh and rip open the artery and I put the other one in his foot and the axe swings wide and hits the wall and Terry goes down with empty hands and Sela has me again and makes for the door as Terry pulls his foot free of the floor and tries to stop the jet of blood from his leg and she takes me out and down the steps and throws me in the waiting white-on-white '78 Thunderbird, ignoring my screams.

—Killhimkillhimkillhimkillhim!

—Joseph, you look like you could use something to drink.

Amanda scoots across the huge rear bench seat.

—Of course, you also look like you could use a bath.

She opens the compartment built into the middle of the seat back and takes out a glass and pours bourbon into it from a full bottle of Wild Turkey and puts it into my hand and wraps my fingers around it.

I try to bring it to my lips and the glass slips from my fingers and spills over my lap.

Amanda picks it up.

—Light*weight*.

She refills the glass and holds it to my mouth and I drink and the alcohol burns the cuts in my lips and tastes good.

Sela opens the driver's door and climbs back into the car.

—No one coming after us.

—Good job, baby.

Amanda takes the empty glass from my lips.

—More?

But she's already put the glass aside.

—Not what you really need, is it?

She eases closer, her thigh against mine.

—No, not what you need at all.

She reaches a hand into the front seat and Sela places a butterfly knife in her palm.

I shove myself into the corner of the seat.

Amanda puts a hand on my wounded knee.

—No, it's *OK*, Joe. It's really OK.

She flips the knife and twirls it and the blade and the handles flutter and she snaps the handles tight under her fingers and shows me the blade.

—Sela taught me that. Cool, huh?

She looks at Sela.

—Is there time?

—There's time.

Amanda lifts a black denim-wrapped leg and swings it over my lap and settles there.

—That OK? Hurt anywhere?

I pull my face back, away from her and her smell.

She twirls the knife and stabs it into the white leather upholstery I've already smeared filth over. She grabs the bottom of her sweater and pulls it off and tosses it aside and draws the knife free of the seat back.

She adjusts the strap of her black tank top and looks down at the knife.

—It's not *that* weird, Joe. It *isn't*. You did something for me once. I just want to do something for you. I just want. *Well*. Just let me do this for you. *Please*.

She puts the blade to the palm of her hand and slices across it and the blood comes and she puts it in front of my face.

—Please, Joe. I'll beg if you want. Please.

But she doesn't have to beg, I'm already drinking.

And when I start to bite and try to widen the wound and she gets scared and pulls free and tumbles off my lap, it's only because Sela is in the car that I don't break her in half and drink the rest.

Amanda plays with the ivory cameo hanging from the black velvet choker around her neck, the bandage Sela applied wrapped tight over her hand.

—She *must* have a thing for you. Lydia must have a *thing* for you.

I look forward and catch Sela's eyes in the rearview and she looks back out the windshield, starts the T-bird and pulls out of Shinbone onto Great Jones.

Amanda reaches out and squeezes Sela's shoulder.

—Laugh if you *want* to, baby, but dyke or no dyke, she just *must* have a thing for Joe. I mean, come *on*, this is *what*, like the second time she's bailed him out? And that's *not* even counting when she hid *me* from Dexter Predo. She's got a *total* straight crush on him.

Sela pats the girl's hand.

—Sweetheart, the woman wouldn't know what to do with a man.

Amanda takes her hand away.

—That's just *stupid*. She would *too*. And you can act like she'd never go there, but people are weirder than that. I mean, look at *us*. And I *don't* mean me. I'm a poor little rich girl orphan whose father was a pederast and whose mother was a tramp, of *course* I fall in love with a chick with a dick. But all you ever *wanted* was a boyfriend who'd treat you like a *woman* and instead you end up with a little girl who treats you like, well, Joe doesn't want to *hear* what I treat you like.

She ruffles her hair.

—Any*way*, that's not the point. The *point* is she likes him. Whether she wants to or not. *That's* how it works. I mean, come *on*, would you have fallen for me if you could have helped it? *Please* don't tell me it didn't fill you with just a little self-loathing when you first realized you had a thing for me. The little *lost* girl. The innocent you had vowed to protect.

Sela maneuvers the long car around a double-parked delivery van.

—I got over it.

Amanda scratches the back of Sela's neck with her fingernail.

—Yes you *did*.

She takes a jar of olives from the bar compartment and twists the lid off.

—Me, I never *had* any question about what I felt. First time we were in the sauna together I *knew* I had to have you.

She plucks an olive from the jar and pops it in her mouth.

—My *God*, Joe, have you ever seen her naked? You are missing *out*.

Sela ducks her head.

—Stop it.

Amanda wiggles her finger into the hole of one of the olives.

—Am I embarrassing you, baby?

She leans forward and wraps her arm around Sela's neck and puts the olive at her lips.

—Are you blushing?

Sela sucks the olive from her finger and Amanda giggles and falls back in the seat.

She holds the jar out.

—Olive?

I don't say anything and she shrugs and closes the jar and puts it away.

She moves close and leans on me.

—You'll *get* over it.

She perches her chin on my shoulder.

—*Not* just drinking my blood, I mean.

She puts her cheek to my arm.

—I mean family. I mean what it's like to have *family*. That's what we're gonna make, Joe. Family. Sela and me, we talk about it *all* the time. Right, baby?

—That's right, hon.

—Like, how the Clans, they're *just* organizations. They treat everybody like they need the *Clans* more than the Clans need *them*. Which you *don't* even need to think about to see that it's *so* wrong. But we're gonna be different. We're gonna treat everybody like family.

Sela has the car pointed east, taking us back the way we fled, heading for the avenues that will run us to the Upper East Side.

She brakes for a stoplight.

—It's true, we're going to start a new Clan. No dogma. No enforcers. No racial barriers. No superstitions. Just support. Just a place for everyone who needs family to have it. Know why it's gonna work? Because Amanda and me are going to be running it. Infected and uninfected. Together.

Amanda tilts her head back to look up at me.

—It's going to be called *Cure*, Joe. That's what we're calling the Clan. So everyone will *know* what we're doing. What we're working for. Cuz there're *so* many that need it. And not just for the *obvious* reasons. Think about it. *Sela*, if she ever went to go post-op and get her *equipment* changed. And *I* am voting *against* that. If she ever did, know what would happen? They'd cut her dick off and do *all* that work and the Vyrus would treat it like a *wound* and heal it. Not, like, grow her a *new* one, just close up the hole between her legs. Leave her with, like, a *patch*. Gross. So, yeah, infecteds want a cure. *Lots* of them. But they also want other things.

She wraps her fingers around my arm and squeezes.

—We'll be a family. We'll all *take care* of each other. And I'll have more money than *God* pretty soon and can make sure *everyone* has the blood they need. And in a few years, I'll have a cure. Because there *has* to be one. It's *just* a virus. No matter how you *spell* it. It's biological and science can explain it. And I can cure it. You just have to isolate it and study it. You have to know it. Be with it. Get inside it. I can *do* that. *Daddy* couldn't. But I can.

She reaches up and runs a finger over the healing cuts that cover my face.

—Lydia *told* Sela what you did. That you tried to save your *girlfriend*. That's *got* to suck. And now you're alone again. But you don't *have* to be. Nobody should be *alone* if they don't *have* to be. So *what* if we're not *normal*? Normal bites. We can have our own kind of family. All we *have* to be is strong enough. I think you're strong enough, Joe. I *really* do. And you don't have to be my daddy or anything. Just, what*ever,* my big brother or something.

She plants her face tight against my arm.

—I just, *gah,* I *love* you no matter *what.*

I look at her.

She's young and healthy and rich and brilliant and beautiful. And her blood is tonic. She'll spoon-feed it to me if I ask because she's as crazed as her parents ever were and I helped her once and she thinks that's love.

Shit. Maybe it is. Like I'm a fucking expert.

It would be easy. An easy life. Can you imagine such a thing?

But Evie would still be in the warehouse.

And I've had a family. One was enough.

I shrug off the girl and push the passenger seat forward and lean and yank the door handle and the door swings open and Sela is rounding onto Park Avenue South and I roll from the car onto the pavement and find my feet and limp into Union Square and hide in the tent city of the homeless until Sela pulls the crying girl back to the car and drives off with her.

On the border of Society and Coalition, the park is not safe.

I walk back onto Society turf.

No one will be looking for me. I couldn't be so stupid as to come back here after what happened at the Society safe house. They'll be locking up tight and stripping the house and piling out the back, leaving wreckage that cops will read as a drug deal gone bad. They'll be busy setting up shop at one of the buildings Terry bought with the Count's money. The money he no longer has.

I have time.

I believe that right up until I stand at the corner of Second Avenue and 10th Street and see the fire engines two blocks away and the flames pouring out the windows of my apartment.

Exile, I head south, away from home.

—A nail in the leg?

I take the beer Christian offers me and suck half of it down.

—And one in the foot.

A few Dusters move around the clubhouse garage. One cracking the gearbox on his Indian, another throwing knives at a paper cutout of bin Laden, two are rewiring an old component stereo system they found scrapped in a dumpster.

Christian sits down on the edge of a fat, balding tire from an old dune buggy he's been tinkering with for a year.

—And she really shot Hurley?

—Yeah.

—And took a crack at Terry?

—Yeah.

—And left them both alive?

—Yeah.

He drinks some beer.

—Jesus. Dead she-male walking.

—Yeah.

The guys with the stereo twist a last couple wires together at the back of a speaker and open the clamshell top of the turntable and drop a vinyl disk on the spindle. It's Television's *Marquee Moon*. "See No Evil" plays.

We listen to the song.

Christian taps the heel of his boot.

—The classics.

—Sure.

He stops tapping his heel.

—A *nail*.

—*Two* nails.

—Fuck me.

—Yeah.

He works a hand inside his leathers and pulls out a pack of Marlboros and offers it to me. I take one and break the filter off and find my Zippo and light up.

He takes a light from me and blows a smoke ring.

—You're fucked.

—Yeah.

—Tenderhooks made a run up to Fourteenth right before dawn. Said the fire was out at your place. Said partisans were out.

—Yeah. No doubt.

He's not wearing his top hat. The crown of his head is bald and weathered. He scratches it.

—Seem to you like it's getting weirder out there, Joe? Scarier?

I look at the big roll-up doors that block out the killing sun on the other side.

—It's getting weirder. Scarier? I don't know.

He spits between his boots.

—Feels scarier to me. Like shit that's been building up is about to cut loose.

—Terry says there's war coming.

He smears the saliva across the floor with the toe of his boot.

—Shit.

—Yeah. Shit.

He looks over at me and smiles.

—He mention that before or after you stuck the nails in him?

—Must have been before. He wasn't waxing too conversational after.

He leans in and clinks his bottle against mine.

—Tell you, man, I would have liked to see that. Smug bastard that he is. I would have liked to see his blood.

—Just like anybody else's.

—Would have liked to see it for myself.

We drink another couple beers and someone flips the album.

I flex my knee and it hurts like hell, but not as bad. The ribs are burning as the Vyrus heals. Some are gonna knit crooked. The cuts and holes are all coming together, along with whatever Lydia did inside my gut, and I'm starting to see some blurs from my burned eye. Still, I only got two pints off the girl. Enough to get me going and to make her talk crazy talk, but I could use some more.

Who couldn't use some more? We all want more.

I think about her. Young and hungry. I know how that feels. Even if it was a long time ago.

*Clan Cure.*

God I hope the name is all about what she's trying to do and not about the fucking band. I hate that band.

Like the name matters.

They'll never let her get away with it.

But.

More money than God. Business and legal hooks deep in the straight world. Knowledge of things she has no right to. That no one has a right to. And a woman like Sela at her side. Love at her side.

No one will be able to take them head on.

So maybe they'll make a run.

Figure once word gets out what she's planning, what she's selling, the bill of goods, they'll get plenty who'll want to pledge. Young and desperate and feeble and alone, they'll take in the dregs. And the sly and the lazy who smell a good thing in her money, and her promise to feed everyone.

Yeah, figure they'll make a run.

Figure they'll run till everyone realizes that a cure is a dream and she's out of her skull. A run till Predo and Terry start sending in their people to infiltrate and fuck shit up.

Figure it will end bad.

Like there's any other kind of ending.

Christian takes two more beers from the case and cracks them open and hands one over.

—A war. That's a hell of a thing. Think we'd all be together, what with how much we have in common.

He blows across the mouth of his bottle.

—You think about it much, Joe?

I tap my Zippo against my bottle.

—What part?

He points at a scabbed gash on the back of my hand.

—What it is. If any of the looneys are right. Like maybe it's not a virus at all. Maybe it's a chemical. Something the government experimented with and lost control of. Or maybe they are in control of it, and they're watching us all the time to see how we cope with it. Or a curse. Not like some Dracula bullshit, but a real curse from a real God. Like in the Bible. In the Bible, a curse is usually a test. So maybe it's a test. And the ones that pass it are the ones who don't give in to it. Like the only way to win is to let yourself die. Or the Enclave and that stuff. What if they're right? Or is it the next step in evolution or a failed step or is it because somewhere in our past all our grandmoms took the same medication or we stood too close to an X-ray machine or all screwed the same monkey. Shit, I don't know.

He makes a fist, loosens it.

—Do you ever think about what we are?

I finish my beer.

—Well, Christian, way I figure it, either you're a Vampyre created by the Vyrus, or you're a vampire created by a something else. It makes any fucking difference which it is, I haven't noticed.

He looks down the neck of his bottle, drains it.

—Yeah, guess that's so.

He tosses the bottle into a garbage can against the wall and it shatters.

—But still, I'd like to know someday.

I toss my bottle after his.

—Don't hold your breath.

More beer. More good music. The sun is moving across the sky out there. Things will be happening soon.

Things are already happening.

He points at the knife-thrower's target.

—Remember that?

I look at the photocopied face of the Arab on the target.

—Sure.

He shakes his head.

—That smell. When they went down. Man, that smell. Blood. Gallons. Everyone went berserk. Rogues. Clan members. Losers came out of the woodwork and swarmed down there for days. Man. Looking at the missing-person posters after, I used to wonder how many went in the towers and how many just got taken off the street. Chaos.

—It was a mess.

He nods.

—But you were righteous. You and Terry. Saw right away it had to be stopped. Went down there and cracked skulls. Closed it down. All the cops and emergency services, they had come across a couple of us feeding in that rubble, first thing we would have been rounded up and thrown in camps. Man.

He laughs.

—Would have been all the proof they needed which side the devil was on. Would have thought we were flying the planes.

He stops laughing.

—But it was a mess. You came and told me you needed us down there. We rode. But, man, that was some killing we had to do, wasn't it?

I pick at the edge of my beer label.

—That was some killing.

He looks at me.

—You can't stay here, Joe.

I take a drink.

—I know.

—Hate to have to make it that way.

—I get it.

—Kind of always thought you'd end up down here with us. Just didn't think it'd be after you shot Lydia and stabbed Bird. We can stand some heat. The local odds and ends down here below Houston, they cause trouble, we can hold our own against any of them. But a real Clan? We just don't have the soldiers for it, man.

—Sure.

He points the neck of his beer bottle at the guys goofing in the garage.

—And I'm club president, man. I got a responsibility to the members. I say we're riding into war, they ride. But there has to be a reason. Has to be some profit. You had joined up back when I offered, it might be different.

—Sure.

He looks at me.

—A war, man. Bird tells you there's a war coming, I have to take that serious. Sure, man, we like to crack skulls. We want to ride free and do what the hell we please, but there's shit I don't need to see again. You, Joe, trying to keep you here, at the Society's back door, that's gonna raise things to an instant boil. There's a war on the way, I can't stop it. But I have no percentage in hastening it along. Or asking it in.

I get tired of hearing what I already know and take him off the hook.

—I'm not asking you for anything. Sun goes down, I'm gone.

He lets some air out.

—We'll give you some wheels. Something to wear doesn't smell like shit. That's about all we got to spare.

—I'll take them.

I stand up.

—Mind if I use the phone?

—All yours. You remember how?

—Yeah.

I limp over to the old pay phone mounted on the wall next to a collage of *Hustler* pinups. I take the handset from the cradle and hit the side of the phone a couple times until I get a dial tone.

I punch in some numbers.

Tenderhooks takes the tarp off a well-used '75 850cc black Norton Commando.

—Gonna beat your kidneys to hell.

I feel the broken ribs in my back.

—Great.

We get some gas in the tank and dribble a little in the carb and Tenderhooks kicks it a few times and it coughs black smoke and shudders awake. He revs it up, twisting the gas with the chrome pincers at the end of his prosthetic arm, and it settles into a nice, even idle and he lets it run for a minute and kills it.

He wipes some dust from the tank.

—She'll do ya.

—Thanks.

I finish my last beer and tuck the empty bottle in the inside pocket of my leather jacket. Even after a good sponging and a spray with Lysol it's rank and stained. But Evie gave it to me, I won't leave it behind.

The only guy big enough to give me some pants is nicknamed Tiny. So it's a given I have to cinch the belt tight around my waist to keep the jeans from falling down. I opted for one of Tenderhooks's sweaty thermals. It's snug and smells almost as bad as the jacket. But someone had some old combat boots my size. So there's that.

Christian comes back with the piece of rubber hose I asked for.

—You don't want a full can? We can stick it in the saddlebags.

I stuff the tube into one of the jacket pockets.

—This is fine.

—Got a couple pieces in the armory, you want one.

—Keep 'em.

Tenderhooks hauls on a chain and it rattles through a pulley and the door rolls up.

I push the bike out to the street and lean it on its stand.

Christian hands me a pair of goggles.

—Hey, man, the Van Helsing. You ever figure that?

I swing a leg over the seat.

—Yeah. That was a bunch of crazy Hebrews out in Brooklyn.

—Brooklyn? No shit?

—Yeah. Way I clock it, Solomon was selling them blood that wasn't kosher. They found out.

—Serious?

—Yeah.

—What was with all the chopping?

—They like to cut people into twelve pieces. It's a thing they do.

He shakes his head.

—Some fucking people, man.

—Yeah.

I kick the bike and trip it into gear and ride.

I ride Pike to Division and veer south into Chinatown. Wall turf. Not that there's much left of the Wall. At Confucius Place I cut down to Pearl, and from there under the Brooklyn Bridge to Water and Slip.

The limo is there.

I pull up behind it and wait for a hail of bullets. It doesn't come. I let the bike idle and climb off and put it up and limp over to the car and a tinted rear window zips down and Dexter Predo looks at me.

—You look worse for wear, Pitt.

—You look like a rat-faced shit fucker.

He nods.

—Well, now that we've exchanged secret passwords to assure each other of our real identities, we can converse freely.

He gets out of the car and the driver's door opens and his giant squeezes out.

I light one of the Marlboros Christian gave me and blow smoke in his direction.

—Fuck you.

He flexes the muscles in his nostrils.

Predo points down Slip toward Front.

—Shall we?

—You gonna take my arm?

He rakes his fingers across his forehead, brushing aside the sweep of his bangs.

—It's a busy evening, Pitt. One that promises no end of complications. Most, I have already gleaned, having to do with you. Well, that comes as no shock. But I am pressed. You offered information. Very well. I am intrigued. We can proceed, or Deveroix here can thrash you for bringing me out under false pretenses, and I will depart.

I look at the giant.

I look back at Predo.

—Yeah, sure, let's talk. I've been beat on enough.

He raises an eyebrow.

—Well, you were bound to reach your limit sooner or later.

So we walk.

And I spill.

I give him the whole thing.

The Docks. The Freaks. The Chosen and the lost Tribe of Gibeah. Shooting Lydia. Daniel in the sun. My death sentence. Sela and her machine gun. Stabbing Terry.

I give him everything but Amanda and her plans.

And Evie. I don't give him Evie.

And when I'm done he looks up at the underside of the bridge.

—A compelling tale. One I can't help but feel has gaps. Sizable gaps.

He looks at me.

—Still, value given.

He nods and I follow him back to the car where he waves at Deveroix, who touches a button on his key chain and the trunk eases open, and Predo reaches inside and takes out a small leather case and flicks the clasps and shows me the contents.

—As agreed.

Several tight bundles of cash. Several pints of blood. And a loaded .38 Detective Special. All of it nestled in smoking dry ice.

—Value paid for value given, yes, Pitt?

I take the case.

—Yeah.

He closes the trunk lid and waves Deveroix down and the giant crams himself back into the car.

I take the revolver and tuck it in my belt and put the case in one of the saddlebags.

Predo comes over.

—And now?

—None of your fucking business.

He pinches his lower lip.

—But it could be.

I wait.

He cocks his head at the limo.

—Deveroix. I think you were right about him. And his ambitions.

—And?

—He'll have to be replaced.

I get on the bike.

—I just quit a job.

—I know. It amused me to ask more than anything. And to imagine the look on Bird's face if you had been smart enough to accept.

He turns and walks toward his long black car.

—But you're not smart enough, Pitt. And that's almost a pity.

—Predo.

He stops with the door open.

—Yes?

—Just wondering, when I came to see you and you let it slip that you knew exactly how many pints the Candy Man had in stock, was that on purpose? To test how smart I am?

He's perfectly still, nothing moves, not an eyelash.

I move my mouth.

—Or was that a mistake? 'Cause you'd rather no one know you were supplying him?

He blinks.

I don't.

—Where do you get all that blood, man? Where do you guys get all that fucking blood?

He touches the knot of his tie.

—Don't overreach, Pitt.

He slides into the car.

—Good night.

The door closes and the engine starts and the lights come on.

I rumble the bike up alongside the driver's window and knock on it.

The giant tightens his lips and rolls it down.

I shake my head.

—*Deveroix?* You made that up, right? Come on, you can tell me. I mean, Joe's not *my* real name.

He squints.

—You're on the outside now, pissant.

He makes two fists and places them end to end and twists them apart like he's ripping something in half.

—Watch your back.

—Yeah, yeah.

I pull the revolver and empty it in the giant's face.

I look at the shadow in the backseat.

—That was a freebie.

I toss the gun in the limo and ride up Slip to Pearl and north.

A guy like that, it doesn't pay to have him around when you're out in the cold. Besides, not like I didn't tell him I was gonna do it.

* * *

A couple miles away I park the bike and unscrew the cap from the gas tank and slip the hose inside and suck on the other end until the gas flows. I fill the empty beer bottle and raise the end of the hose and the rest of the gas runs back into the tank. I toss the hose aside and screw the cap into place and walk over to a dumpster and find a rag and stuff one end into the neck of the bottle.

Back on the bike, I ride around the corner and stop in the middle of the block and straddle it. I look up and measure the distance as I remember it and light the rag and heave the Molotov in a high arc up over the Enclave warehouse, and above the sound of the Commando, I hear shattering glass.

Fire.

It will do little.

But I want him to know.

That I'm alive. That's it's not over.

And that I'll be coming back for her.

Thirty minutes later I'm crossing the Broadway Bridge at the northern tip of Manhattan. Onto original turf. Unhallowed ground. Home.

The Island is done with me. Closed its doors and cast me out.

That's just fine. I wasn't born there. Only made.

And soon enough the city will be burning.

And I'll be going into the flames.

To get my girl.

Dreaming of fire and love and an enemy's blood, I ride into the Bronx.

# EXTRAS

www.orbitbooks.net

# About the Author

**Charlie Hutson** is a novelist. He lives in L.A. with his wife, the actress, Virginia Louise Smith. Visit his website at www.pulpnoir.com

Find out more about Charlie Huston and other Orbit authors by registering for the free monthly newsletter at www.orbitbooks.net

*An interview with*

# CHARLIE HUSTON

**Can you tell us a bit about your background? How did you get into writing?**

I wrote my first novel, *Caught Stealing*, while I was bartending and managing an Italian restaurant in Brooklyn called Noodle Pudding. As these things go, it's the best job I've ever had.

I'd get up in the morning, go to the gym, then come home and write until I had to go to work. Pretty much the same schedule I keep now, except for that last part. I never meant to write a novel. My feet hurt. And that sounded like the first line of something. When I got to page 100, I knew it was a novel and I knew I really wanted to finish it. The night I did, I saved it on a disk, took the disk to a bar and had a drink with some friends. It was nice.

Later, after work one night, me and a buddy were having a tallboy of Bud before grabbing the train back to Manhattan. I told him about the book. Nobody really knew until then. A couple weeks later he told me about a friend of a friend, a film and TV agent looking for writers, and asked if I wanted to pass it on to her. Everything I've sold started that night with that beer. I still drink Bud.

**You began your career writing crime novels without any supernatural elements. What was the impetus for introducing vampires to the mix?**

More than anything, I wanted to have a little more fun. The Hank Thompson books are stylized, but still rooted in a world that's meant to be quite close to ours. I was looking to cut my imagination loose a bit more. Vampires let me do so.

**Have you always been a genre fan? Who are some of your favourite/most influential authors in that area? How do they affect your writing?**

The first genre work I fell in love with was *The Lord of the Rings*. When I was really little I had a cousin who would tell me the story of the trilogy in instalments. After that I fell for fantasy and SF. As a kid I was a sucker for Poul Anderson, Larry Niven, John Christopher, Lloyd Alexander, stuff like that. These days I don't read nearly as much fantasy and SF. Anything William Gibson writes. Jonathan Lethem, Jack Womack. As far as the Joe Pitt books go, the writer who influences them the most is Raymond Chandler. The whole point is vampires in a Chandler world.

***Already Dead* and the subsequent Joe Pitt novels fit into the classic noir tradition. Did the character of Joe Pitt come out of wanting to create a noir novel or was it the other way around?**

I didn't go for a straight noir approach out of the gate, but about halfway through *Already Dead* I started finding a voice for Joe that really echoed classic noir style. I fought it at first, but once I relaxed and went for it, things started to click.

**If Joe Pitt is your classic noir gumshoe, a lot of the characters that surround him are a little less easy to place. You've**

**got hippie gang leaders, hilariously spoiled students and truly freakish freaks in the cast of characters. Where did they all come from?**

It's the Max Allen Collins line I've quoted before, "They're all just us with guns." Characters, they all get drawn from who we know, what we've witnessed, read, watched. can't pinpoint where these folks come from. A character like Chubby Freeze had his genesis in a sign I saw in Oakland, a soft serve ice cream place called Chubby Freeze. Once I saw that, I knew it was a great character name. But it's hard to say where all the components come from.

**By setting the novels in New York, you've incorporated a lot of contemporary issues (racial divides, religious divides, drug use, AIDS). How important was it for you to incorporate these sorts of 'real world' conflicts into the narrative?**

I didn't set out to try and work that stuff in. HIV became an element because I wanted to heighten the romance between Joe and his girl Evie. Giving her a blood disease wasn't exactly original, but it worked for the story. Other elements are more a reflection of what may be on my mind and any particular time. One of the strengths of genre fiction is that it's a strong frame that you can dress in any number of ways. I can let whatever happens to be on my mind slip into these stories, not so much because I'm trying to make a point, but because it helps me to focus certain ideas for myself.

**Much of the critical praise for the Joe Pitt novels has mentioned what an original take you have on the vampire mythology. Do you purposely keep away from other vampire sources or do you have significant influences?**

I'm not very well read in horror fiction. And the number of vampire books I've read is quite limited. It's not a conscious effort, just a matter of what kind of material I'm naturally drawn to. Really, after I spend six months of every year working on my own vampire books, spending more time reading other people's doesn't sound relaxing. As for any originality, that's entirely random. I wasn't thinking consciously about Richard Matheson's *I Am Legend* when I made a virus the agency for vampirism in the Pitt books, but I had read it. Obviously that idea came to me from him. Likewise, a vampire with a mortal girlfriend is hardly new. Dracula met his end because of his love for Mina. Genre is a stew pot; you're always serving up mysterious bits and pieces left over from previous meals.

**Finally, *Half the Blood of Brooklyn* really progresses Joe's story, and the story of those around him. Have you had a story arc planned from the beginning? Can you tell us a bit about what we can expect in the next Joe Pitt novel?**

When I first began I had no plan at all. By the time I had sold *Already Dead* I knew the series would run to five or six books and that it would culminate in finding out the nature of the Vyrus, and the end of Joe and Evie's love story. At this point I know that book five will be the last. Most of the character arcs are mapped, but I've changed my mind before. As far as what's to come, I'm sure it will be no surprise that readers can expect some major characters to die before this is all over. Some scores will be settled, other will not. At the end of *Half the Blood of Brooklyn* Terry Bird says there's a war coming. Believe it.

**If you enjoyed**
**HALF THE BLOOD OF BROOKLYN,**
**look out for**

# WORKING FOR THE DEVIL

***by***

***Lilith Saintcrow***

# 1

My working relationship with Lucifer began on a rainy Monday. I'd just settled down to a long afternoon of watching the holovid soaps and doing a little divination, spreading the cards and runes out on the hank of blue silk I'd laid out, when there was a bashing on my door that shook the walls.

I turned over a card, my lacquered fingernails scraping. The amber ring on my left middle finger sparked. The Devil card pulsed, landing atop a pile of flat runestones. I hadn't touched it. The card I turned over was blank.

"Interesting," I said, gooseflesh rippling up my back. Then I hauled myself up off the red threadbare carpet and padded barefoot out into the hallway. My rings flashed, a drift of green sparks snapping and popping down my fingers. I shook them off, frowning.

The lines of Power wedded to my front door twirled uneasily. Something nasty was on my front step. I hitched up my jeans, then reached over and curled my fingers around the sword hanging on the wall. I lifted it down, chucked the blade free with my thumb against the guard.

The peephole in the middle of the door was black, no light spilling through. I didn't bother looking. Instead, I touched the door, spreading the fingers of my right hand against smooth iron. My rings rang and vacillated, reading the flow of whatever was behind the door.

*Oh, gods above and below*, I thought. *Whatever it is, it's big.*

Bracing myself for murder or a new job, I unlocked the door and stepped back, my sword half-drawn. The blue glow from Power-drenched steel lit up my front hall, glimmering against the white paint and the fulllength mirror hung next to my coatrack. I waited.

The door creaked slowly open. *Let's have some mood music for effect*, I thought sardonically, and prepared to sell myself dear if it was murder.

I can draw my sword in a little under a second and a half. Thankfully, there was no need to. I blinked.

Standing on my front step was a tall, spare, golden-skinned man dressed in black jeans and a long, black, Chinese-collared coat. The bright silver gun he held level to my chest was only slightly less disconcerting than the fact that his aura was cloaked in twisting black-diamond flames. He had dark hair cut short and laser-green eyes, a forgettable face and dreamy wide shoulders.

*Great. A demon on my doorstep*, I thought, and didn't move. I barely even *breathed.*

"Danny Valentine?" he asked. Well, demanded, actually.

"Who wants to know?" I shot back, automatically. The silvery gun didn't look like a plasgun, it looked like an old-fashioned 9mm.

"I wish to speak with Danny Valentine," the demon enunciated clearly, "or I will kill you."

"Come on in," I said. "And put that thing away. Didn't your mother ever teach you it was bad manners to wave a gun at a woman?"

"Who knows what a Necromance has guarding his door?" the demon replied. "Where is Danny Valentine?"

I heaved a mental sigh. "Come on in off my front porch," I said. "*I'm* Danny Valentine, and you're being really rude. If you're going to try to kill me, get it over with. If you want to hire me, this is *so* the wrong way to go about it."

I don't think I've ever seen a demon look nonplussed before. He holstered his gun and stepped into my front hall, peeling through the layers of my warding, which parted obediently to let him through. When he stood in front of me, kicking the door shut with one booted foot, I had him calculated down to the last erg of Power.

*This is not going to be fun*, I thought. *What is a Lord of Hell doing on my doorstep?*

Well, no time like the present to ask. "What's a Lord of Hell doing on my doorstep?" I asked.

"I have come to offer you a contract," he said. "Or more precisely, to invite you to audience with the Prince, where he will present you with a contract. Fulfill this contract successfully, and you will be allowed to live with riches beyond your wildest dreams." It didn't sound like a rote speech.

I nodded. "And if I said I wasn't interested?" I asked. "You know, I'm a busy girl. Raising the dead for a living is a high-demand skill nowadays."

The demon regarded me for maybe twenty seconds before he grinned, and a cold sweat broke out all over my body. My nape prickled and my fingers twitched. The three wide scars on my back twitched uneasily.

"Okay," I said. "Let me get my things, and I'll be happy to attend His Gracious Princeship, yadda-yadda, bing-bong. Capice?"

He looked only slightly less amused, his thin grim face lit with a murderous smile. "Of course. You have twenty minutes."

If I'd known what I was getting into, I would have asked for a few days. Like maybe the rest of my life.

# 2

The demon spent those twenty minutes in my living room, examining my bookshelves. At least, he appeared to be looking at the books when I came downstairs, shrugging my coat on. Abracadabra once called me "the Indiana Jones of the necromantic world," high praise from the Spider of Saint City—if she meant it kindly. I liked to dress for just about any occasion.

So my working outfit consists of: a Trade Bargains microfiber shirt, dries quickly and sheds dirt with a simple brush-off; a pair of butter-soft broken-in jeans; scuffed engineer boots with worn heels; my messenger bag strapped diagonally across my torso; and an old explorer coat made for photojournalists in war zones, with plenty of pockets and Kevlar panels sewn in. I finished braiding my hair and tied it off with an elastic band as I stepped into the living room, now full of the smell of man and cologne as well as the entirely nonphysical smell of demon—a cross between burning cinnamon and heavy amber musk. "My literary collection seems to please you," I said, maybe a little sardonically. My palms were sweating. My teeth wanted to chatter. "I don't suppose you could give me any idea of what your Prince wants with me."

He turned away from my bookshelves and shrugged. Demons shrug a lot. I suppose they think a lot of what humans do deserves nothing more than a shrug. "Great," I muttered, and scooped up my athame and the little jar of blessed water from my fieldstone altar. My back prickled with fresh waves of gooseflesh. *There's a demon in my living room. He's behind me. I have a demon behind me. Dammit, Danny, focus!*

"It's a little rude to bring blessed items before the Prince," the demon told me.

I snorted. "It's a little rude to point a gun in my face if you want me to work for you." I passed my hand over my altar—no, nothing else. I crossed to the big oak armoire and started flipping through the drawers. *I wish my hands would stop shaking.*

"The Prince specifically requested you, and sent me to collect you. He said nothing about the finer points of *human* etiquette." The demon regarded me with laser-green eyes. "There is some urgency attached to this situation."

"Mmmh." I waved a sweating, shaking hand over my shoulder. "Yeah. And if I walk out that door half-prepared I'm not going to do your Prince any good, am I?"

"You reek of fear," he said quietly.

"Well, I just had a gun shoved in my face by a Lord of Hell. I don't think you're the average imp-class demon that I very rarely deal with, boyo. And you're telling me that the Devil wants my company." I dug in the third drawer down and extracted my turquoise necklace, slipped it over my head, and dropped it down my shirt. *At least I sound good*, I thought, the lunatic urge to laugh rising up under my breastbone. *I don't sound like I'm shitting my pants with fright. Goody for me.*

"The Prince wishes you for an audience," he said.

*I guess the Prince of Hell doesn't like to be called the Devil.* On any other day I might have found that funny. "So what do I call you?" I asked, casually enough.

"You may address me as Jaf," he answered after a long crackling pause.

*Shit*, I thought. If he'd given me his Name I could have maybe used it. "Jaf," however, might have been a joke or a nickname. Demons were tricky. "Nice to meet you, Jaf," I said. "So how did you get stuck with messenger duty?"

"This is a sensitive situation." He sounded just like a politician. I slipped the stiletto up my sleeve into its sheath, and turned to find him watching me. "Discretion would be wise."

"I'm good at discretion," I told him, settling my bag so that it hung right.

"You should practice more," he replied, straight-faced.

I shrugged. "I suppose we're not stopping for drinks on the way."

"You are already late."

It was like talking to a robot. I wished I'd studied more about demons at the Academy. It wasn't like them to carry guns. I racked my brains, trying to think of any armed demon I'd heard of.

None sprang to mind. Of course, I was no Magi, I had no truck with demons. Only the dead.

I carried my sword into the front hall and waited for him. "You go out first," I said. "I've got to close up the house."

He nodded and brushed past me. The smell of demon washed over me—it would start to dye the air in a confined space, the psychic equivalent of static. I followed him out my front door, snapping my house shields closed out of long habit, the Power shifting and closing like an airlock in an old B movie. Rain flashed and jittered down, smashed into the porch roof and the paved walk. The garden bowed and nodded under the water.

I followed the demon down my front walk. The rain didn't touch him—then again, how would I have noticed, his hair was so dark it looked wet anyway. And his long, dark, high-collared coat, too. My boots made a wet shushing sound against the pavement. I thought about dashing back for the dubious safety of my house.

The demon glanced over his shoulder, a flash of green eyes in the rain. "Follow me," he said.

"Like I have another option?" I spread my hands a little, indicating the rain. "If you don't mind, it's awful wet out here. I'd hate to catch pneumonia and sneeze all over His Majesty."

He set off down my street. I glanced around. No visible car. Was I expected to walk to Hell?

The demon walked up to the end of the block and turned left, letting me trot behind him. Apparently I *was* expected to hoof it.

Great.

# 3

Carrying a sword on the subway does tend to give you a certain amount of space, even on crowded hovertrains. I'm an accredited and tattooed Necromance, capable of carrying anything short of an assault rifle on the streets and allowed edged metal in transports. Spending the thirty thousand credits for testing and accreditation at the Academy had been the best step I'd ever taken for personal safety.

Although passing the final Test had turned a few of my hairs white. There weren't many accredited Necromances around.

The demon also granted me a fair amount of space. Although none of the normals could really tell what he was, they still gave him a wide berth. Normals can't see psychic power and energy shifts, but they *feel* it if it's strong enough, like a cold draft.

As soon as we started down the steps into the underground, Jaf dropped back until he was walking right next to me, indicating which stile to walk through and dropping two old-fashioned tokens in. I suppressed the shiver that caused—demons didn't usually pay for anything. What the bloody blue blazes was going on?

We got on the southbound train, the press of the crowd soft and choking against my mental borders. My knuckles were white, my fingers rigid around the scabbard. The demon stood slightly behind me, my back prickling with the thought—*he could slip a knife between my ribs and leave me here, gods protect me.* The whine of antigrav settled into my back teeth as the retrofitted train slid forward on its reactive-greased rails, the antigrav giving every bump a queer floating sensation.

Whispers and mutters filled the car. One little blonde girl in a school uniform stared at my face. She was probably examining the tattoo on my left cheek, a twisted caduceus with a flashing emerald set at the top. An emerald was the mark of a Necromance—as if anyone could have missed the sword. I smiled at her and she smiled back, her blue eyes twinkling. Her whey-faced mother, loaded down with shopping bags, saw this and gasped, hugging her child into her side a little harder than was absolutely necessary.

The smile dropped from my face.

The demon bumped me as the train bulleted around a bend. I jumped nervously, would have sidled away if the crowd had allowed. As it was, I accidentally elbowed an older woman with a crackling plastic bag, who let out an undignified squeak.

*This is why I never take public transportation*, I thought, and smiled an apology. The woman turned pale under her gray coif, coughed, and looked away.

I sighed, the smile again falling from my face. *I don't know why I even try. They don't see anything but my tat anyway.*

Normals feared psions regardless—there was an atavistic fear that we were all reading normal minds and laughing at them, preparing some nefarious plot to make them our mental slaves. The tats and accreditation were supposed to defray that by making psions visible and instituting tight controls over who could charge for psychic services—but all it did was make us more vulnerable to hatred. Normals didn't understand that for us, dipping into their brains was like taking a bath in a sewer. It took a serious emergency before a psi would read a normal's mind. The Parapsychic Act had stopped psions from being bought and sold like cattle, but it did nothing to stop the hate. And the fear, which fed the hate. And so on.

Six stops later I was heartily tired of people jamming into the subway car, seeing me, and beating a hasty retreat. Another three stops after that the car was mostly empty, since we had passed rapidly out of downtown. The little girl held her mother's hand and still stared at me, and there was a group of young toughs on the other end of the car, sallow and muttering in the fluorescent lights. I stood, my right arm wrapped around a pole to keep my hand free to draw if I had to. I hated sitting down in germ-laden subway seats.

"The next stop," Jaf-the-demon said. I nodded. He still stood very close to me, the smell of demon overpowering the canned air and effluvia of the subways. I glanced down at the end of the car and saw that the young men were elbowing each other and whispering.

*Oh, great*. It looked like another street tough was going to find out whether or not my blade was just for show. I'd never understood Necromances who carry only ceremonial steel to use during apparitions. If you're allowed to carry steel, you should know how to use it. Then again, most Necromances didn't do mercenary work, they just lived in shitty little apartments until they paid off their accreditation fees and *then* started trying to buy a house. Me? I decided to take the quicker way. As usual.

One of them got to his feet and stamped down the central aisle. The little girl's mother, a statuesque brunette in nurse's scrubs and Nikesi sneakers, her three plastic bags rustling, pulled the little girl into her side again as he passed.

The pimpled young man jolted to a stop right in front of me. He didn't smell like Chill or hash, which was a good thing; a street tough hyped on Chill would make the situation rapidly unbearable. On the other hand, if he was stone-cold sober and still this stupid—"Hey, pretty baby," he said, his eyes skittering from my feet to my breasts to my cheek and then back to my breasts, "Wassup?"

"Nothing," I replied, pitching my voice low and neutral.

"You got a blade," he said. "You licensed to carry that, sugar?"

I tilted my head slightly, presenting my cheek. The emerald would be glinting and winking under the harsh lights. "You bet I am," I said. "And I even know how to use it. So go trundle back to your friends, Popsicle."

His wet fishmouth worked a little, stunned. Then he reached for his waistband.

I had a split second to decide if he was armed or just trying to start some trouble. I never got to make the decision, though, because the demon stepped past me, bumping me aside, and smacked the youngster. It was an open-handed backhand strike, not meaning to do any real damage, but it still tossed the kid to the other end of the subway car, back into the clutch of teen toughs.

I sighed. "Fuck." I let go of the pole as soon as I regained my balance. "You didn't have to do that."

Then one of the punk's friends pulled out a Transom 987 projectile gun, and I crouched for nonexistent cover. The demon moved, stepping past me, and I watched events come to their foregone conclusion.

The kids boiled up from their seats, one of them yanking their injured, pimply-faced friend to his feet. They were all wearing black denim jackets and green bandannas—yet another minigang.

The demon blinked across intervening space and slapped the illegal (if you weren't accredited or a police officer) gun out of the boy's hand, sent it skittering against the floor. The nurse covered her daughter's ear with her hand, staring, her mouth agape. I moved forward, coming to my feet, my sword singing free of the sheath, and slid myself in between them and the gang, where the demon had broken one boy's arm and was now in the process of holding the gunner up by his throat, shaking him as negligently as a cat might shake a mouse.

"You want to get off at the next stop," I told the mother, who stared at me. "Trust me."

She nodded. Her eyes were wide and wet with terror. The little girl stared at me.

I turned back to find the demon standing in the center of a ring of limp bodies. "Hello!" I shouted, holding the sword in my right hand with the blade level across my body, the reinforced scabbard reversed along my left forearm to act as a shield. It was a highly unorthodox way to hold a katana, but Jado-sensei always cared less about orthodox than keeping alive, and I found I agreed with him. If the demon came for me, I could buy some time with the steel and a little more time with Power. He'd eat me alive, of course, but I had a chance—

He turned, brushing his hands together as if wiping

away dust. One of the boys groaned. "Yes?" Same level, robotic voice.

"You didn't kill anyone, did you?" I asked.

Bright green eyes scorched the air. He shrugged. "That would create trouble," he said.

"Is that a yes or a no?" I firmed my grip on the hilt. "Did you kill any of them?" I didn't want to do the paperwork even if it was a legitimate kill in response to an assault.

"No, they'll live," he said, glancing down. Then he stepped mincingly free of the ring of bodies.

"*Anubis et'her ka*," I breathed. *Anubis, protect me.*

The demon's lips compressed into a thin line. The train slowed, deceleration rocking me back on my heels. If he was going to attack, this would be a great time. "The Prince requested you delivered unharmed," he said, and sidled to the door, not turning his back to my blade.

"Remind me to thank him," I shot back, swallowing against the sudden dust in my mouth. I wondered what other "requests" the Prince had made.